A KNIGHT OF HONOUR

Anne Herries

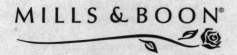

MILLS & BOON®

MILLS & BOON and MILLS & BOON with the Rose Device are registered trademarks of the publisher.

First published in Great Britain 2005
Harlequin Mills & Boon Limited,
Eton House, 18-24 Paradise Road, Richmond, Surrey TW9 1SR

© Anne Herries 2005

ISBN 0 263 84372 6

Set in Times Roman 10½ on 13¼ pt.
04-0605-90407

Printed and bound in Spain
by Litografia Rosés S.A., Barcelona

Anne Herries, winner of the Romantic Novelists' Association's ROMANCE PRIZE 2004, lives in Cambridgeshire. After many happy years with a holiday home in Spain, she and her husband now have their second home in Norfolk. They are only just across the road from the sea, and have a view of it from their windows. At home and at the sea they enjoy watching the wildlife and have many visitors to their gardens, particularly squirrels. Anne loves watching their antics, and spoils both them and her birds shamelessly. She also loves to see the flocks of geese and other birds flying in over the sea during the autumn, to winter in the milder climes of this country. Anne loves to write about the beauty of nature, and sometimes puts a little into her books, though they are mostly about love and romance. She writes for her own enjoyment, and to give pleasure to her readers.

Recent titles by the same author:

THE SHEIKH
A DAMNABLE ROGUE*

Winner of the Romantic Novelists' Association's Romance Prize

and in the Regency series
The Steepwood Scandal:

LORD RAVENSDEN'S MARRIAGE
COUNTERFEIT EARL

and in
The Elizabethan Season:

LADY IN WAITING
THE ADVENTURER'S WIFE

and in
The Banewulf Dynasty:

A PERFECT KNIGHT

*Look for Alain de Banewulf's story
in HER KNIGHT PROTECTOR
in August 2005*

Chapter One

'My lady, have a care!'

Elona, daughter of Lord John de Barre, glanced back at her companion, the light of laughter in her eyes. Her long red hair streamed out in the breeze behind her for she wore no head covering. She was a beautiful girl and had the delicate colouring of her mother, a Scotswoman who had married at seventeen, given birth to a son and then a daughter and died, leaving her husband distraught. Elona also had her mother's temper, which could flare easily and disappear as swiftly as if it had never been. But she was undoubtedly a woman of compassion, loving and loyal to those she cared for, and the person she cared for most in the world was her father. Lord John de Barre.

'Catch me if you can,' she called to her squire in a spirit of defiance.

This past year had been hard to bear, for first the shocking murder of her beloved brother Pierre, and then the natural death of her kind and loving stepmother Elizabeth, had left her saddened and concerned for her ailing father.

The lady Elizabeth had been English, a good kind woman

who had seen to Elona's welfare and loved her as a mother. Both Elona and her father had mourned her sincerely when she'd died earlier that year, but Pierre's death had broken Lord de Barre's spirit, leaving him aged and ill. Elona had feared for him these past months.

Now, however, she glanced over her shoulder at the young man, bending over her horse's neck as she recklessly urged it to go faster. She had always ridden fearlessly, taught by both her father and brother who were proud of the lovely girl.

'You should have been a boy!' Pierre had teased her unmercifully as a young girl, but he had loved her. She missed him terribly and had turned in her loneliness to the young squire, William de Grenville, who was accompanying her that morning.

Seeing that he had no hope of catching her on his horse, which was a sluggard compared to her own, Elona slowed, allowing him to come up with her.

'One day you will take a tumble and break your neck,' Will said, giving her a stern look. 'And your father will blame me for not taking better care of you.'

'Poor Will,' Elona said, her eyes sparkling. 'That would be unfair since I do as I please and you have no power to compel me.' Yet she sighed, knowing he was right to urge caution. 'You do well to chide me, sir. My father suffers enough as it is. He would be alone if I died.'

'He would not be the only one to mourn for you, my lady.'

Will's dark eyes seemed to smoulder with passion as he looked at her and Elona smiled. She was well aware that he loved her and sometimes she was sure that she loved him. Of course, he was not a knight and, unless he earned his spurs, could not expect to marry the daughter of John de Barre. Yet there was time enough. She was but seventeen and in no hurry to wed.

A frown wrinkled her smooth forehead. Elona knew that her father had recently received an offer for her hand. He had refused it at once, for it came from Baron Danewold, a man both she and her father disliked intensely. They knew that the Baron coveted the rich lands that marched side by side with those belonging to his first wife, and the two men had argued over boundaries before now. Although there could be no proof, Lord de Barre believed that the Baron was behind the brutal murder of his son, possibly in the expectation that he would die and leave his daughter unprotected. However, despite increasingly frail health, Elona's father had clung to life and hoped to continue until his daughter was safely married.

They had reached her father's fortified manor house and Will came to help her down from her mount, his hands lingering a little longer than necessary about her waist and bringing a flush to her cheeks. She smiled at him, but said nothing; she was not yet certain of her own feelings regarding the young man. It might suit her to wed him and yet it might not.

'Thank you, Will,' she told him. 'If it is fine, we shall ride again tomorrow.'

'Yes, my lady. You know I wait only to serve you.'

The look he gave her burned so deep that Elona felt an odd sensation low in her abdomen. He had a soft kissable mouth and she had oft wondered what it might be like to be held in Will's strong arms. If only he had earned his spurs, she might then look upon him with favour without fear of her father's reproach.

She ran into the house, her fine leather slippers making no sound on the flagstones in the great hall where a fire was kept burning, even in the heat of summer, for the house was never truly warm. Today it struck cold, though outside it had been a warm spring day. In this northerly region of France the spring might be as warm as summer or cold, but today was somewhere between the two.

Elona turned towards the curving stone staircase that led to her solar and bedchamber, but her father's steward called to her as she put her foot upon the first stair.

'Ah, well met, my lady,' Griffin said and smiled at his lord's daughter. He found her a lovely woman, spirited and sometimes reckless, but generous and caring towards her father, who, though fond of her, had often neglected her in favour of her brother. Daughters were not sons, after all, and, while he lived, Pierre had been his father's favourite. 'Lord de Barre requests the pleasure of your company in his private chamber. I was about to come in search of you, but you have saved me a journey.'

'Then I am glad of it,' she replied with a smile. Like her father, the steward was well past his youth and suffered with aching joints, particularly in the wet weather. 'I shall come at once. I know my father has been expecting news. Perhaps it has arrived.'

'He will tell you himself, lady,' the steward said, wondering how the lady would take the news that her father had decided upon a marriage for her. It was the custom for a father to make these arrangements, but the Lady Elona did not always take kindly to being told that something was signed and sealed without her consent. Griffin had advised caution, but his lord was in truth of much the same temperament as his fiery daughter. 'I dare say 'tis best that he does.'

'That means I shan't like it,' Elona said and pulled a wry

face. She did not waste time in answering her father's summons, however, for that would avail her nothing. She must listen first and then plead her case if need be. She was well aware of what the probable news would be, but did not yet have any idea of who might have been chosen to be her husband.

Griffin did not reply. He was ever the diplomat, she thought and did not press him. It was not his decision, after all, but her father's.

John de Barre smiled at his daughter as she entered the small room that served as his private chamber. Situated just off the great hall it allowed him to be aware of what was going on and yet seek the solitude he needed more and more these days.

'The ride has done you good, child,' he said as she went to kiss his cheek. 'You look beautiful—but then you always do, just like your mother.' A sigh escaped him. He had never ceased to mourn his first wife, though he had never blamed Elona for her death. A child must be born by her parents' consent and could not be blamed if the mother died.

'Are you unwell, Father? You look tired?'

As well he might, since the letter from England had arrived the previous evening, keeping him awake throughout the dark hours. Yet he had wrestled with the selfish emotions that told him to keep his daughter by him and won. It was for her sake that he had written, for he sensed that his time was near and she must be protected from the evil that he feared might come to her if he were dead.

'I am a little tired, but my health is the same as always,' he replied and took her hand, leading her to the solid bench beside his fire. Cushions sewn by Elona herself for his comfort were piled against the hard back, but he chose to remain standing, motioning her to sit down. 'Please rest, my dear. I have something to tell you. Shall I send for wine and biscuits to refresh you before I begin?'

A slight smile touched her mouth. 'Do you hope to sweeten the taste, Father? Was your letter to my kinswoman successful?'

'Yes, indeed. Lady Alayne de Banewulf was everything that is kind and generous in her letter. She was sorry to hear of your stepmother's death and…of other things.' The Lord de Barre paused as he fought his grief, which shook his thin body and threatened to overcome him. He recovered and looked at his daughter, standing there so young and proud, and wilful as her mother before her. Her husband must be a man he could trust, otherwise she would find life too harsh outside the protecting walls of her home. He loved her dearly, though he knew that he had neglected her in the past. 'I told her why I wanted to arrange a match for you and she asked me to send you to her, Elona.'

'Shall you come with me, Father?'

He shook his head. 'I fear the journey might be the death of me, Elona. I shall send your ladies and Will de Grenville with you, but I shall stay here. You will be safer with your kinswoman until I have set up certain precautionary measures here. I intend to make you a ward of Duke Richard until your marriage. He will know how to act if anything happens to me—if, for instance, I should be murdered like your brother. He will control your lands then, Elona, and none may gainsay him and escape with their life. But that will take time and until it is done I fear that you may suffer some harm.'

'I do not want to leave you, dearest Father. You have not been well. You need me with you, to care for you and keep you company.'

'It is for the best, child,' he said and sighed. 'I do not wish to part from you, Elona, and I shall miss you sorely, but if anything should happen to me before the Duke has agreed to this contract, you would be at the mercy of unscrupulous men. Lady Alayne has promised to send her son to fetch you and he will bring an armed escort to add to those that I am able to provide. I cannot spare my best men for my manor would then be vulnerable, and I will fight to my last drop of blood to prevent the lands of Barre from falling into Danewold's hands.'

'Oh, Father,' Elona said and held back the sob of grief that rose to her lips. If Pierre had not been so brutally killed, her father would not have had to send her away. 'Must I truly go to England to be married to a man I do not know?'

'Lady Alayne has not promised a match with her son Alain de Banewulf,' John de Barre said. 'She says that she will be your guardian and guide you in the matter of your marriage. She and her husband see no reason against the match, but she says it would be kinder to let you young people get to know each other first; then, if it seems suitable, you will wed. If not, she promises that she will arrange another match of the same worthiness for you. It is the best I can do for you, my child. Had Elizabeth lived, I could have left all to her…' Again he sighed. 'We have been unlucky this past year, Elona. I would ask that you do not add to my burdens by refusing this match for no good reason. The young man is personable and of good family. What more could you ask?'

Elona could have told him but did not, holding her tongue, though it cost her to remain silent. To refuse outright at this moment would provoke a quarrel and her father looked very tired. She was afraid that if she quarrelled with him, she might be the unwitting cause of a relapse; if she seemed to give way at first, there might yet be a chance of escape for her.

As soon as she could, she sought out her squire to ask him what he knew of the man to whom her father hoped she would be married.

'I know nothing of Alain de Banewulf,' Will told her. 'But I have heard of his brother, Sir Stefan.'

Something in his tone made Elona shiver. 'Tell me, what have you heard?'

'Some say he is a religious man,' Will said, looking thoughtful. He had heard that the English knight was a man of abstemious habits who neither drank nor sported with wenches excessively. 'He dedicated himself to the service of Duke Richard when he was but fifteen and hath won honour and fame by his deeds—though some think him dour and stern.'

Elona frowned. Alain de Banewulf's brother sounded cold and humourless to her and she was thankful that it was not he she was to marry.

'At least I shall never need to think of him,' she said. 'For, if he serves the Duke, it is unlikely that we shall ever meet…'

'We are almost there, Orlando,' Stefan said as they emerged from the great forest that edged his father's manor. He reined in his mount to look at the house. It was impressive, being well maintained and fortified in the new way, but seemed smaller than when he'd last seen it. Many years had passed since he'd last visited his family, for until recent months he had not returned to England since taking service with Duke Richard of Aquitaine. 'Tell me what do you think of it—speak as if we meant to lay siege as we did at Taillebourg.'

Sir Orlando of Wildersham smiled, his eyes crinkling at the corners as he recalled the siege of Taillebourg. Stefan had been just seventeen then, young, eager and one of the bravest fighters he had ever seen. Orlando owed his life to Stefan that day, and since then they had been the best of friends.

His critical eye moved over the improvements made at Banewulf; like Stefan, he was trained to assess the vulnerability of a fortress and the best way of broaching its defences. In 1179 he had seen Taillebourg raised to the ground; a fortress that had been thought impenetrable proving all too easy to subdue.

'It will do, Stefan,' he said in his low deep voice. 'In Henry's England. But if things were to change… there are more improvements that might be made.'

'Yes, you are right,' Stefan agreed. 'England has been fortunate these many years, safe and peaceful under King Henry II—but as you and I know, the King and his sons often quarrel amongst themselves.'

Sir Orlando gave a wry smile. The Plantagenet brood were an unruly mob, father against sons, brother against brother. More than once the brothers had rebelled against the King, and there was a dispute between Henry and Richard even now. Who could tell what would happen if the old King died?

'My father, Sir Ralph de Banewulf, has ever been loyal to Henry,' Stefan said. 'But on whose side would he stand if there were a dispute between the King's sons—a struggle to take the throne that Henry's death would leave vacant?'

'Surely on that of the rightful heir—Duke Richard.'

'Perhaps…'

Stefan frowned as he realised he had no idea of his father's loyalties. How should he when he'd been sent away to his kinsman's house at the tender age of five years? Harald of Wotten was a good man, who had seen to his education in all the ways necessary, but Stefan had been devastated at his exile from the father and home he had loved. His father's re-marriage to a beautiful lady and the birth of first a half-brother, then a half-sister, had made his hurt all the sharper.

However, he had learned to conquer his bitterness over the years. He had won both fame as a mighty warrior and great wealth in the service of Duke Richard, and, since his return to England some three months earlier, had purchased the rich manor of Sanscombe for himself. Duke Richard had knighted him after Taillebourg, but he was also entitled to call himself Baron Sanscombe by reason of title to the manor.

'Does your father expect you?'

'I sent word a few days ago,' Stefan replied. He smiled rue-fully at his friend. 'They will scarce remember me.'

'I doubt they will forget you next time,' Orlando said and was rewarded by a soft laugh from his companion. Some thought Stefan dour, but those who knew him were aware of lurking humour in those grey eyes. Though he could not be called a handsome man, he had something about him that drew others to him, and, it was oft said, the strength of a bear.

'I have certainly grown these past years.'

'What made you decide to return?'

Stefan looked at him thoughtfully. In truth, he was not sure what had drawn him back to England after ten years of sol-diering abroad. Was it a desire to see his family? His father was no longer a young man, his half-brother must be grown to man-hood by now, and Marguerite almost a woman at fifteen.

'If I speak honestly, I do not know. I had thought never to return.'

Stefan lapsed into silence as he and his companions clattered over the drawbridge. Just what had drawn him back to Banewulf in the spring of 1187? His father had cast him out because his birth had killed his mother. He knew that from his nurse, who had told him when he could scarce understand the significance of her words.

What would it avail him to return now?

Yet deep within himself Stefan felt a need he could not identify. The desire to visit Banewulf had grown too strong to resist.

'It has been too long, Stefan.' Alayne went to greet her stepson with a smile, her hands outstretched. 'We are delighted to have you with us and hope you will stay for as long as it suits you.'

She seemed hardly to have changed in the last ten years, Stefan thought, lifting her right hand to salute it with a chaste kiss.

'You are kind to welcome me so warmly, lady,' he said. 'May I introduce Sir Orlando of Wildersham—a good friend who is on his way to London and was pleased to accompany me thus far. I hope it will not inconvenience you to give him shelter for the night?'

'How should it?' Lady Alayne said. 'A friend of yours must always be welcome in my house, Stefan.'

'I thank you, lady,' Orlando said and swept her an elegant bow, his eyes moving to the face of the girl standing a little behind her. How beautiful she was!

'How often we have all talked of you, Stefan,' Alayne cried. 'You were but a lad when you left us and now you are grown to a fine, strong man.' Her eyes went over him appreciatively. His tunic and gown were plain and of sober hue compared to that favoured by most men of wealth, but in that he was much like his father. Both men chose black or grey rather than the peacock colours so beloved of the courtiers. 'Your fame has spread, Stefan. We know of your brave deeds in battle and as a trusted counsellor to Duke Richard.'

'Aye, and I can vouch for it that he deserves every word of the praise heaped upon him, lady,' Orlando said.

'Too much is said with too little cause.' Stefan dismissed their praise carelessly. He could see the young man and girl waiting to greet him. Both were cast in the image of their mother: fair, slim, eyes of a greenish-blue shade; attractive and lissom, they seemed to radiate content to the eyes of a man who had always felt a stranger to his family. They looked at him curiously, seeming pleased to welcome him after so long, but there was no sign of his father and he felt the sting of disappointment that Sir Ralph had not bothered to be there for his return. His eyes narrowed as he looked at Alayne. 'My father is not here?'

'Unfortunately, he had business elsewhere he could not avoid. We were not certain when to expect you, but he will be here to feast with us in the hall this evening.' Alayne turned to beckon her offspring forward. 'Here are your brother and sister to greet you.'

'Alain—Marguerite,' Stefan said. He saw the eagerness in his half-brother's eyes and smiled inwardly. It was not the first time he'd seen that expression in the eyes of a young man keen to hear details of battles. The girl held back shyly, but when he smiled at her she answered him with her own. She was already bidding fair to rival her mother's beauty, he thought. 'It is good to see you both.'

'We have longed to see you,' Alain said. 'You have done and seen so much.'

'Welcome to Banewulf,' Marguerite added softly. 'We are happy to have you here.' She glanced shyly at Sir Orlando. 'And you, sir.'

'Marguerite speaks for us all,' Alayne confirmed. 'Come, Stefan. A chamber is prepared for your comfort. Alain will take you there and see that you have all you need. Sir Orlando, you will take a cup of wine with me while my servants prepare a chamber for you.' She smiled and lowered her voice. 'I would hear more of my stepson's brave deeds and we need not put him to the blush.'

Stefan did not hear his friend's reply. He allowed himself to be drawn away to the part of the house occupied by young, single men. Though most would sleep on the floor of the hall, family and honoured guests had always been provided with their own chambers at Banewulf.

'Your chamber is next to mine as it always was,' Alain told him. His pleasure in the visit was obvious. 'It means we shall be able to talk. I want to hear about all the battles you've fought, all the men you've killed.'

'I am not proud to have killed men—apart from a few who did not deserve to live,' Stefan told him. 'It is necessary in battle, for one must defeat the enemy, but wherever it is possible I show mercy. Duke Richard is the same, though he can be ruthless.' There had been times when his justice had been merciless, but it needed a strong hand to keep the unruly nobles in check, otherwise there would be no law.

'They say he is fearless!'

'Yes, I have heard it said. He may be Duke and a prince of England, but his name is linked with that of kings. Some say he has the heart of a lion.'

'And that you have the strength of a bear.' Alain grinned,

a boyish mischief lurking in his eyes though he was a man grown. 'Do you remember when we wrestled as boys? You could have beaten me easily, but you often let me win.'

'You were still a child. I already had a man's strength. It would have been unfair of me to use it against you.'

'We must put ourselves to the test again one day. I think you would not find it so easy to beat me now.'

Stefan assessed him quietly. His brother appeared slight compared to his own heavier build, but he suspected a wiry strength beneath that elegant exterior of fine clothes. Alain wore blue and silver with deep slashes in the full sleeves of his tunic and a girdle of leather chased with silver. He smiled inwardly. Seldom had he seen such finery except at the court of Aquitaine!

'Have you been recently to court?' he asked, avoiding the challenge, though he was not sure why. Alain looked disappointed, as if he felt himself rebuffed.

'You think me too fine a fellow to test you? Do not mistake me for a weakling, brother.'

Stefan relented, a glint of humour in his eyes. 'Well, we shall put that to the test tomorrow. Do you care to train with me, Alain?'

'Aye! Right willingly.' The younger man's sunny smile was restored at once. 'Tell me, is Duke Richard a good man to serve?'

'Yes, I have found him so. You do not think to serve him?'

'I have given it some thought.' A look of frustration passed across Alain's face. 'I must make my way in the world somehow. I cannot remain always in my father's house.'

'You are unhappy here?'

'No, of course not. I have been the most fortunate of youths to have the love of my parents and our father has trained me well. Yet I long for adventure.'

'Life has perhaps been too easy for you?'

'I would not say that exactly. Father spared me nothing. I worked as hard as any man at Banewulf. I might have been knighted by the King after winning the joust as his champion, but asked that I might be allowed to earn my spurs more worthily.'

'You have not yet been knighted?' Alain was two years older than Stefan had been when he received his own, but he had earned them in battle. 'Perhaps you should go abroad, brother. Yet I dare say Father could arrange it if he chose?'

'I must earn my honours,' Alain insisted. He smiled at his brother. 'I shall not plague you with questions now for you must wish to rest and refresh yourself—but we shall talk more of these things?'

'But of course, as often as you like,' Stefan replied and clasped his shoulder. 'I hope we shall be friends?'

'We always were,' Alain said, looking slightly puzzled.

Stefan frowned as the door closed behind his half-brother. Was that the truth? Had they been friends? Perhaps. He had forgotten. He hoped it was true, for it meant that he had never caused Alain to be aware of his jealousy, which he knew to be unworthy. Alain was not to blame for his exile—that sin was his alone to carry.

Nor had his stepmother wanted him sent away, Stefan admitted. She had always been kind to him. No, it was his father who had shut him out. He could not help feeling hurt that even now Sir Ralph had put his duty before his son's homecoming, but he fought the bitterness. It was time to put such things behind him. He had come to Banewulf to make friends with his family. The realisation had come slowly, but his half-brother's warmth had brought home to Stefan that he needed the feeling of belonging. He had shut himself off for too long.

'You will forgive me for not being here when you arrived?' Ralph asked later that afternoon as he clasped his eldest son's hand firmly. Though nearing his fiftieth year he was still a strong man, similar in build and looks to the man he welcomed. 'It was duty. One of my loyal retainers was dying and wanted me to witness his last words. He had served me faithfully for years. I could not do less for him.'

'No, nor should you think of it,' Stefan assured him. In his father's place he would have done the same and understood completely. His feeling of resentment melted at once 'Your lady, my brother and the Lady Marguerite made me feel welcome, sir.'

'And why not? This has always been your home, Stefan.'

Then why did you send me away? Why did you break my heart? The questions remained unspoken. A child had asked them, but Stefan was no longer that child.

'I have come only to visit, Father. I have purchased the manor of Sanscombe.'

'And the title that goes with it.' Sir Ralph nodded. 'You have done well, Stefan, but Banewulf is your birthright as my eldest son. Alain has his mother's lands and a small estate I purchased for him.'

'Banewulf is yours, Father. I trust you will enjoy many years as its lord.'

'Mayhap.' Sir Ralph shrugged. 'I wanted to be sure that you understood.'

Stefan nodded. As the eldest son he could claim the manor

by law. Yet his own manor was larger and richer, though he would not boast of that to anyone. He was entitled to be called the lord of his manor, but preferred his own name, and the knighthood he had earned in battle.

'It may be that I shall have more than one son. I would have lands enough in such a case.'

'You are thinking of taking a bride?'

'Perhaps. There is no one special—but a man reaches a time when he begins to think of sons.'

'Yes, that is true,' Ralph agreed. 'But I would not have you marry only for that reason. Choose your lady with care, Stefan. Wealth and beauty are tempting but there are other qualities that mean more.'

'I have yet to meet a lady I admire sufficiently for marriage.'

'You should consult your stepmother. She accompanied your brother to the joust last summer and may know of a suitable match for you.'

'You did not go with them?'

'I was laid low of a putrid fever earlier in the month. I had recovered or they would not have left me, but I felt too tired to make the journey.'

'You are not ailing, sir?' An odd pain clutched at Stefan's heart. Had he left this reconciliation too long? If his father were to die before they had had a chance to know each other…but that was foolish and he would not let the thought take root in his mind!

'No, no,' Ralph said and laughed. 'It is a fever that strikes every few years. Alayne cured me but, if truth be told, I no longer care for the court and used it as an excuse to stay at home.'

'A man may weary of fine trappings,' Stefan agreed. 'I have

seen much of the life and find it no longer holds the appeal it once had.'

'You are wise,' Ralph said. 'You have known your share of fighting and can now enjoy the spoils. Find yourself a wife, Stefan. I would see my grandsons before too many years have passed.'

Stefan's mouth curved in a wry smile. He'd had no thought of marriage before this moment and hardly knew why he had spoken of sons. Yet perhaps it was what he had been unconsciously looking for these past months.

His brother had shown that he bore him no ill will and was eager for the wrestling contest that was to take place between them the next day. Stefan knew that he must not hold back this time, for Alain would not forgive such a slight. There was no doubt in his mind who would win, but it must be fair and good-humoured, and they would remain friends.

'Perhaps I shall seek your lady's advice, Father. It can do no harm to ask, after all.'

'Your father tells me you would take a bride?'

Stefan was walking in the manor gardens with his step-mother. He glanced at her, a gleam of humour in his eyes. Her expression was alert, almost eager, and he guessed that she had thoughts of making a match for him.

'If I could find a lady as beautiful, wise and good as you, my lady, then I might be persuaded.'

Alayne's laughter was husky and delightful. It was little wonder that some had called her an enchantress in her youth.

'You flatter me, Stefan. The older I become, the more I realise my failings.'

'I do not believe you have ever failed my father.'

'I almost lost our first child in a fall. He scolded me for that. I believed it was the child he loved and not me—but I wronged him. Your father was not given to pretty speeches when he was younger. Indeed, you are much alike in your manner, Stefan. He has grown softer with the years and the right wife could do the same for you—show you how to find happiness, my dear.'

'Shall you find her for me?'

'I shall do my best,' Alayne said. 'But I also have a favour to ask of you. There is a lady, a kinswoman of mine—I have promised her sanctuary here. It may be that she and your brother will marry, though nothing is settled.'

'But you hope for it?'

'I hope to protect her. She has been threatened by the shadow of a beast. Baron Danewold wants her and he is evil. I know how that feels; something similar happened to me before I was fortunate enough to wed your father. Elona's father is ill and unable to protect her for the moment and he looks to us for help.' She gazed up at him. 'Would you bring her here to us?'

'Where does she live?'

'In Normandy. I know it is much to ask of you, Stefan.'

'Not so very much since I must visit that country on business myself quite soon. There are many leagues between Aquitaine and Normandy, but I could attend on Duke Richard and then return here with the lady.' Stefan frowned as he thought of something. 'But would not my brother wish to go—since that lady may be his bride?'

'I do not wish him to feel obliged to wed Elona simply to please me. If he went to fetch her, he might feel honour bound to offer for her. Alain is a sensitive man, Stefan. I want him to know his wife before he commits himself.' She sighed deeply. 'Sometimes I fear for him. He is not like you or his father—and he is restless.'

'Yes, I have noticed that he is easily hurt,' Stefan admitted. 'Not physically, for he has a wiry strength and I was hard put to best him when we wrestled together. Indeed, he is a skilled fighter in every way, but inwardly it is another matter.'

'It worries me that he should be so tender. Perhaps I have spoiled him. Ralph wanted to send him away for his education as he did you, but he was always delicate as a boy and I begged to be allowed to keep him with me. Your father gave me my way, but I have wondered if I was wrong to ask it.'

'My brother does not suffer ill health now?'

'Oh, no, he grew out of it as children will. He grew strong and confident under his father's eye—but I think now that he lost by the arrangement. He longs to travel and I fear that we shall lose him before long.'

'You cannot keep him always with you, lady.' Stefan thought she was still over-protective of her son, but liked her too well to hurt her.

'You do not think he would resent my bringing the lady Elona here?'

'There may be danger for Elona,' Alayne said, looking anxious. 'It would relieve my mind if you would go. You are a soldier. You will know how to protect her.'

'Very well,' he said. 'I shall bring her to you—and in the meantime you will try to find a lady who would be willing to marry a rough brute like me.'

'You are a little stern at times, it is true,' Alayne said with a smile to soften her words. 'But so was your father when I first met him. The right lady will teach you to smile more, Stefan.'

'When I find her!' He gave her a rueful grin. 'I rely on you, my lady mother.'

'And I shall do my best for you, dear son.'

'I shall return within two months. You have my word. After all, it cannot be so very difficult to escort a lady from her home to yours—can it?'

He little knew how soon he would learn to rue those words!

Chapter Two

Elona was walking in the gardens of her father's house, her head bent in thought. Try as she might, she could find no way of persuading her father to relent. Another letter had come from England, and now her father was insisting that she go to England with this man—this Sir Stefan de Banewulf!

She had begged Will to find out as much as he could about this English knight, but so far he had little to report other than what he had already told her. An image had taken root in her mind of a stern, cold man, and she had begun to focus her resentment on him. If he had not promised to escort her, she might have remained at home, for it seemed that his brother could not be bothered to fetch her.

What kind of a man was content to let his brother escort his promised bride for him? He could not wish for the match, surely? Perhaps he too was being forced into it?

A surge of rebellion went through her. She would not let them marry her to someone she disliked! And yet to refuse stubbornly might cause her father distress.

He was so weary these days, his eyes sunk into his head and dark shadowed. How could she leave him knowing that she might never see him again? It would break her heart to do so, but it was his wish.

Her defiant spirit was torn between a desire to please her father and the need to somehow escape this unwelcome marriage. What could she do? If only there were someone to help her!

Her gaze fell upon her young squire. Will was untried, though brave and strong—but she was afraid that her father would never agree to a match between them.

And even if he would agree—did she really want to marry him? Yet it might be better than being forced into a marriage with a man she did not know and was determined to dislike.

'Oh, Will,' Elona cried as they walked together in the warm sunshine that morning, 'my father says that Stefan de Bane-wulf will be here within a few days and then I am to leave for England. They will marry me to Lady Alayne's son and I shall never see my home again.'

Tears stood in her lovely eyes as she gazed up at the young man, whose company had been her only solace of late. She was aware of a deep reluctance to leave all that was so familiar to her, and, though she would never have admitted it, there was also fear of the unknown. To travel to a strange land and marry a man she'd never seen! It would daunt even the bravest heart.

'You have tried to persuade your father to let you stay here?' There was shock in his eyes and something more—something close to despair.

Elona shook her head, her throat tight with emotion. 'In truth, I cannot. He is happy that he has arranged for me to live with my kinswoman. As you know, Father's health does not improve. Who knows what might happen if I defied him? I do not wish to harm or worry him by my defiance.'

'Shall I go to the Lord de Barre and ask for your hand, Elona? I swear I would defend you both with my life. You would have no need to fear Danewold if I commanded your forces here.' Will's voice rang with passion, a light flaring in his eyes as he dared to speak of his hopes for the first time.

For a moment hope flared in Elona's breast. If she was married to Will, she would be able to stay near her father. She need not go to England—and yet how could the young squire assume command of her father's men? Until he had proved himself as a brave knight, the men would not follow him.

'You have not been knighted, Will,' she reminded him gently, the hope dying as she realised it was impossible.

'Your father could arrange it if he chose. I swear Danewold would not threaten you if I were your husband, nor yet your father.'

If only it could be! He was such a kind, generous man and she thought sometimes that she could easily love him; indeed, she was more than passing fond of him. How happy she would be to wed him and stay here with her father. And yet in her heart she knew that the Lord de Barre would refuse such an offer for her. He would not consider Will her equal.

'I do not think my father would listen, Will.'

'You know that I love you?' Now there was a hint of desperation in his voice.

Elona gazed up at him, seeing something in his intense eyes that she had not been aware of previously. His love for her was no light thing—not a boy's tenderness, as she had imagined, but a man's burning passion. Her soft mouth quivered as he closed the gap between them, taking her into his arms to kiss her with a hungry yearning that startled her by its fierceness. Yet she clung to him, finding comfort in the strength of his devotion as she realised that this man was truly hers to direct as she willed. The power that gave her as a woman was a little frightening for she had never experienced the feeling before.

'You must not speak to my father,' she said as he released her. 'For then he might send you away. No, stay close to me, Will, be my friend and protector. If I find that I cannot bear to marry my kinswoman's son, then—I shall run away with you. If we married and returned to my father, he would surely not turn us away.'

'Would it not be better to speak openly of our feelings?' Will was an honest man and did not care for the idea of deceiving his lord, yet he found the thought of her wed to another almost unbearable, especially if that marriage were against her wish.

'I think he would be angry,' Elona said. 'We must try to think of a way for you to earn your knighthood, Will. My father would welcome you then.'

In truth, it was her father's place to secure that favour for him, Will thought somewhat ruefully. He had served his lord faithfully and well and the honour might have been sought from Duke Richard's hand long since. He came of a good but poor family and had hoped to rise in the service of John de Barre, though of late he had begun to think that he must look elsewhere if he would win honour or wealth. It was only his devotion to the Lady Elona that had held him here.

'I am yours to command as always,' he said and knelt before her, taking up the hem of her gown to kiss it. 'I swear to die before allowing Danewold or any other to harm you.'

Elona's cheeks were heated as she begged him to rise. His

declaration had made her feel a little foolish and yet it also excited her. Until this day she had not realised the depth of his devotion to her. It gave her confidence. She was not alone, for Will would never desert her, and if need be she would run away with him.

'You are my dearest friend,' she said. 'But we must do nothing too soon, Will. For the moment we must wait and see…'

Standing as they did at the edge of the woods bordering the north side of her father's lands, they could be clearly seen by any riders approaching the manor house from the north. Yet neither of them had thought for others. Caught up in each other as they were, neither noticed the small party of horsemen in the distance, nor the lone rider who had come on ahead of his men and was close enough to see and hear Will's pledge to his lady.

A frown creased the man's brow as he watched the pair turn and walk slowly back towards the house. Just what had he witnessed and what were the two plotting now?

Stefan watched as, nearing the house, they broke apart, the young man walking now a few steps behind the lady. Were his suspicions correct? Had he just seen a lovers' tryst—and was this the woman he was supposed to take back to Banewulf as his brother's bride?

Anger flared inside him. He would not stand by and see Alain offered soiled goods. If this woman had given herself to a lover…but he must not judge her too harshly. The man's devotion had been clear enough, but the lady was less easy to read. She would bear watching, Stefan decided. He had promised Lady Alayne to take her kinswoman safely to her at Banewulf and this he would do—heaven help any callow youth that tried to stop him!

If he suspected that the lady was not as pure as she was beautiful—and she was undoubtedly lovely—he would inform his brother and stepmother of her shame.

For the moment he must watch and wait, and reserve his suspicions to himself. Before he rushed to judgement, he must speak with the lady's father and discover what kind of a man he was, and from that he might better judge the lady herself.

Later that afternoon, when she came down to the great hall to greet her father's guests, Elona was dressed in a gown of deep emerald silk. The material was thick and rich, embroidered with silver thread, which shimmered in the light of the torches that lit the hall, as did the scarves of the same hue she wore at her creamy throat and in the cap of silver threads that held her bright hair. A plain silver cross hung from a chain to mid-waist, a simple ornament but one that suited her regal bearing.

She looked what she was, the proud daughter of a wealthy lord, her eyes gleaming with defiance. In the smoky light of the torches her hair was a flame that no veil could quite hide, her face beautiful but cold, showing none of the churning emotion inside her

'My Lord of Sanscombe,' John de Barre said, pride stirring in his breast as he looked at his lovely daughter and knew her a prize for any man. Had he thought of it, he might have sought an alliance with this eldest son of Ralph de Banewulf, for there could be few in France who had not heard of his brave deeds, in battle and the joust. 'It is my pleasure to introduce you to my daughter, the Lady Elona de Barre.'

'Lady, I am honoured to meet you,' Stefan said as he bent

over the hand she offered, but his expression was stern, his eyes cool as he greeted her—she was indeed the woman he had seen earlier that day. By heaven! She was a proud beauty, but she had not looked so coldly upon the lover who had plighted his troth to her. 'I know that the Lady Alayne is eager to welcome you to Banewulf.'

'Thank you, sir. I am happy to welcome you to my father's house, but I fear we must delay our journey for a few days.'

'Why is that, Elona?' John de Barre was puzzled by both her manner and that of his visitor; they seemed to have taken an instant dislike to one another, which was a pity.

'My nurse is sick and cannot travel yet and I cannot go without her—it would break her heart.'

'You make too much fuss of an old woman,' her father scolded. 'If Melise cannot accompany you, she must stay behind. Sir Stefan will not want to linger here more than a day or so; he is a busy man and has other calls on his time. We are fortunate he has come all this way to escort you, daughter.'

Elona frowned and bit her lip, but said no more. Stefan caught a flash of something in her eyes—was it distress? If so, it was quickly hidden. Yet perhaps she was not the faithless wanton he had taken her for; a woman as lovely as she might have many admirers and remain pure of heart and body. He must not rush to judgement too soon.

'I can give your nurse three days,' he told her, 'and then we must leave. I have a message to carry from Duke Richard to his father the King and may not tarry too long.'

Elona knew she was beaten. She inclined her head, assenting to his command. Her father was not to be swayed. He was determined that she must go to England and she could not disobey him—though once she had left his lands it would be a different matter. She would ask questions of this man who had come to escort her, try to win his confidence, though that would be no easy thing—and if she decided that she could not bear to wed his half-brother, she would ask Will to take her away.

Her decision reached, she felt calmer and began to study the man who had come to take her to England. He was a large man, powerful and stern with long dark hair and eyes the colour of wet granite. He was not a handsome man, but neither was he ill favoured or repulsive to her gaze.

Stefan de Banewulf's eyes were icy cold as they dwelt on her face and she felt as if he were probing her mind, trying to see her thoughts. There was suspicion in his face, as if he did not quite trust or like her—now why was that? They had only just met. Surely she had done nothing that could arouse his dislike?

A shiver ran through her and she thought that if this were the man she was intended to marry, she would flee from her home this very night and seek sanctuary with the nuns. Nothing would persuade her to marry a man like him!

And yet she must find a way to break down his reserve if she wanted to discover what kind of man his brother might be.

'You are kind to give me so much of your time, sir,' she said and forced a smile to lips that were too stiff. Inside her emotions churned, but she fought them down. She must govern her temper and her tongue if she wanted his confidence. 'Perhaps my nurse may be ready before the three days are up. Melise is very strong, though old and reluctant to leave the home she has known all her life.'

'I dare say it will be a wrench for her—and for you, lady,' Stefan replied, feeling a flicker of sympathy for her. He knew what it was like to be wrenched from those he loved and

could understand her feelings. 'To leave the home and people you love behind is never easy, but I believe you will find
an honest welcome in Lady Alayne's house. She bid me tell
you that you are very welcome and she looks forward to seeing you at Banewulf.'

'And your brother, sir? Will he also welcome me to his
home?'

'I believe he may,' Stefan said his eyes watchful. What was
in her mind now? 'But that will be for him to say when you
meet. I am merely your escort. Banewulf is not my home,
though I have been visiting there for a few weeks prior to this
journey.'

'You have lived for many years in Aquitaine, I believe?'
Elona moved away to stand a little closer to the fire. For some
reason she felt shivery, though the day had been warm enough.

'I returned to England some months ago to make my home
there and have purchased a manor of my own. My father is
still a strong, healthy man and I hope it will be many years before I inherit his manors, therefore I have made my own plans.'

Why did his eyes seem to see into her very soul? Elona
turned away to hold her hands to the fire. She was a little afraid
of this stern man, though she believed he meant her no harm.

'You have been too busy to think of settling before this. Your
name has become illustrious, Sir Stefan, linked with Duke
Richard's as both a fearsome warrior and a man of honour.'

Stefan's expression did not alter. 'You are too kind, lady.
I have merely served my lord as I ought.'

'Yes, some would say that,' she agreed, determined to press
on no matter how many rebuffs she met. 'But I have heard
that, though you are a brave and skilled soldier, you have
shown mercy to your enemies whenever it was possible.'

'It gives me no pleasure to take a man's life,' Stefan told her and his voice grated harshly on her ears. 'But if necessary I would do it and not think twice.'

Elona turned and looked at him, her knees quaking as she saw the look of iron about his mouth, his eyes hard and unforgiving. She knew then that he was not a man to be crossed by man or woman and an arrow of fear pierced her heart. This man carried a deep hurt inside him; she felt it instinctively, felt also his inner loneliness that he kept hidden, and something inside her reached out to him. Yet her mind shied away from these feelings. She did not want to like or trust him, for she meant to use him and then betray his trust if she chose.

Her eyes moved round the room and found Will de Grenville. He was watching her, a mixture of anxiety and—was that jealousy in his eyes? She smiled at him, wanting to reassure him. He need not fear that she would turn to this man for comfort instead of him; there was no softness in Stefan de Banewulf that she could see.

When she looked at the English knight again, she saw that the cold look was back in his eyes and her heart caught with fright. Had he seen her smile at Will? Had he guessed her secret? Yet how could he? No one could know, for she did not know for certain what was in her own heart and mind.

'Come, my daughter,' John de Barre said. 'It is time that we dine. Sir Stefan has travelled many leagues this day and will want to rest, his men also. Tomorrow we shall hold a feast, but this evening we sup quietly together.'

'Yes, Father.' Elona went to him, noticing that he had shadows beneath his eyes and looked tired himself. Her heart caught with fear for him. She must do nothing that might has-

ten his death, for it would grieve her all her life if she
did. 'I shall do as you bid me…'

'And how are you this morning, my lady?' Stefan asked as
he chanced upon Elona walking in the garden the next morning. It was a fine day, the air warm, the sun just beginning to
break through the clouds of early morning. He had been up
with the dawn, exercising with his men as usual, but it was
early for her to be abroad. His gaze dwelled on her lovely face
for a moment, noticing faint shadows about her eyes. 'I trust
you slept well?'

Elona's head went up, a flash of pride in her eyes. 'I slept as
always, sir,' she answered, for she would not have him know that
she had been restless throughout the night—and because of him!

'Then you were not kept awake by fears for your nurse,'
Stefan said, a smile flickering at the corners of his mouth. 'I
hope she is no worse today?'

'No worse, but no better,' Elona said, annoyed that she had
let him trap her into the admission. 'She needs several more
days to be ready for the journey.'

'We must hope that she recovers soon,' Stefan said, 'for I
fear I cannot wait for her. My business will not brook delay.'

Elona looked at him with dismay. He was a cold, hard man
and she heartily disliked him!

'Your business is your own, sir. Had I been born a man and
at liberty to please myself, I should not have placed myself
in your hands and might have travelled as I pleased.'

'Alas, such things cannot be changed,' Stefan replied. 'Pray
believe me when I say that I have given my promise to others and will do my best to carry out the task they have asked
of me—despite your efforts to thwart me.'

'I do not understand you, sir.'

'Do you not?' For a moment she could have sworn that there was laughter in his eyes, but in another second it had gone and the harsh look was back. 'Then perhaps I wrong you? Excuse me, I have wasted enough of the morning in dalliance. I have business I must discuss with your father.'

Elona watched him walk away, her foot tapping. What was she supposed to make of that? She had been wasting his time with her foolishness perhaps? Or was there some deeper meaning behind his words?

What was it about this man that disturbed her so?

Three days passed without Elona finding an excuse to delay their journey further and on the morning of the fourth she was forced to take a tearful farewell of her father. In the end she had decided to leave Melise behind; the old woman would find the journey too strenuous.

'I shall never see you again, my child,' Melise said as tears trickled down her cheeks. 'There is naught left for me but the grave.'

'Pray do not!'

Elona's heart wrenched with grief as she saw the nurse's distress. They were standing in the courtyard, their backs turned against the others for privacy as they made their farewells. The chill of early morning was upon them as they tenderly embraced.

'I feel this parting as much as you,' Elona said, her eyes moist with tears. 'But do not despair, dear heart. It may be that I shall return and sooner than you think—' She ceased her impassioned speech abruptly as she sensed someone close by and turned to see Stefan behind her. The man moved with the stealth of a cat! She had not heard him approach.

Why must he creep up on her? She glared at him, her eyes darting flames of fury. She did not know why he looked at her so disapprovingly despite all her attempts to break down the barriers between them, and she vowed she would do so no more. It had grieved her to see Melise so distressed and she was even more determined to return to her home before too long had passed. Surely her father would welcome her if she were married to a man who could protect both her and the de Barre lands?

'Forgive me if I intrude, lady,' Stefan said, eyes narrowed and wary. What was she plotting now? She was clearly a troublesome wench and he would have to be alert. He had seen her in deep conversation with her squire three times since his arrival, and Will de Grenville's feelings were on display every time he looked at her. The young man was besotted with her and no doubt willing to do whatever she asked of him. 'I know this parting pains you, but we must begin our journey. I cannot tarry longer.'

He implied that he had already delayed too long for her sake! Elona burned with anger as she darted a last kiss at her nurse's cheek. Would that she could dismiss him with a word or a glance, but this was not a man to be trifled with!

'Remember that I am thinking of you,' she said to Melise, and turned away before the tears turned to sobs of grief. She had already spoken to her father that morning in private and merely nodded at him as he stood watching with the others while she was helped to mount her palfrey. Had she gone to him now, she might have begged him to allow her to stay, but neither her pride nor her concern for her father would let her give way before the man she was beginning to think of as her enemy.

'I am ready now, sir.'

Her head lifted, her face becoming cold and proud. It was clear that Sir Stefan found her a nuisance if nothing worse. She had seen hostility and sometimes suspicion in his eyes when he looked at her. Why should he dislike her? What could she possibly have done to make him treat her so coldly?

It did not matter. He was nothing to her!

Elona rode with her back straight and stiff, looking directly ahead. To glance back might overset her and she must not weep. To show weakness would make her vulnerable to this man with the stern face and hard eyes. She would meet ice with ice. Let him see that she was no mere girl to be treated as a piece of baggage!

As they left the courtyard of her father's manor, Will came to ride beside her. She glanced at him and nodded, but not even for him could she raise a smile. It felt as if her heart was being torn from her body, and in her mind she blamed the man who rode ahead of them for causing her such terrible pain. It was he who had taken her from her home, he who had forced her to part from her beloved Melise, for had he waited another week or so the old nurse might have been able to withstand the journey.

Elona had a growing determination to thwart those who would marry her off to a man she had never seen, and began to think of ways to escape her fate. And then Stefan turned his head to look at her and a shiver went down her spine. She would swear that those chilling eyes could see her into her soul! Something told her that he suspected what was in her mind, though how he could have guessed she had no idea. Yet his manner warned her to be wary of him.

He had been given the charge of delivering her safely to her kinswoman and he was not the kind of man who would be easily denied. She would have to be very careful that he did not guess what was in her mind.

It was clear that the young squire was devoted to his lady, Stefan thought, watching as Will de Grenville stood talking with Elona after helping her dismount. It was his duty to assist her, of course, but he took every opportunity of touching her, and his eyes followed her like an adoring puppy. Did the foolish young man have dreams of wedding her? It was impossible—he was too far beneath her in rank and the wedding would never be permitted.

Stefan looked about him. They had made camp for the night and the servants were busy preparing the tents and pavilions for their comfort. He had ordered that his own tent should be close to Elona's so that he could keep an eye on her. He did not trust the wench, for she had a temper and a stubborn way with her. He had attempted to reach an understanding with her on two occasions before they left her father's house, but she had given him one of her haughty stares and taken refuge in her dignity, something that made him think her father might have done better to take a strap to her when she was younger.

Noticing the animation in her look as Elona spoke to the young man, Stefan wondered what was in her mind. He had caught a snatch of her conversation with the old nurse before they left her father's manor and had been disturbed by it. Had she been lying to comfort Melise—or was she truly planning to return to her father's house?

Yet if she was against the marriage, why had she not spoken out long before this? The Lord de Barre was not an unkind man and when he and Stefan had spoken together he had seemed to care only for his daughter's future.

'She must not fall into Danewold's hands,' John de Barre had warned. 'She would fare ill as his wife, for he cares only for wealth and advancement. My poor daughter needs someone who will love and protect her. Is your brother such a man, Sir Stefan? I have heard good of your father, and the world knows of your deeds, but little is said of your brother.'

'Alain is a good brave man,' Stefan said. 'He has not yet been knighted, though the King would have done it at the tourney last summer, when he stood as Henry's champion. My brother asked that he might earn it in battle or some brave deed, but as yet there has been little opportunity. However, should he be ready to take a wife, I have no doubt that my father will arrange for Alain to receive his spurs.'

'Is he capable of protecting her?' the anxious father asked. 'There are others who would treat her kindly, some who truly love her—but you know that a man must be strong to protect his lands and his lady. Is your brother such a man?'

'My brother is untried in battle, though a victor in the tourney many times. Yet I believe there is strength in him…'

Stefan had not added that he thought his brother sensitive, perhaps too gentle and good a knight for the proud beauty Elona of Barre. She needed another kind of man to tame her!

At that point Stefan had realised where his thoughts were leading him and checked them instantly. She was one of the most beautiful women he had ever seen, and something in the way she looked at him stirred him in a way no other had—but she was not for him. Any feelings he might have for the proud beauty must be crushed ruthlessly. She was destined to be his brother's bride and in all honour he must deliver her safely and untouched to Banewulf. To have lustful thoughts of her would be to betray the code of honour by which he lived.

Perhaps it was because he found her more attractive than he cared to admit that Stefan had withdrawn into himself even more. Far better that she should dislike him than that he should be tempted to betray a sacred trust! Yet there were moments when he had felt…but that was mere lust. Any red-blooded man might feel as he had for a woman as lovely as she.

It would be a matter of a few weeks before they reached Banewulf. He would be a poor excuse for a man if he could not control his baser instincts for that long!

He would allow no woman to make him betray his honour. Even one as beautiful as Elona de Barre.

'I tell you, I do not trust him,' Elona said in a soft voice that was not meant to carry. They must be constantly on their guard that they were not overheard. 'The way he looks at me…watches me…' Indeed, every time she turned around his eyes seemed to follow her.

'Sir Stefan is a man of honour,' Will said, for he had mixed with the English knight's men and heard stories that gave him nothing but admiration for him. 'I believe that he means only to protect you, my lady.'

'He does not like me. I feel his hostility—his suspicion. I have tried to break down the barrier, Will, believe me. I thought to discover what manner of man his brother might be, but he says little of anything. Trying to learn anything from that man is like drawing blood from a stone!'

'They say Alain de Banewulf is very different to his brother—a merry man who smiles and dresses in the manner of the court. Yet he has also won the tourney on several occasions and they say that only his brother can best him in a wrestling match. But then, there are few men who could beat Sir Stefan in that sport. He has the strength of ten men, so they say.'

'He is a great bear and I hate him,' Elona said passionately. 'He knows all of fighting and war, and nothing of kindness or love. You must help me escape from him, Will.'

'Are you sure?' Will's heart raced and his eyes leaped with excitement. He wanted her for his wife and yet he was afraid that she might regret his lowly status. 'Do you not think it might be better to visit Banewulf first? You need not agree to a marriage and within a few months I may earn my knight-hood—then I could claim you in all honour.'

'You have changed your tune,' Elona cried with a flash of temper in her eyes. 'Only a few days ago you begged me to fly with you.'

'I have not changed my mind. I merely wondered if it might be better if I sought service with Duke Richard for a while. In his service I might quickly earn my honours…' Honours that had been denied him in the service of John de Barre.

'But if you seek service with Duke Richard…' Elona frowned. He could not take service with another lord for a few months and then return to her father. 'But that would mean we might have to—' She broke off as she saw Stefan striding towards them. As usual he was frowning and a shiver of fear ran down her spine. 'Hush, Will,' she said as he began to speak. 'We will talk of this further another time. Leave me now. I would speak to Sir Stefan alone.'

'Your pavilion is prepared,' Stefan said to her, his face as expressionless as his tone. 'Your maids await you. I dare say you would like to refresh yourself before we eat.'

Elona looked at him, her thick lashes flicking down an in-stant later to veil her eyes. Was he suggesting that she join him for their evening meal? She saw that the two largest tents had been erected side by side—one of them hers, she presumed. Clearly one of them belonged to Stefan de Banewulf. Was it his intention to stay close to her so that he could watch over her, prevent her from escaping?

'I shall require only a light meal in my pavilion,' she told him icily. 'I am tired and would be alone, sir.'

'As you wish,' he said, his look of disapproval deepening. 'I must warn you not to wander abroad after dark, lady. My men have strict instructions to keep a close guard over the camp and anyone found wandering would be dealt with severely. I would not care for you to receive rough handling by mistake.'

'I think your men know me well enough, sir!' Head up, she challenged him.

'Have you not heard the saying that all cats look alike in the dark?' Stefan's white teeth gleamed in the dusk as he grinned suddenly. 'Some enemies are cunning and send women to do their spying for them—nor would I have you mistaken for a camp follower. You might find that embarrassing, if not worse, my lady.'

Elona's cheeks flushed dark red. 'You dare to insult me, sir? You would not have done so in my father's house!'

'I meant only to save you from insult,' Stefan said and there was a hint of amusement in his eyes. 'Men sometimes drink of an evening if they are not on duty and the blood heats—I would not have you offered insult by any of my men. Besides, there can be no reason for you to leave your pavilion after dark—can there?'

'No, of course not,' Elona snapped. Could he read her mind? She had hoped to slip away with Will while his men slept, but it seemed that there would always be someone to guard them. 'So you might have saved your breath.'

She swept past him, her shoulders straight and proud, but inside her heart was hammering wildly against her ribs. There had been something different in the way he looked at her for a moment, something that had frightened her. Had he guessed that she was considering a plan to escape his escort and return to her home?

Surely he could not know? She had been uncertain of her feelings at first; even now she had her doubts as to the wisdom of putting herself in Will's care. She knew he was devoted to her—but Sir Stefan's words had brought home to her how vulnerable she was in this world dominated by men. He himself was reputed to be a man of honour, a man who fought bravely and yet showed mercy when it was possible—but there were others who did not live by the rules of honour that governed a true knight's life. The laws of chivalry that decreed a lady must always be treated with courtesy and respect, the laws that governed a man's honour demanding that he cling to that above all else, did not apply equally to all those who called themselves knights. Baron Danewold was one of those—and Elona knew that she would rather die than be his bride.

Once again she was torn with indecision as she went into her tent and allowed her women to come to her. She sat on the stool provided while they unbraided her hair, brushing it until it shone as it fell about her shoulders in silken tresses.

'They say that Alain de Banewulf is very handsome,' Julia said and giggled as she assisted her mistress from the gown she had worn all day, replacing it with the softest silk nightrail. 'He sings like a nightingale and his hair is the colour of ripe corn, his eyes like a summer sky.'

'Where have you heard that, Julia?'

'Oh…from one of Sir Stefan's men,' the handmaiden said with a faint blush. 'He spent some time at Banewulf and he says it is a fine house.'

'But Banewulf belongs to Sir Ralph and will belong to his eldest son one day,' Elona said, looking thoughtful. 'Alain is merely a second son, though I believe he inherits his mother's lands in France, which are quite considerable.'

'But Sir Stefan is the wealthier of the two,' Bethany pointed out as she removed the fine leather riding boots from Elona's feet and then brought her scented water in a silver basin to wash her face and hands. 'He is such a fine, handsome man— so strong and brave. I think he would make a worthy husband for you, my lady.'

'Do not even think it!' Elona cried and looked horrified. 'I would as soon wed Baron Danewold as that cold fish! Besides, I do not think him handsome.'

'Sir Stefan is not cold,' Bethany said with a little smile at the corners of her mouth. 'He may not have the pretty looks of some men, but he is attractive. He has such noble bearing and when he smiles his face is altered. You have only to see the way he looks at you, my lady, to know that there is fire beneath the ice.'

'May God have mercy!' Elona said and crossed herself. 'I would cut off my hair and cover myself in sackcloth if I thought he looked at me with desire. No, no, Bethany, you are quite wrong. Sir Stefan despises and distrusts me.'

'I wish he might look at me the way he does at you sometimes,' Bethany insisted, but was quietened by a look from her mistress. 'Forgive me, it was merely a jest.'

'Then think before you make another such,' Elona said.

The last thing she wanted was for Sir Stefan to look at her with lust—and yet there had been something different in his eyes earlier. She had noticed it herself. He could not secretly desire her? No, no, it was unthinkable! Elona thrust the idea from her mind.

Her serving woman was foolish, as was the way of such girls; they thought of little else but handsome knights and love, their heads filled with tales of courtly love and the legends of Queen Eleanor's Court of Love, which had begun the tradition.

It was pleasant enough to pass a winter's night with such stories of daring feats performed in the name of love, but Elona knew only too well that love was seldom found within marriage. Marriage was something arranged between powerful men for their advantage, women merely the pawns they moved at will. Even her father had not consulted her wishes, though she knew he had been thinking to protect her from a worse evil. Yet, had he once asked her what she wanted, she might have been safe at home and married to Will.

Was there a tiny voice in her head that told her she did not truly wish to be Will de Grenville's wife? If there were, she would not listen to its prompting.

'Will my lady eat something?' Bethany brought her a dish of fruits, setting it by her as she retired to recline upon her couch. 'A cup of wine to help ease the strains of the day?'

'Yes, thank you,' Elona said and smiled to show that she was not angry with the girl. It was not Bethany's fault that she was so sorely troubled in her mind. Oh, why had her father not seen fit to arrange for Will to be knighted long ago?

Yet even if that honour were his, was he truly the man she had dreamed of marrying as young girls will?

Smiling inwardly at her foolishness, Elona sipped her wine and bit into a large ripe plum, the juice running down her chin until she wiped it away with a kerchief. Julia was playing a lyre and singing a song of love, and Elona closed her eyes, letting the softness of the melody lull her to sleep.

She was tired after riding so far, for Sir Stefan had not let them rest for more than half an hour during the day. What a tyrant he was, she thought with her last waking moment, drifting towards sleep as Julia's song came to an end.

The women prepared their own pallets on the ground at the foot of her couch. Outside the campfires were still burning brightly, men taking it in turns to patrol the boundaries, ever watchful for sudden attack. They were a large party and would not meet with attack from the bands of beggars that roamed the forests, nor would wolves dare to approach the camp. However, there were others who might know of the prize they guarded and seek to snatch it from beneath their noses, and their lord had bid them to be vigilant.

Dare she try to slip away now? Elona pondered the thought. Some of Sir Stefan's men would be watching her tent, but she could crawl underneath the back and find Will. She knew that he would be sleeping somewhere near the horses. They could take their horses and go while most of the camp slept.

No, perhaps not this night, she thought. It would be best to alert Will to be ready. She would go tomorrow night… Surely if she returned home and threw herself on her father's mercy, all would be well? He might be angry at first, but if she told him she could not bear to leave him he would understand—wouldn't he?

Within his own tent, Stefan ate and drank sparingly of the food offered him, his brow creased as he thought about the

Lady Elona. It was clear that she disliked him. He had had sufficient time to observe her with her women and with the young squires who served her. She had smiles enough and warm words for them, though none quite as warm as she gave to Will de Grenville.

Was he wrong in thinking they were plotting to elope together? Stefan had seen the young squire kissing her the day he arrived at her home, and since then he had noticed them whispering together on more than one occasion. Did the foolish young man believe that if he gained her as a wife he would gain all that belonged to her father?

Not if Stefan was any judge of men! Lord de Barre would not stomach such a marriage; he would prefer to hand over his lands to Duke Richard and live as his dependent than see his daughter the wife of a man he would consider beneath her.

Curious about the relationship, Stefan had mentioned the question of Will de Grenville's knighthood and been told more of the young man's history.

'Will is brave enough,' John de Barre had confided to him. 'His mother was a girl of good family—a kinswoman of mine—but she was deflowered by a rogue and her father married her to a man beneath her in rank so that her child would have a name. William must earn his honours in battle if he will have them, for I cannot in all conscience seek them for him.'

'Does he know the truth of his birth?'

'No—nor any in my household,' the Lord de Barre replied. 'I am aware that there is a fondness between Elona and the young man and, had he not been the bastard of a baseborn rogue, I might have looked kindly on the match, but he has bad blood and I will not see him wed to my daughter. That is why I wrote to Lady Alayne. It will be better if Elona lives away from her home until she weds. Here she has no chance to make a good marriage and I am too ill to take her to court. In England she will find contentment.'

It was clear to Stefan that he must prevent any elopement with the young squire. John de Barre would not thank him if he saved her from Danewold only to allow her to fall into the hands of a man who was too far beneath her in rank.

Besides, she was all but betrothed to Stefan's brother and he must see she reached her destination safely. At first he had thought that she and the squire might have been lovers, but he had changed his mind. She was proud and haughty, it was true, but there was something innocent and untouched about her. Will de Grenville looked at her with love mixed with respect, but none of the intimacy that lovers were apt to show to one another. He had been wrong to suspect her of betraying her modesty.

No, she was still pure at the moment, and he must make certain she remained that way until her wedding day. Which meant that he must ignore this burning in his groin that told him he desired her—and desired her with an intensity he had seldom known before. Nay, if he were truthful he had never felt quite this way for any other woman.

It must be because she treated him with disdain. Women had been only too eager for his attentions in the past. He had matured early, bedding his first wench as an untried youth in the hayloft of Banewulf; there had been others since, of course, some of them sophisticated, beautiful women from the court at Aquitaine. Far fewer than there might have been had he wished it, especially of late. His last entanglement with the scheming Isobel de Montaine, wife of Lord Alfredo Montaine, had soured his taste for women who were too eager for his loving.

He recalled the poisoned words Isobel had dripped into his ear as she lay panting with lust beside him on their silken couch. She had begged him to rid her of her husband, who she said bored her and could not satisfy her lusts, offering to share her wealth with him.

He paced the floor of his pavilion, his mind tormented with thoughts that had ceased to trouble him long since. Why was he thinking of Isobel? She was not worth a moment's discomfort on his part.

Stefan had recoiled in horror at her suggestion that he might kill her husband in the joust, almost throwing her from the bed so that she lay on the floor, looking at him venomously as he told her he did not bed with serpents.

'You are a fool,' she had cried, hatred replacing the languishing looks she had been used to bestow on him. 'One day you will meet your match, Stefan de Banewulf. No woman can touch your heart—did you know that is what they say of you? They call you a true knight, a knight of honour, but I think you are afraid to love—afraid to take what is yours by right. With me by your side you might have been one of the most powerful knights in Christendom—but one day you will reap your just deserts. One day a woman will prick at you with thorns you cannot tear out and then you will know what it is like to suffer rejection.'

'Indeed, it may happen, Isobel,' Stefan had replied, his eyes slaying her with his disgust. 'But if I suffer for love it will not be for you.'

No, it would not be for Isobel!

She had vowed to have her revenge one day, but he had merely smiled. He smiled now as he set down a wine cup from which he had drunk but a few sips. How delighted Isobel would be if she could guess that her prophecy was beginning to come true—that he was burning up with desire for a woman that could never be his.

He would never feel the thorns of despair because of Isobel, but he might for want of another. Cursing, Stefan dismissed his fevered thoughts. He was a fool! Elona de Barre was not for him and the sooner he accepted that the better.

Chapter Three

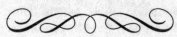

'Are you sure that you want to risk it?' Will looked at her uneasily. 'I do not believe Sir Stefan would take kindly to being made a fool of by any woman, my lady.'

'He will not know,' Elona said. 'Last night he invited me to dine with him and I refused. Tonight I shall invite him to my tent for supper and ply him with strong wine. I shall drink only sparingly, and when he leaves I shall slip out under the back of my tent and join you. You must somehow have our horses ready.'

'But what of your women?'

'Oh, they may follow us when it is learned that I have fled,' Elona said with a frown. 'It is my only chance, Will, for if we go now we shall soon be at my father's manor.'

'I do not think the Lord de Barre will be pleased with us.'

'He will understand when I tell him that it was breaking my heart to leave him, and that I want to stay at home and marry you.'

'Supposing Sir Stefan pursues us?'

'Why should he? He is in a hurry to take his message to

the English King. He will shrug his shoulders and forget me—why should he bother to come after me?'

Will looked at her doubtfully. He did not think that she would find it as easy to slip away from the camp as she imagined, but he was too much in love with her to refuse.

'I shall wait until you come,' he promised. 'But be careful, my lady.'

'I shall make certain the English knight sleeps well,' she said, a scornful smile on her mouth. 'Once he has drunk deeply of my wine, he will not lie awake watching for me.'

Stefan's eyes narrowed as he saw the smile of welcome on the lady's face and heard her invitation to sup with her that night. Her sudden change of attitude made him suspicious and something in the manner of Will de Grenville had put him on his guard. The young squire had seemed edgy and ill at ease when he had spoken to him only moments earlier.

Now what was the foolish wench plotting? Well, for the moment he would go along with her.

'You are gracious, lady,' he said and inclined his head. 'I shall look forward to dining with you.'

'And I with you, sir.'

She was definitely up to something!

Stefan dressed in the best tunic and hose he carried with him, donning a dark blue gown over all so that his appearance would do justice to the occasion. He had slipped away to the stream to bathe in the icy water, as was his custom whenever the chance occurred, and he knew that Elona's women had carried water to her tent so that she might cleanse herself of the day's dust.

She was wearing a gown and overmantle of blue and gold,

which she had worn on the evening before their departure from her home, and which he believed was her best. He had noticed that her clothes were of good quality cloth, but she did not seem to have as many as he might have expected a lady of her status to possess. It was a little strange since he knew her to be the heiress to a considerable fortune, and had thought her the Lord de Barre's spoiled daughter.

He must learn more of her circumstances, Stefan decided.

He took a seat on the padded stool provided for his comfort as her serving wenches began to bring food and wine. As was his habit, Stefan ate and drank sparingly. The wine was a good red burgundy, which had been supplied by Elona's father for their journey, but which he found a little strong for his taste. He would normally have taken it with water, but did not ask for it to be changed, merely sipping at it before setting the cup down.

Elona smiled at him winningly. 'Will you not have more wine, sir? Is it not to your taste? Would you prefer ale?'

'I do not drink wine to excess,' Stefan told her. 'I see that you do not drink much either. Do you not like your father's wine?'

'It is well enough,' she answered, seeming annoyed by his answer. 'But more to a man's taste, I think?'

'Perhaps,' he said and smiled oddly. 'If you are hoping I shall become intoxicated and forget to order a watch tonight, you are mistaken, my lady. And if I should it would avail you nothing. The men who guard you do not drink while they perform their duty; it is a rule we live by, for it has kept us safe in many a battle. You would need to drug their food if you wished to be sure of slipping away—and your foolish squire has been warned not to try stealing horses if he wishes to spare himself a birching.'

'How dare you threaten me or my squire!' Elona said and leapt to her feet. 'I am not your prisoner and if I wish to return to my home I shall. You cannot prevent me.'

'Oh, I believe that you will discover I can do much as I will with you,' Stefan said, rising to his feet more slowly. He smiled inwardly as she flung herself at him in a rage, attempting to strike him with her fists. He caught her wrists as she struggled helplessly, his grip such that she had no chance against him. 'However, my intentions towards you are entirely honourable, lady. Were it otherwise, I might show you another side of my nature.' The gleam in his eyes made her breath catch in her throat. What did he mean? She took refuge in haughty disdain.

'I hate you! You are nothing but a rough soldier.'

'Indeed, you speak truly, mistress.' Stefan laughed and let go of her wrists. His smile died as she rubbed at them, and winced. 'Forgive me if I hurt you. I am not always aware of my own strength.'

'It is nothing, but you are a brute,' she snapped. 'What difference could it make to you if I went home? Why should you care what becomes of me?'

'In truth, I care nothing for you, lady, but I have given my word to escort you to the Lady Alayne,' he said, answering like with like. 'Your father asked me to take care of you, and whether you approve of me or not, that is exactly what I intend to do.'

'Stay!' she cried as he turned towards the entrance to her pavilion. 'You have not punished Will? It was not his idea.'

'I know well where the idea came from. I give Master de Grenville credit for having more sense,' he said and grinned at her, revealing a side of him she had not seen previously. 'I fear you will have to do better than this if you wish to escape me, my lady. And now I wish you sweet dreams. Do not stay awake all night, Elona, we have a long journey ahead of us, and I would not have you wear yourself out with worrying about something that may not be changed.'

'Get out of here!' Elona cried, and seizing a pillow from her couch, threw it at him. 'I hate you! You are an arrogant, self-satisfied bear and I wish I had never seen you!'

She heard him laugh as he went out and gave a little scream of frustration. How could he have known what was in her mind? Was she so easy to read?

Oh, damn him, damn him! She would like to tear his eyes out and feed him to the hunting dogs alive…at least the thought was comforting, though she doubted she had the stomach to do it. But he was so arrogant and she felt helpless.

Surely there must be some way to escape from him?

They were nearing the coast, having ridden at what seemed to Elona to be a furious pace. At times she had thought that her escort's haste was because he could not wait to complete his task and be rid of her. However, when she complained to Will, he told her that it was because some of Baron Dane-wold's men had been seen following them, and that one of them had been taken prisoner.

'He was spying on us?' Elona felt cold all at once. Until this moment she had believed that the Baron would accept his dismissal with a good grace. 'Why would the Baron do that, Will? Surely he must know there is no chance of a marriage between us? My father was clear in his rejection of the offer.'

'He believes that your father would relent if…' Will hesitated, a faint flush in his face, for it was not fitting to speak of such things to a lady of gentle birth—a lady he knew to be innocent.

'You mean if he abducted and then deflowered me?' Elona was not so innocent that she did not understand the perils that could befall an unprotected maiden. Although sheltered and protected by her family, she knew what had happened to unfortunate village maidens, for she and her stepmother had helped them when they could. 'But surely he would not dare to attack Sir Stefan's men?'

'Not while he keeps such a close guard over you,' Will admitted with reluctant admiration. 'His men watch over you all night long. It would be difficult to infiltrate the camp—at least this side of the English sea. In England he may relax his guard, though the Baron has lands there as well as here.'

Elona was aware of her perilous situation in a way that she had not been before. If the Baron was determined to have her at all costs…it did not bear thinking of! 'What are you saying to me, Will?'

She had thought long and hard these past days for she felt it would be best to escape sooner rather than later if she meant to do it, but she knew Will was right. She was constantly observed, though not intrusively, but enough for her to realise that if she tried to slip away she would be seen and questioned. Sir Stefan guarded her so closely that it would be impossible for her to run off with her young squire without being challenged. And since her attempt to get him drunk had failed, she had not been able to think of a way to fool him.

'I do not believe it is possible for us to escape, my lady,' Will said as if to confirm her fears. 'We are both watched, and I was warned not to attempt to steal the horses. I would give my life to serve you, but alone I have no hope of winning a fight for you.'

'So you are giving up all hope of me?' There was disappointment and anger in her lovely face, though it was unfair to blame him when she had been unable to think of a way to escape herself. And now that she realised how dangerous such a venture might prove, it had lost some of its appeal. For the two of them riding alone might easily fall prey to the Baron's men. Yet in her frustration she blamed the squire for what she knew was no fault of his. 'I had thought more of you, Will. But it seems that you do not care for me at all.' She was close to tears as she faced the truth that her plans had always been merely a foolish girl's fancy.

They were strolling beneath the shade of some trees. Stefan had been forced to halt their progress for long enough for his men to make repairs to one of the baggage wagons, which had broken a leading pole soon after they set out that morning. It was not the first time a small accident had caused them delay, and Elona knew that her stern guardian would make up the time lost if he could.

'You know that I adore you,' Will cried, stung by the hint of scorn in her voice. 'I do not give up so easily, Elona, but perhaps there may be more chance when we get to England—perhaps to Banewulf itself. They may not guard you so strictly there. Why should they? They will not be expecting you to try to run away…'

Elona nodded but made no answer. She was being unfair and she knew it, but her spirit rebelled at being so closely confined. Why should they not take their chance now? They were at the edge of the camp. If they were to disappear into the woods this very minute…but Sir Stefan was watching them, his eyes hooded and veiled with thick dark lashes.

He had the eyes of a hawk, she thought angrily. As keen

as any bird of prey—and she was his victim. One unwary move on her part and he would swoop on her and then… She did not know why the thought of Stefan swooping on her like a hawk on its prey was so disturbing, but it made her breathless all of a sudden, her heart racing. Anger swelled like a rising tide inside her as she walked towards him, head up, shoulders straight, every inch the proud lady. Clearly she could look for no help from Will. He seemed to have fallen under Sir Stefan's spell as deeply as her foolish serving women! So she would vent her frustration on the man who was the cause of all her troubles.

'How long before we reach the coast?' she demanded imperiously.

'It was my hope to reach the ship and board her before dusk.'

'I am pleased to hear it. I grow weary of this journey.'

'I am sorry it has taken so long, my lady. But I had not thought you in such a hurry?'

'The sooner we reach our destination, the sooner I may be free of your company!'

'Ah, I see…'

Stefan's eyes narrowed. Now what was she up to? Had she some new plan to deceive him? It had not escaped his notice that she had seemed displeased with her squire. A faint smile touched his mouth. It seemed his precautions against Danewold were a two-edged sword, proving as effective at keeping the lady and her admirer inside the camp as Danewold's men out.

The spy they had caught had talked readily when given the alternative of having his tongue split if he did not. Such barbarity was against Stefan's principles as a Christian knight, but the threat had been sufficient, reducing the man to a gibbering fool ready to betray his own mother if need be.

Danewold's men were under orders to watch and follow, nothing more. Clearly the Baron was too wise to risk an all-out fight with men trained and battle hardened as Stefan's men were. Yet Danewold was like a dangerous snake hiding in the undergrowth, waiting his opportunity to strike the unwary. He would snatch Elona from under their noses by stealth if he could—but he would not get the chance. Nor would she take flight with the young squire if Stefan could prevent it.

'This delay is tedious,' Elona complained, irked by his silent brooding look into further speech. His mind was a closed book to her. She never knew what he was thinking. 'Why do your men not take better care of the wagons?'

'Accidents will happen,' Stefan replied, but knew it was not the whole truth. One of his men had told him that he believed the pole had been deliberately weakened.

Perhaps Danewold had hoped to catch them at a disadvantage? If so, he had been sadly disappointed. Yet Stefan suspected another culprit. William de Grenville had had more opportunity to cause such accidents than Danewold's men. But what purpose did he hope to achieve by these small delays? No serious harm was ever done, no man or beast injured; they were at worst a delaying tactic—but why?

There seemed no reason for them. Unless they were meant to give Danewold a chance to prepare a trap on the road ahead?

Stefan had sent two men on ahead to scout and warn him of any such plot, but so far there had been none. Danewold seemed content to bide his time, more like a scavenger waiting for the remains of prey left by a ravening wolf rather than a predator himself. Stefan's reputation as a fearsome warrior was enough to hold off all but the stoutest hearts.

So if it was not Danewold and not Will… All his own men

were loyal to him, he would swear to it. However, he would be extra-vigilant in future. The small mystery would be solved in time.

'How many days shall we be on the road once we reach England?'

Elona's question broke into his thoughts, causing his attention to centre on her once more. She was in a rare mood, clearly frustrated and choosing him as her whipping boy. Well, his shoulders were broad enough, and she was magnificent when she was angry. Gazing at her lovely face, he was seized with a desire to take her in his arms and kiss away the hurt and frustration he knew to be inside her—but that was forbidden him.

'Three before we reach Henry's court,' Stefan told her. 'We shall rest there for a few days. As you know, I have a message for the King from Duke Richard. Besides, I thought it might please you to visit the court, lady. Your father said you might want to order some silks from the merchants in London.'

'Perhaps…'

It would please her very much to visit both the court and the silk merchants, Elona thought. But why should *he* want to please her? His usual expression was so cold and harsh when he looked at her…though she had seen him laughing with his men—and at her the night she had thought to get him drunk!—that she was certain he disliked her. Suddenly, her anger drained away and she felt close to despair, a small sigh escaping her.

'Are you very weary?' Stefan asked and the softer note in his voice made her heart jerk. 'Once we are on the ship you will be able to rest. I fear I have pushed you too hard in my haste?'

'No, I am not weary,' she replied. Did he think her such a poor thing? Her head lifted with unconscious pride, banishing the momentary despair. 'Merely sad. I am glad I did not bring my nurse. My poor Melise could not have stood the journey. It was for her sake that I left her behind.'

'Do you miss her very much?'

'Yes…' Elona choked as the unexpected gentleness in him brought a tide of emotion welling up, filling her throat so that it felt tight and painful. Her situation was easier to bear when she was angry with him. 'She loves me as much as any mother and I love her. I think it broke her heart that I was forced to leave her at my father's house.'

'There is no reason why you should not send for her once you are settled at Banewulf. She could travel with a small escort at her own pace. I dare say it might be easier for her if she were carried in a wagon with a straw pallet to lie on and a young woman to care for her needs.'

Now the tears were very close. Elona was almost overcome. 'You show an unexpected concern, sir. I did not think you understood my feelings on the matter.'

'You thought me an unfeeling tyrant, I dare swear.' Stefan laughed deep in his throat. It was a strangely pleasing sound, husky and warm. 'Well, you are not entirely wrong, my lady. I can be impatient and harsh at times—but I have it in me to be generous. When we are safe on board the ship bound for England, a man shall return to your home and arrange for the old woman to be brought to you. It is an easy enough matter.'

'Thank you. You are generous indeed.' Elona turned away quickly, afraid that she would weep. Such a thoughtful act of kindness had unsettled her. Why had she not thought of the solution for herself?

She had been too angry with Sir Stefan, and, indeed, her father also. Besides, in her innocence, she had imagined it would be an easy matter to slip away with Will. How little she had understood the man who was to be her escort!

Wandering away from him, Elona realised that she still did not understand the man. He had seemed so stern and hard, but now he had offered her a precious gift. She had been told he was a brave, true knight, but she had not wanted to believe it. Now she began to see him as others must—and how weak and shallow some men appeared in comparison.

The scales of self-deception had begun to fall from her eyes and she realised that she had been fooling herself to believe that her father would ever countenance a marriage between William de Grenville and his daughter. In truth, when she looked deep into her heart, she did not really wish for it herself...

Then what did she wish for? Elona could not answer the questions her mind immediately threw up. When viewed calmly and sensibly, it seemed unlikely that she would be able to return home, at least until she was married and no longer at risk of abduction—but did she wish to marry Alain de Banewulf? From what she had heard of him from the crumbs gleaned by her women and from Stefan himself, it seemed that he was a pleasant young man, though untried and perhaps no more capable of commanding a garrison than her squire.

The knowledge that Baron Danewold had been shadowing them, that he was intent on snatching her from beneath Stefan's nose if he could, had somehow unsettled her. It seemed that women were always at the mercy of men, some more unscrupulous than others, and she was coming to the conclusion that her father had been right after all. Because of the rich lands she would inherit one day, she must either wed a man strong enough to hold them for her or enter a convent.

A life spent in fasting and prayer held no promise for her and, being a sensible girl at heart, Elona saw that she must make up her mind to marry. But the matter of her husband's identity was still to be resolved. Why should she let others choose for her—why not take her destiny into her own hands? No one could force her to marry against her will for her father had signed no contract.

But if she did not wish to wed Alain de Banewulf, or Will—who did she picture as a husband she could respect and admire? The man who would stand by her side, her equal in birth and wealth, her champion and trusted protector. Her eyes moved slowly over the men gathered about the clearing, noting that the wagon had been repaired and that they were almost ready to leave.

How disciplined the men were, she thought. She had reprimanded Sir Stefan for their carelessness, but in truth she knew that accidents must happen. These men were respectful and worked with a show of eagerness to please the man who commanded them. Her father was respected by his people—but they did not worship him as Sir Stefan's men did their lord.

Surely she was not thinking…? Elona pulled her thoughts together with a sense of shock. Only a few moments ago she had been hating him and now… But no, that was not quite true, she realised, a little smile curving her soft lips. She had resented his attitude, her feeling of being his prisoner, but she did not hate him. Indeed, she had come to respect him during these past days of their journey. In some strange way, she had enjoyed pitting her wits against his, taunting him to see the glint of anger in his eyes, and sometimes a smile that turned to laughter.

And now that he had shown her his softer side… After all, if she must marry for her safety, she would clearly do better to choose the strongest man she could find. And if rumour spoke true, there was none stronger or more respected than her escort.

How foolish she was! Elona laughed inwardly at her own thoughts. Sir Stefan…no, Stefan, for they had gone beyond formality…found her nothing but a nuisance. She had believed that he disliked her but, if that were true, why should he promise to bring Melise to her?

And there was an odd look in his eyes at times. Elona had thought it temper or some strong displeasure, but now she wondered if its cause was very different. Was it possible that he felt attracted to her? Not love, perhaps, for she did not see him as being a sentimental man—but certainly desire. Yes, he was certainly a man of strong passions, even if he kept them under strict control.

Yet he had given her no hint of his feelings and she doubted her own senses. Will had offered her a gentle tender love, though she sensed a deeper passion hidden beneath the surface—but, she imagined, Stefan's feelings would be fiercer, lustier. If he desired a woman, he would put his mark on her. His wife would belong to him, body and soul. Let Danewold and all others beware if she was his…

No, no, she was imagining things! Where were her wits? Bethany's foolish talk had turned her head. Stefan de Banewulf did not see her as a desirable woman; he was merely acting the part of her guardian, taking her to his home to be his brother's bride.

She turned as she heard his voice call her name.

'We are ready to leave, my lady. I hope that you are ready to continue?'

It was the first time he had asked rather than simply commanding. She smiled at him and for a moment fancied she saw fire leap in his eyes. He looked at her now as a man dying of hunger might look at a feast—a feast at a rich man's table that he might not taste. She could not be mistaken this time!

Romantic love might not be in this man's thoughts, Elona thought, but she certainly was. She was sure that Bethany was right—he did desire her. Yet even as she gazed up at him, her heart beginning to thud madly against her ribs, she saw the fire dim and he turned from her abruptly, barking an order at one of his men to bring her palfrey forward.

When he turned back to her, she saw that his face was wearing its usual look of icy reserve, but she was not deceived. She *had* seen that look and she was sure that she understood what was in his mind—an honourable man could not steal his brother's bride. Even if he wanted her, she was forbidden to him. But she had no such reservation. She was not promised to Alain de Banewulf, and if she had decided she would have Stefan instead of his brother… But had she?

'Will you help me mount, sir?' she asked, a husky note in her voice as her palfrey was made ready. 'Persimmon was a little restive this morning. If your man could hold her while you help me…?'

Stefan seemed to hesitate, then took two steps towards her. Instead of offering his hand for her to place her small foot in it, his hands seized her about the waist and he lifted her easily to the saddle with one flowing movement that left her breathless.

How strong he was and powerful! Perhaps not handsome in the way that Will was, and yet now she had begun to see that the squire was almost too pretty to be a man. Indeed, compared to Stefan, he was still a youth.

A faint flush touched her cheeks as Stefan remained by her side looking up at her, and she knew that he had been as affected by what had just passed between them as she. Yes, he did want to bed with her—but was she playing with fire? Was her wilful nature leading her towards something dangerous?

Stefan de Banewulf would be the master in any marriage. He would dominate and his wife would be expected to give all that he demanded. She knew that and her pulses quickened as she wondered what it might feel like to lie beside him…to feel the touch of his hands on other, more intimate parts of her body, his lips on hers.

'If your mount is restive, I will get one of my men to lead you on a rein,' he said, breaking into her thoughts and bringing her back to earth with a bump. All sign of his softer side had gone so that she thought she must have imagined it. He was glaring at her as if he hated her now.

Had he read her thoughts somehow? Had she given herself away—was that why he had withdrawn once more?

'I need no leading rein!' she retorted, angry now. 'Would you insult me, sir? I am perfectly able to manage my horse.'

'As we both know,' he said, an irritating gleam in his eyes. 'This new behaviour will avail you nothing, lady. If you think to blind me to your wiles, you are mistaken. I have given my word to deliver you safely to Banewulf and that is what I intend. You will be given no chance to run off with your squire.'

Elona gasped, feeling as if he had slapped her in the face. She flicked her reins and moved past him, wishing she dared to ride at him and knock him to the ground, to let her horse trample on him. What a fool she had been to imagine for one second that she could ever find content as this man's wife! He was an arrogant bully and she would think no more of him!

Oh, how she wished she might die! Would this torment never be done?

Elona rolled on to her side as another wave hit the ship full on and caused it to shudder; it seemed to lift into the air, hover, and then fall back down—so far that she felt her stomach lurch and the vomit rose in her throat once more. She leaned over her cot and vomited on the wooden floorboards, groaning as she felt pain in her stomach; she had vomited so much that it hurt her now to move.

'Ohhh,' she muttered miserably. 'What have I done that I should be punished thus?'

Her father had sought to protect her, but instead he had sent her to her death, for, if the storm did not soon abate, she feared she would never survive it. If this sickness did not kill her, the ship would surely sink!

She was aware of movement beside her and wondered which of her serving women had managed to stagger to her side, for both were similarly afflicted, though not as violently as she herself.

'Is that you, Bethany? Go and rest yourself. There is nothing you can do for me. I am dying…'

'I doubt that, Elona,' a strong, too-cheerful voice said at her side. 'You are suffering from sea sickness, but it will pass when we reach land.'

'If we ever do,' she muttered resentfully as she realised who had come to her. The ship rolled yet again and her stomach lurched. Would this terrible voyage never cease? 'Why are you here? Have you come to gloat over me?' How she hated him! Her annoyance was such that she was able to raise her head and look at him. He looked disgustingly fit and well. She might have known that he would not be affected by the weather. Nothing touched him. She closed her eyes again, sinking back with a groan.

'No, not to gloat—to give you something that may ease you, foolish one.' His hand was on her brow, soothing the damp hair back from her forehead and she found his touch comforting.

Elona opened her eyes as she felt his body close to hers, and then his strong arm was beneath her, lifting her clear of the cushions, holding a cup to her lips. She set them against him, sure now that he meant to poison her. In her distress she blamed him for her sickness.

'Leave me…' She made the mistake of trying to order him away from her and found that a vile-tasting potion was immediately poured down her throat, making her gag and spit. 'You beast!' she cried when she had stopped choking. 'Have you killed me with your poison?'

Stefan's laugh was warm and amused, coming from deep down inside him as he stood looking at her.

''Tis foul stuff, Elona,' he said. 'But it will stop you retching on an empty stomach. Try to sleep now and when you wake we shall be in England and this will seem but a bad dream.'

'Go away. I hate you! You did this on purpose.'

'I cannot order the storm or the wind,' Stefan said, laughter in his voice once more. 'I thank you for the thought, Elona, but you make me too powerful. Yet blame me if it eases you, for I can do no more to help you, my lady.'

Elona groaned and rolled on to her side, hiding her face in the pillows and cushions. Her stomach was still heaving, but it already felt calmer and there was not the urgent need to vomit every few seconds.

'I shall leave you to rest, lady,' Stefan said. 'But I wanted you to know that I have kept my promise and a man has been sent to fetch Melise.'

'Thank you, that was kind.' Elona was too wretched to lift her head and the words were muffled, but he heard them and smiled to himself as he went on deck.

He was not certain that she would be pleased with him when she discovered the identity of the man he had sent to fetch the old woman!

'You did what?' Elona stared at him in shocked disbelief. Oh, what a cunning fox he was! She saw it all now. What she had taken as kindness had been merely an excuse to get rid of her squire. 'You have more than thirty men to serve you and yet you sent my squire! That was not generous of you, sir. You knew that I relied on him for so much.'

Her hands curled at her sides and she itched to strike him. Only the knowledge that she might as well batter at a stone wall kept her from flailing at him with her fists.

'I hate you! I wish that I might have you at my mercy for only a minute and I would make you suffer.'

'I see that you are recovered from the effects of the storm,' Stefan said, but his eyes were not filled with laughter now. Their colour was darker than the stormy sea over which they had just passed, his mouth drawn into a thin line. 'I thought it a sensible precaution to make sure you could not do anything foolish. Will was happy to serve you, my lady. He knew how much it would mean to you to have Melise with you, and he agreed that she would feel safer with someone she knows to escort her.'

They were standing on the shore, having been rowed to land from the ship, which was sailing again for France that very afternoon. It was several degrees cooler than it had been before they left her homeland, and the breeze was swirling about her, plucking at her thick cloak. She suppressed a shiver, refusing to show any weakness.

'You did it to thwart me,' Elona challenged, eyes flashing with temper. 'You are determined that I shall be delivered to Banewulf and forced into a marriage I do not want! You are cruel and uncaring and—I wish that I had died in the storm.'

Stefan's eyes narrowed as he looked at her. 'I think no one has mentioned forcing you to marry Alain. Indeed, I know your kinswoman has it in mind to let the pair of you decide for yourselves.'

'And if we do not suit I shall be given to whoever asks, I suppose? And he may be older than my father! Why does no one care what I feel?'

Elona knew that she was being unreasonable, for there was no reason to accuse Lady Alayne of planning any such thing, and, besides, she knew that she must marry sooner or later. Had she not already decided that for herself?

'Perhaps none will ask,' Stefan replied a wry twist to his mouth. 'Many might prefer a bride with a gentler tongue, Elona. Some would not take a shrew to wife no matter how rich her father's lands.'

'A shrew!' Elona glared at him, her hands itching at her sides as she longed to administer the slap he so richly deserved, and yet as she saw the gleam in his eyes, she knew that he had deliberately provoked her. He was merely teasing her. How dare he? 'I hate you, Stefan de Banewulf.'

'As you told me last night, I seem to recall—and several times since. It is a shame that you were not taught more variety in your speech. Repetition loses its sting. I know that I am a mannerless oaf and a rough soldier—can you not do better? Last night you accused me of wanting to poison you—that at least had the merit of being original.'

'You…you!' She had the grace to blush as she recalled that his cure had eased her, giving her rest. 'I did not realise…I must thank you, sir. Your vile potion eased me.'

'I am glad I was able to help,' he told her, smiling despite her grudging manner. 'It is made from a herb given to me by an Arab physician while I was in the Holy Land.'

'You went there?' She was surprised for she had not known it.

'I visited a garrison of knights there just before I decided to return to England. Duke Richard wanted news of them and I offered to make the journey as a pilgrimage.'

'Oh…' Had he felt the need of spiritual comfort? Had he committed some terrible sin and gone to seek forgiveness?

Stefan saw the look in her eyes and laughed. 'No, Elona, I did not go there to repent of my wicked ways or in the hope of a miracle cure for some dread illness. I wanted to see for myself what it was that inspired the men who take up the Cross.'

'And did you?' She was genuinely interested despite herself.

'I saw dedicated men who fight for a cause they believe in,' Stefan said. 'But I did not feel the call to join them.'

He had been looking to find himself, but whatever it was he needed to fill the emptiness inside him, he had not found it in that austere gathering of knights.

Elona nodded, but made no comment. Was there no end to the surprising traits in this man's character? It seemed that she was learning something new of him every time they spoke, and, she admitted reluctantly, coming to respect him more with each passing day. Yet she could not quite forgive him for sending Will away; it made her more vulnerable, more reliant on him for all her needs.

'I have appointed a youth to take Will's place,' Stefan said and again it seemed almost as if he had read her thoughts. 'Dickon is a willing lad and good natured. He will serve you as faithfully as your own squire.'

'I believe I have seen him about the camp,' Elona said and nodded, feeling pleased by his choice. The youth could not be more than fifteen, but he was strong and seemed to take the jesting of his companions with a smile and a shrug of his broad shoulders. 'He is strong and tall for his age, I think?'

'Dickon is much as I was at his age,' Stefan replied with a wry twist of his lips. 'If I am fair to him, I shall send him to Duke Richard in another year or so in order that he may win honours for himself.'

'As my father should have done for Will de Grenville? I have oft thought it unkind in him to neglect poor Will for he hath given loyal service to my family.'

'Perhaps,' Stefan replied. He would not betray her father's confidence. 'Perhaps your father had his reasons, lady.'

'I thought it was because he needed all his men about him, especially after my brother was so foully killed.'

'Yes, I heard of that,' Stefan said and his mouth hardened. 'It was murder and the culprit should be brought to justice— if it could be proved.'

'But how could such a thing be proved? 'Twas done in secret and under cover of darkness. He was riding home when he was set upon, beaten and left to die alone.' A sob caught at her throat and suddenly the tears welled up and spilled over, for it was her brother's terrible death that had led to her banishment from her home. 'I loved him so…'

Stefan hesitated, but the sight of her in such distress was too much for him. He moved towards her, taking her into his arms, holding her tight as she sobbed out her grief. His lips were warm and soft against the fragrance of her hair.

'Sweet lady,' he murmured huskily, 'do not weep so. It grieves me to see you in such distress.'

'Does it?' Elona lifted her head to look up at him, her eyes wide with wonder as she saw the look of unmistakable tenderness in his own. 'I miss him…and my father.'

'You will find happiness again,' Stefan vowed and then, hardly knowing why he did it, he lowered his head, touching his lips to hers in the softest, sweetest kiss any maiden had ever received of him. 'My poor little one…'

The tenderness in his voice and the touch of his lips acted powerfully on Elona, and her arms surged up about his neck as she clung to him, returning his kiss with such eagerness that his hold tightened, and his kiss changed suddenly to one of hunger and desire. It was only as he felt her willing response, the way she melted into his body, seeming to surrender to him, that Stefan recalled his wandering thoughts and drew away from her. He was stung by remorse as he saw the swollen pink pout of her mouth, revealing the thoroughness with which she had been kissed, and the brightness of her eyes. Her cloak had come unfastened and had fallen open. Beneath the thin silk of her gown her breasts were taut, the nipples hard and pressing against the material in a way that told him of her arousal, which had matched his own.

In another place, at another time, they would have been swept away on the tide of passion that had mounted between them.

But he was at fault! He was a man and older; he ought to have known what might happen if he let down his guard.

'Forgive me,' he muttered gruffly. 'That was unpardonable. I had no right to force my attentions on you, Elona. I meant only to comfort you and was carried away.'

She had thought his kiss meant he loved her, and the cool reserve of his tone struck her like a douche of icy water. She had thrown herself at him and he was angry with her for making him drop his guard.

'No, no,' she faltered, a flush in her cheeks as she felt the sting of shame. 'It was merely a moment of madness, because I was weeping all over you like a foolish child.'

'Not foolish, Elona,' he replied stiffly. 'I am the one who should know better.' He saw some of his men gathered a short distance from where they stood and realised that the kiss had been noticed by more than one. There was much curiosity and some amusement, which was only to be expected. 'Damnation!'

'What is it, Stefan?'

'I was seen to kiss you,' he said. 'I must take care it does not happen again or my brother will believe that I have betrayed his trust by stealing his bride.' He raised his hand, summoning the youth he had told her of. 'Dickon—attend to your mistress. She is in some distress.'

The young lad came running and the other men turned back to their business, which was the unloading of goods and horses from the boats that had just landed on the beach.

'I have done my best to comfort the Lady Elona,' Stefan

said in a voice loud enough to carry. 'But I am a rough soldier and I do not know how to ease her hurts. I shall leave her in your charge, Dickon. I charge you take good care of her and respond to her as you would to me. Indeed, she is your mistress now. You are to obey her wishes in everything.'

Stefan walked away, leaving the youth to help Elona as best he could. He was aware of hidden smiles as he approached the small group of soldiers and knew that his impulsive behaviour had been noticed. All the more so since none of them would ever have seen him behave so tenderly towards a lady before.

His reputation for living almost as a monk had been exaggerated, but since he chose his women carefully and conducted his affairs in private, few would know of them. And there had been none since Isobel. Her scheming had so disgusted him that he had thought it impossible a woman should reach the inner core of him again, but he had been mistaken. Elona had touched him in a way that no other woman ever had, and he was afraid to look too closely at his own heart.

Elona de Barre was not for him. She of all women was forbidden, for she was all but betrothed to his brother. He must put his sinful thoughts of her away, forget the sweetness with which she had melted in his arms, offering herself in a way that had almost caused him to forget his honour. Had they been alone…but he must guard against that happening!

He was stung with remorse at the memory of his behaviour. Had he prevented her from eloping with her squire only to seduce her himself? How could he have betrayed himself by giving into temptation, even if only briefly?

It must not happen again!

He did not look back at her as she talked to the young

squire. Somehow he must conquer this lust that had come upon him since the first moment of seeing her!

'You are sad, lady,' Dickon said as he saw the way her eyes followed Stefan. 'May I do anything to comfort you? I could play my lute or sing for you an' it pleases you.'

'Thank you, Dickon, but I shall be better in a moment. I was thinking of my brother and my father—and of my home, which I may never see again.'

'It always hurts to lose those you love,' Dickon agreed, his smile soft and understanding as he saw her expression and guessed what she would not say. 'My father sent me away from home when I was but five, and I served the Duke until I was eleven, when he gave me to Sir Stefan.'

'Oh, you poor thing,' Elona said, forgetting her own worries as she looked at him in sympathy. 'How could they treat you like that—as if you were a mere possession?'

'I was, my lady,' Dickon replied, but seemed untroubled by the fact of his servitude. 'My father was poor and he sold me into the Duke's service. But when Sir Stefan received me as a gift he set me free. I am a freeman now and may seek service where I please—though I would never leave my lord.'

'Would you not leave him even to win honours in the Duke's service?'

'Not unless my lord bid me to it,' Dickon said. 'It is my pleasure and my duty in life to serve Sir Stefan—and now you, lady, since he asks it of me.'

'I am pleased to have you serve me, Dickon,' Elona said and smiled at him. He reminded her of her brother when he was of the same age and gladdened her heart. 'But I shall not forget that you are your own man and may leave me if I displease you.'

'I do not believe that any man would willingly leave you, my lady,' Dickon replied sincerely, bringing a faint flush to her cheeks. 'I hope that I shall serve you well, now—and in the future.'

Elona nodded, but she wondered a little at the look in his eyes. He was one of those who had observed that kiss…the kiss that had set her whole body aflame with a strange sweet sensation that she had never felt before, and that she realised must be desire. It was the overwhelming power of that new sensation that had made her cling so wantonly to Stefan. Little wonder that he had turned from her in disgust. And yet he had wanted her; she had felt it, sensed it as he held her. But perhaps it was not fitting for a lady to show her feelings so openly. She ought to have pretended to a maidenly reserve.

Dickon clearly believed that she was destined to be in his lord's life for more than the short time that it would take to deliver her to Banewulf. But Stefan seemed determined that she was promised to his brother. Had the betrothal been signed and sealed it could not have been broken, of course, for it was almost as sacrosanct as a marriage ceremony, but there had been no vows taken, no marks made on parchment and sealed to hold her to her promise.

Stefan was at times the most infuriating man—cold and harsh when he chose—and yet he could be so thoughtful, so tender. There was something in him at times that made her think they were more alike than they yet guessed, as if there was an inner thread that bound them whether they willed it or not. His kiss had awakened the sleeping woman inside her, stealing something from her that could never be returned, for it was her love, and once given she could not take it back.

She would have no other to husband, Elona decided. She

was not promised to Alain de Banewulf and she was certain from what she had heard of him that he would not suit her. No, it was Stefan she wanted—Stefan she loved, though foolishly, for she was sure her love was not returned. What he felt for her was the lust of a red-blooded man for a woman he found attractive, nothing more.

But she would have him or no one, she thought, and a little smile curved her mouth as she began to wonder how best to make sure that he desired her to the point where his need overcame his reserve.

'Tell me more about your lord, Dickon,' she said. 'Is he a good man to serve?'

'Oh, yes, my lady,' the youth said and a grin split his face. He pushed back his long, sandy hair as he helped her to mount her palfrey and stood looking up at her, holding the reins until her horse settled. 'There is none better despite his frowns and his stern manner. It will be my pleasure to tell you all you need to know…'

The look he gave her was clearly conspiratorial and Elona knew that he had guessed her secret. She had no fear that he would betray her, for he was obviously on her side.

'Then you may ride beside me,' she said. 'For I would learn as much of your lord as you can tell me.'

Chapter Four

Stefan had taken a house for them within the city walls, but Elona was dismayed when she saw how small it was. Just the kitchens and a small hall below and three chambers above that, put together, were hardly the size of her bedchamber at home.

'I do not believe that this will accommodate us all,' she said, feeling puzzled. Surely he could not expect her to stay here? 'Are there no larger houses to be hired in London?'

'None to be had for love or money,' Stefan said with a rueful expression. 'The city is full to bursting, for the King has summoned his knights to a tourney and their ladies oftimes come with them. It is a holiday, a time of celebration. Fear not, Elona. The house is for you and your servants. Four of my men will sleep on the floor downstairs to guard you, but the upper chambers are for your own use.'

'What of you and your retinue?'

'We shall set up our camp outside the city walls. It is, after all, the way we have followed for many years and will be no hardship for us.'

'Oh…' Elona was aware of a sense of loss. For some days

he had slept no more than a few paces from her pavilion and she had grown accustomed to the sight of his powerful figure about the camp. She thought that she would have preferred to remain with him, but would not say so and was unconscious of the wistful tone of her voice as she asked, 'When shall I see you?'

'Not for two days,' Stefan told her, his eyes dwelling briefly on her lovely face, noticing the uncertainty reflected there. 'My business with the King will occupy me until then. I shall come to escort you to the tourney, but you must find your own amusement in the meantime. I imagine there are merchants enough to keep you from straying into mischief.'

'Visit the silk merchants?' Elona frowned. Once she would have flown into a temper at his teasing, but now she knew it meant nothing. She had not previously met with a sense of humour in a man and scarcely knew how to react. 'How shall I pay them? My father always attended to such matters.'

'You may tell the merchants to apply to me for payment.'

'But will they accept such an arrangement?' Elona was hesitant as she looked at him, trying to read his expression and failing.

'Oh, yes, I believe you will have no difficulty. However, I shall give Dickon a letter of authority and you may leave him to settle with the merchants on your behalf. It is his business to serve you and save you such inconvenience. All you have to do is choose whatever you wish and as much as you please, for it may be some time before you are again in London, and it is best to choose enough now rather than send for the wares you need.'

Elona accepted that her father had given Stefan a sum of money to defray her expenses and put the matter from her mind. She would miss seeing him every time she looked around, but it was only for two days and in the meantime she would enjoy visiting the merchants of this city.

Yet a little voice in her head told her that she would have enjoyed it so much more if he had accompanied her.

The bedchamber was strewn with bales of beautiful silks and damasks; a bewildering array of colour and the finest cloths available. Elona had discovered such treasures at the merchants she had visited that she had bought recklessly.

'Do you think I have spent too much?' she asked her women as she ran her fingers reverently over the gorgeous fabrics. 'I did not intend to buy so much, but the merchant kept showing me more and I could not resist.'

'Such is the way of merchants,' Bethany said. She picked up a pair of dainty slippers. They were made of soft leather and embroidered with beads. 'These are particularly fine, my lady.'

'I prefer these…' Elona pointed to a pair of yellow shoes with heels made of painted wood. 'Or perhaps these…' She had bought ten pairs in all and matching girdles, some of them jewelled or adorned with gold and silver. 'Oh, mercy, I fear Sir Stefan will say that I have bought too much! How will he ever get all these things on the wagons? They were already filled to bursting point.'

'I dare say he will have to hire another wagon,' Bethany said with a giggle. 'You will not need to visit another merchant for years.'

Elona bit her lip, beginning to regret her reckless spending. How could she have been so very extravagant? It was just that she had never seen so many lovely things. At home the merchants had brought samples of their wares to her father's house and her stepmother had advised her on what she ought to purchase. They had normally chosen cloth for two or three gowns each from the selection shown them.

Discovering a row of cloth-merchants' shops, all of them with vivid, tempting signs hanging outside, had been like walking into a magical world of enchantment for Elona.

At first she had found the city daunting. It had seemed noisy, dirty underfoot and the streets smelled awful. Beggars with dreadful sores sat in the filth at the roadside and begged for alms until they were driven off by some honest burgher with a stout stick; painfully thin dogs hunted amongst the rubbish for rotting food, and it was difficult to ignore the horrid stench. Elona had wondered why anyone would choose to live within the city, and it was not until she came to the cloth merchants that she had begun to enjoy herself.

Each shop was a part of the merchant's home. There were huge wooden shutters that were let down during the day and boarded up at night, and it was possible to see through to the wares on display inside. Some of the cheaper wares were on display in the street, but the more expensive goods were inside.

Elona had spent several happy hours going from one merchant to another. Now, as she saw how much she had bought, she was anxious lest Stefan should scold her—or worse still, tell her she must return some of these wonderful things!

'I think he will be very cross with me,' she said. 'But there, it is no matter. It is my father's money I have been spending, not his!'

'No, of course you have not been too reckless,' Stefan assured her when he came to the house that evening. She might have spent twice as much and he would have thought it worth it for that look in her eyes. He had thought her magnificent when she was angry, but when she smiled at him like that…but he must not let himself think that way! 'If you are to marry, you must be well prepared. Did I not tell you to buy whatever you desired?'

'I hope my father gave you sufficient monies, sir, for I fear I may have spent more than you expected.'

His expression remained unaltered. 'Have you bought all you need? That is my only concern.'

'Oh, yes,' she said, smiling as she saw his indulgent look. 'Besides all the lovely materials I found a new gown at one merchant's shop. It had been made up by his sewing women for a customer who had not collected it, and he was pleased to sell it to me. Bethany has altered it to fit me and I shall wear it to the tourney tomorrow. It is finer than any gown I have in my trunks.'

Her words were more revealing than she knew.

'What colour is your gown?' Stefan asked, his eyes intent on her face. She had such pleasure in these simple things— gifts that many another would have taken as their due.

'Green,' Elona said, her eyes lighting with pleasure. 'A deep leaf green with a girdle of gold threads—do you think that suitable?'

'Oh, yes,' Stefan replied. 'I am glad you chose green, for I believe this chain will go with it.' And the emeralds he had bought for her would match the colour of her eyes, though *they* changed with her moods, becoming darker or brighter as she went from anger to happiness.

Elona stared as he took something from beneath his tunic. He was dressed as always in the plain tunic and hose of a soldier with a heavy hauberk of mail and leather. He had a small silken pouch in his hand, which he handed to her in an odd manner…almost shyly, she thought.

'What is this?'

'You will need some ornament to wear to the tourney, Elona. All the other ladies will be richly dressed. I have noticed that you wear only a plain silver cross. I asked your women and they said you have no other.'

A little defensively, she touched the cross that hung from a silver chain at her breast. 'It was my mother's. I have had no need of anything more.'

'I believe you may feel more comfortable with some ornament tomorrow,' Stefan said. 'Why do you not look and see if it pleases you?'

Elona drew the chain from the pouch. It felt heavy and she saw that the gold was intricately worked and that several dark green stones were set into the metal. It was a thing of beauty and very precious. She frowned, for she guessed that it must be valuable.

'Are you sure my father gave you sufficient gold to buy all these things, sir?' she asked, lifting her bright gaze to his. 'I would not be in your debt, for I cannot pay you myself.'

The Lord de Barre had never been particularly generous to his daughter in the past. Until his son died it had always been Pierre upon whom he lavished his gifts, and Elona who received what was necessary, but that was the way of things and she had not noticed any lack. It was true that she was heir to his lands, but they would pass to her husband once she was married. She knew that it was her father's wish that it should be so ordered, and indeed, it was the custom. A man was a better guardian of lands and wealth than a woman, though Elona knew that some women held lands in their own right.

She had never wished to inherit the de Barre lands. They should have gone to her brother, her own portion something much more modest.

'Your father has been generous, Elona,' Stefan told her, breaking into her thoughts. 'You do not come empty handed to your wedding.'

Elona nodded. Of course, the chain would form a part of her dowry. She had thought for a moment that it was a gift from Stefan, but he would not give her something like this. Why should he? Only a man who intended to wed would give such a gift.

'I understand. I must be grateful to my father—and to you for thinking of me. The chain is beautiful and I am grateful that you took so much trouble to choose it for me.'

Stefan smiled, but said nothing. The chain was a gift from him as were all the other goods he had told her to purchase. Although a dowry would be paid on Elona's marriage, and her father's lands become her husband's in time, the Lord de Barre had provided little for her present expenses. It had been Stefan's idea that she might like to visit the merchants of London. He had made it his business to learn all he could of her life, and he knew that, far from being the Lord de Barre's spoiled daughter as he'd first thought her, she had oftimes been neglected in favour of her brother.

Perhaps it was that knowledge, gained from Will de Grenville and her women, that had made him want to indulge her a little. After all, he was a rich man, well able to spend large sums of money if it pleased him, and it pleased him to give her some happiness. She, too, had known what it was to come second in a father's affections. Forced to leave her home for a strange land, to live with people she had never met, and perhaps to wed a man she did not know, Elona had faced her future bravely.

She had not begged or pleaded, because to make a fuss might have caused her father to suffer. Stefan admired her restraint and the character that led her to put her father's wishes before her own.

He had been aware of her inner struggle. Had she been given a chance, she might have fled with her squire in the hope of being forgiven after the marriage by her father. Stefan believed that she would have been sadly disappointed. The Lord de Barre was more likely to have cast her off as a disgrace to her family and his name.

Stefan had guarded her well, as much for her own sake as any other, and now that they had reached the safety of the English court, he was in the mood to relax and allow her to enjoy herself.

'Have you ever been to a tourney, Elona?'

'No—at least, there was a small one held at my home a few months before my brother died. Pierre was the victor—he was so brave, so clever, that he vanquished all comers, including knights who had won many honours at larger tourneys. I was so proud of him that day…' She sighed. 'Pierre promised to take me to the Duke's court when I was seventeen, but…it was not to be.' She lifted her head proudly, determined not to let her sadness spoil the treat that lay ahead for them. Her brother had loved her and from him she had received much kindness. 'I am looking forward to the tourney very much.'

'As am I,' Stefan said softly. The shadows in her eyes touched him in a way he had not thought possible. He was aware of a need to protect and cherish her. 'It will be my pleasure to escort you. And now I must leave you; the hour grows late. I shall return soon after cockcrow, for we must be early enough to secure you a good place, Elona. You will want to see everything.'

She smiled as he took her hand and kissed it gallantly. After he had gone she held the spot where his lips had touched her to her cheek, feeling a warm glow inside. No one had ever taken such care for her pleasure, not even her beloved brother.

If she had had any doubts they had all fled now. Stefan de Banewulf would be her husband or she would have none at all.

'Oh, it is so exciting,' Elona cried as she saw the pennants flying in the wind, the bright colours of the knights' pavilions that had been set up in the field and the throng of richly dressed ladies and gentlemen. 'I have never seen so many people in one place.'

'Now you know why it was difficult to find a suitable place for you to stay,' Stefan said. 'It is a huge occasion; this tourney is the most important of the year and all the knights will try to win honour here.'

'I do hope that they will not injure themselves,' Bethany said anxiously—she knew that one of Sir Stefan's men had entered the lists of challengers, and, although nothing had been said, there was an understanding between them.

'It happens,' Stefan told her seriously, 'but it is not often that anyone is killed unless he falls badly—or a lance enters his breastplate. If a knight is well prepared, and his armour well maintained, he should suffer nothing more than a few cuts and bruises.'

'You do not fight?' Elona looked at him, a shaft of fear touching her heart. If he were to be in danger all her pleasure in the day would disappear.

'Not this time,' Stefan assured her. 'I have fought and won honours enough, most on the field of battle. Today I am devoted to giving you pleasure, Elona. I shall be by your side and we shall sample all the delights on offer together.'

'What kind of delights?' she asked, giving him a teasing look that brought a gleam to his eyes. When she looked like that she was irresistible!

'Why, from the peddlers and side-shows, lady,' Stefan said. 'Have you not seen them wandering amongst the crowd?'

'Yes, I had noticed,' she replied. She pouted at him, little knowing that it raised a raging desire in him to sweep her up in his arms and carry her off. 'Shall I have my fortune told, Stefan?'

'If it pleases you. My only wish is to give you a day you will remember as being happy—' Liar that he was! His true wish at that moment was to take her into his arms and feel the warmth of her melting surrender, but such thoughts were dangerous and must be quelled. With some difficulty he recalled his wandering thoughts. 'But first I must take you and introduce you to the King. I would warn you that he is not well, Elona. Some say he has ailed from the day that his knights murdered the sainted Archbishop Sir Thomas à Becket, and that he is cursed by the crime that will forever stain his memory—but I think it is merely the curse of age that takes its toll of him.'

'I have heard men speak of that ill deed,' Elona said and looked grave. 'Some say it was a careless word from the King that sealed the Archbishop's doom, causing those knights to foully slay him, but they say also that His Majesty was justly angry with them and has regretted it from that day to this.'

'I am certain that is so,' Stefan said. 'But I do not judge

a man on words spoken in anger. Any man might speak as Henry did when his patience is at an end—just as a blow may be struck in the heat of the moment and then regretted—it is the slow drip of malicious poison that I despise and hate. Liars and those who would use slyness to gain their evil way.'

There was something in his tone then that made Elona look at him. She caught a flicker of anger in his eyes, a hardening of his mouth, as if he was remembering something, and yet in an instant the look had gone and he was smiling at her.

'But we speak of things best left unsaid. The King will hardly notice you, Elona. You have only to smile and curtsy, and it will be over.'

'You will stay with me?' she asked nervously, and felt better as he inclined his head, giving her an encouraging smile. With Stefan by her side, how could she fear anything?

As he had promised, the introductions to his Majesty were brief; the King inclined his head, but gave no further sign of having noticed her. He was clearly weary, his face sallow and sickly, his body slumped in the huge chair that had been set for him on the dais as if he found it almost too much trouble to attend the festivities. Within seconds they had passed on and Stefan was introducing her to his friends as the daughter of John de Barre and kinswoman to the Lady Alayne de Banewulf.

Elona met several knights who greeted her with courtesy, bowing over her hand and smiling. One of them, she learned, was Sir Orlando of Wildersham, Stefan's closest friend, for whom, she guessed, he held a warm affection.

She saw one or two glances between the knights, which seemed to say that they sensed more—that perhaps they suspected an understanding between Sir Stefan and the lovely woman he had brought to the tourney. However, nothing was said to bring a flush to her cheeks.

She was given one of the seats of honour, just five or six places down from where the King's own party was seated. Stefan stood behind her, for all the seats were occupied by ladies, who were laughing and whispering behind their hands to each other, clearly very excited.

'Who do you think will be the champion of the day?' asked a pretty dark-haired girl sitting next to Elona. 'I am Constance Graves. Someone said that your name was Elona de Barre—is that correct?'

'Yes. My father is John de Barre,' Elona replied. 'I do not know who may win. I am newly come from France and this is the first time I have attended such a splendid tourney.'

'Ah, I see.' Constance smiled in a friendly way. 'I have been many times. My father is one of his Majesty's advisers and we travel about the country in his service. Not that he is well enough to travel as he once did. We have been quartered in London for some months now.'

'Does your father take you with him wherever he goes?'

Elona was surprised, for her father would have thought it unsuitable to take her with him. She had always been left at home when he and her stepmother visited the Duke's court at Aquitaine.

'Oh, yes, he cannot be parted from me,' Constance said with a soft laugh. 'My sisters say that it is time I was wed, but my father will have none of it. He will not bear to lose me for another year.'

'What does your mother say?'

'She died some months after I was born. My father has not married again, though he has five daughters. My eldest sister was twelve when our mother died and she has been a mother to us. We are trying to find our father a pretty young wife, for we all love him dearly.'

Elona found her merry smiles enchanting, and wondered at the relationship she was describing with her father, which seemed to be an ideal one. They continued to talk happily to each other until a fanfare of trumpets announced the parade of challengers. As each name was announced there were cheers from the crowd, and, occasionally, some booing or cries of disapproval.

'Everyone has their favourite,' Constance confided. 'Mine is Sir Robin Adair, but I do not dare to give him my favour lest my father disapprove.'

'Of what should I disapprove, child?' a booming voice said from behind them. 'Do not let my daughter lead you astray, lady, for she is always in some mischief.'

Elona glanced back at the man who had spoken. He was fair-haired with a small, neat beard, merry blue eyes and looked too young to be the father of five daughters.

'I think you jest, sir?' Once she would not have realised that he was teasing her—but that was before she had come to know Stefan de Banewulf. Now she knew that jesting was something many knights enjoyed. Her father had seldom laughed, and never since his son died.

'Take no notice of him, Elona,' his daughter cried. 'I was telling Elona that you might disapprove of my showing favour to Robin Adair, Father.'

'Nonsense, child,' he said, his eyes twinkling at her. 'He has only to ask for your hand and I'll have you wed ere you can blink!'

His tone was gently teasing, his smile warm with affection.

Elona liked him immediately and felt a little envious of Constance's comfortable relationship with her father.

'You are Elona de Barre,' Sir Basil Graves said. 'I was told that you were fair. 'Tis a plain lie. You are beautiful, and most welcome in our midst, lady.'

Elona blushed at the compliment, for none so gracious had come her way before. She glanced over her shoulder and saw that Stefan had moved away and was talking with some friends. He had seen that she'd found a friend for herself and left her for a few moments.

The knights had begun a parade in front of where the ladies were seated. Some of them were given favours—scarves and ribbons thrown down to them—which they tied to their armour.

Constance did not give her favour to anyone, though she waved to a knight wearing colours of red and silver.

Elona had no desire to give her favour to anyone. Stefan was not taking part in the lists and she was glad of it. Especially when the mêlée began. For a while it was so fierce and noisy that it looked like a real battle and she was terrified that someone would be killed, as did sometimes happen.

However, despite the thunder of the huge horses' hooves, the clash of metal against metal, and the loud cries of the participants, it seemed that no one was fatally injured that morning. Some knights were winded as the fast and furious contest went on apace and they had to be carried off by their squires, and some prudently retired from the fray after they had been knocked from their horses. Others carried on when the hand-to-hand fighting began, and there were some excellent contests between men of equal skill. Gradually, most knights were either deprived of their weapons or too exhausted to carry on.

At last there were only two. Elona saw that one of them was Sir Robin Adair, the other a knight dressed in black armour whose name she did not know.

'They are well matched, are they not?' whispered Constance, looking excited. 'Oh, I do hope Robin will win—Sir Gavin has won too many times.'

'Do you not like Sir Gavin?' Elona asked and the other girl shook her head.

'He wants to marry me, but he has been wed twice before—and I do not like him.'

Elona glanced at her thoughtfully. She believed there was one knight that Constance liked very well, but before she could question her further there was a gasp from the crowd as Sir Gavin's sword went flying through the air. Sir Robin was the victor and a great cheer went up as the knight he had vanquished saluted him, for the crowd always appreciated a show of gallantry and honour.

'So…' Stefan's voice sounded close to Elona's ear, startling her. She suddenly discovered that her pulses were racing, her breath short as she felt him so close to her. 'Have you found it exciting, my lady?'

'Yes.' She turned to look at him. Today he was dressed finer than she had ever seen him in an embroidered tunic and rich gown, though still in the sober colours he favoured, and she wondered how she could have ever thought that he was not handsome. He was so close to her, his head so near hers that she could have reached out and placed her lips against his. 'Where did you go just now? I looked for you, but could not see you.'

'I knew you were safe enough with Constance Graves and her father, and I had an errand. It is finished now and we can visit the peddlers to see what trinkets they have to please us.'

'I must first say goodbye to Constance, for I may not see her again.'

'Certainly you may say adieu, but she will be at the King's feast this evening and you will see her there.'

'We are going?' Elona was surprised—she had not expected it.

'Of course. All the knights and their ladies will be there. I would not have you miss it.' His eyes were bright with amusement. 'Come, Elona, let us see what trinkets we can find. I imagine we might discover some small treasures if we have good fortune.'

As Elona turned to say goodbye to Constance she saw a lady standing a short distance away. She seemed to be staring very fixedly at Sir Stefan, Elona thought. Although beautiful, her face was hard, her mouth turned downward at the corners.

She noticed Elona at that moment and her eyes narrowed as if in dislike. A shiver went through Elona and she felt as if a chill wind had passed across her heart. Then all at once the woman turned away.

'Did you see her? That beautiful lady with the pale hair, like the silver of the moon…' Elona asked of Constance.

'Who?' Constance looked in the direction she indicated, but the woman had disappeared.

Everyone was moving from their places now, intent on enjoying the rest of the day as they pleased. There were peddlers, stalls selling hot pies and sweetmeats, jugglers performing marvellous feats and entertainers of all kinds from many countries, who earned their living wandering from one village fair to another. Seldom could there be such a gathering as here, Elona thought, feeling a rush of pleasure. She was so fortunate to be present!

'Shall you be at the feast this evening?' Constance asked.

'Oh, yes,' Elona said. 'We shall be there.'

It was all so very exciting. First the tourney and now a splendid feast. Elona's only concern was for the gown she would wear that evening.

'Sir Stefan warned me that you would need a fresh gown for this evening,' Bethany said later that afternoon when she returned to the house to change and tidy herself. 'I went back to the merchant we visited yesterday and bought this silver surcote for you, my lady. If you wear it over your blue kirtle, you will look fine enough for anyone.'

The surcote was a loose tunic and was intended to be worn over a plain tunic or kirtle; this particular one was fashioned of silver cloth with long, full sleeves that had been heavily embroidered with blue beads.

'How clever of you,' Elona cried, delighted with the garment. She had seen it the previous day, but rejected it because she felt she had already spent too much, but after seeing the richness of the ladies' clothes at the tourney she was glad to have it now. 'I must hurry and change; Sir Stefan will be here shortly.'

'It was he who thought of it,' Bethany said. 'He is such a thoughtful man. Any lady fortunate enough to be his wife would be well cared for, I dare swear.'

'Yes,' Elona replied and smiled inwardly as she recalled the way her heart had raced at the tourney when he whispered against her ear. She thought that the woman he married would be fortunate in many ways! 'I shall not deny that you speak truly, Bethany. At first I did not trust him, but I have come to see that he is a true knight.'

'None truer,' Bethany said and their eyes met in shared laughter. 'And I think I waste my breath, for your mind is already set.'

'How well you know me,' Elona said and laughed. 'And now I must hurry!'

The hall was already crowded with knights and their ladies when Stefan and Elona arrived to take their places at the boards. Stefan's rank secured them places near to the high table, though not at it. This evening one of those much-coveted places had been awarded to Sir Robin for winning the tourney, and another, further down, to his vanquished opponent, Sir Gavin. Ladies sat on either side of the King, who seemed less weary that evening, though perhaps bolstered by the wine he drank.

Elona saw that both Constance and her father were seated at the high table and she waved in their direction as she took her own place, then she frowned as she saw that the beautiful woman, who had been staring at Stefan at the tourney, was seated next to Constance's father.

Elona touched Stefan's arm. 'Do you know that lady? She was staring at you oddly earlier today.'

Stefan glanced in the direction she indicated, stiffening as he saw the woman he most detested. She smiled at him, raising her wine cup in mock salute.

'You do know her!' Elona exclaimed.

'I knew her once for my sins,' Stefan said, his face grim. 'Keep a distance from Isobel de Montaine, Elona. She hath a poisonous tongue and I would not have you suffer from her darts of envy.'

Looking at him, Elona was shocked by his expression of

loathing. What could the lady Isobel de Montaine have done to arouse such disgust in him?'

'Why do you dislike her so?'

'It is a story I would fain not repeat,' Stefan replied. 'Believe me when I tell you that she is not the kind of woman you would feel comfortable with—nor would you like her.'

Did he think her a silly child, to be overshadowed by a woman of the court—a woman so beautiful that most others paled into insignificance beside her? The thought brought a swift pain but she smothered it immediately. She would be naïve indeed to imagine there had been no female companions in his life.

She turned away from him, sipping her wine thoughtfully. Why had he looked so angry? Had Isobel de Montaine hurt Stefan—had he once loved her and been rejected? It was a painful thought, but one that Elona could not put from her.

But there was too much to see and enjoy to dwell on such thoughts for long. Some mummers were performing for the company, declaiming fine verse in loud clear voices, and there were fire-eaters, jugglers, minstrels and a fool, who ran around hitting the knights about the knees with his pig's bladder on a stick.

The food was rich and flavoured with spices and herbs, often swimming in delicious sauces or gravy. The bread was crisp and freshly baked, the fruit preserved in honey, which had become crystallised and was so sweet that it made Elona's mouth water. She was careful with the wine she drank, for it was very strong, and she made sure to have it watered; she did not want to become intoxicated as some others were—ladies as well as gentlemen.

The seemingly endless feasting went on for hours. Course

after course of delicious food was brought to table, but some of the courtiers were dancing now, surfeited with food and wine, their cheeks red and flushed. They formed circles within circles, laughing and clapping and then joining hands. Every now and then someone broke from the inner circle and came to drag a man or woman from the outer circle. When that happened, the 'victim' was forced to either sing or declaim a verse before being allowed to join the dance once more.

Elona watched, her eyes bright with amusement as some of those rather more intoxicated than others began to sing rather ribald ditties.

'If you have had enough, I think we should be leaving,' Stefan said with a frown as he caught one particularly scandalous verse. 'You do not wish to dance, do you?'

Elona would have liked to dance earlier when the company was more decorous, but now she shook her head. Some of the gentlemen were much the worse for wine and she did not care to be manhandled as was happening to some of the ladies.

She noticed that Isobel de Montaine was dancing with Sir Gavin, and she saw that knight, who had fought so bravely, glance at her and then at Stefan. He whispered something to his partner, who seemed to find it most amusing.

Isobel's behaviour was almost lewd, Elona thought. The way she looked up at her companion, flaunting herself in the most intimate manner. Stefan had been right to warn her to stay away from that lady, and she would take care to do so. Not that she expected to see her in the future, for they would be leaving for Banewulf Manor very soon.

'Go and say goodnight to your friend,' Stefan said, pointing out that both Constance and her father were also leaving. 'I must speak to someone, but I shall be with you very soon.'

Elona nodded and walked towards her friend, who had paused to wait for her beside one of the huge stone pillars that supported the arched roof of the banqueting hall.

'My father says we must leave,' Constance said. 'Sometimes the knights go too far in their jesting and some ladies forget their modesty—and it seems it will be that way this evening, so we are leaving.'

'Sir Stefan has someone to see and then we are also leaving,' Elona said. 'I had hoped we might get a chance to talk this evening, for I am not sure if we shall meet again.'

'But you cannot leave the city yet,' Constance said. 'Tomorrow most of the men will go on a hunt, but I shall stay behind as will several ladies I know. Come and join us, Elona. We are going for a meal by the river if it is fine. My father will be there and Sir Robin, for he says he will not hunt.'

'I should like to join you,' Elona said. 'But I am not sure that Sir Stefan will allow it.'

'But I am sure he does not intend to leave us yet. He told my father that you would be in London for several more days.'

'Did he?' Elona's face lit up with pleasure. Remembering his haste to leave her father's house, she had not thought he would delay long at court. 'Then I shall be pleased to join you tomorrow, Constance.'

'I am glad, for my father likes you, I know.' Constance raised her brows, a teasing look in her eyes. 'He does not like many of my friends—but he likes you, Elona. He says you are the most beautiful lady to come to court in many years.'

'I am not beautiful—not compared to Isobel de Montaine.'

'Oh, her…' Constance pulled a face. 'She does not count. No sensible man would want to wed with that serpent. They say…but I must not repeat that kind of malicious talk. My father forbade it and he is right. I cannot know the truth.'

Elona was curious and sure that with a little prompting Constance would tell her more, but, before she had a chance to press her, she saw that Stefan had finished his business and was about to join them.

'I have asked Elona to join us for an outing tomorrow,' Constance cried as he came up to them. 'Do say that you will come too, Sir Stefan!'

'If it is fine, I can think of nothing more pleasing,' he said and smiled at her. 'We thank you, lady, and perhaps I may arrange a trip upon the river if it pleases you?'

'That would set the seal upon the day,' Constance said, pleased by his entering into the spirit. 'You are good to think of it, sir.'

'It was on such an errand that I was bent a few seconds ago, for your father had already invited us to join you,' Stefan told her. He glanced at Elona and a tiny shiver of pleasure went through her, making her tremble. Sometimes when he looked at her she was sure that he cared for her—that he desired her. 'I have arranged for Lord Fernhaven's barge to be at our disposal the whole day, and for his minstrels to play us over the water.'

The Lady Constance clapped her hands, clearly delighted. Glancing over her shoulder at that moment, Elona saw that Isobel de Montaine was watching them, a look almost of hatred in her eyes. A shiver went through her and she turned quickly back to her friends.

'Tell me, what may I bring to the feast tomorrow?'

'Only yourself,' Constance said. 'My father's steward will arrange it all.' She moved impulsively towards Elona, kissing her cheek. 'I am glad that we are to be friends, and I shall look forward to seeing you tomorrow.'

'And now I must see you home,' Stefan said, taking her arm. The touch of his hand sent tingles down her spine and she caught her breath. How was it possible that she had gone from hating to loving in so short a time? But she knew without doubt that her love for this man had become a living flame inside her. 'The hour grows late, Elona, and the streets of London are not safe in the dark hours. It is as well that my men are waiting to escort us home.'

A little chill touched the nape of Elona's neck. For some reason she was remembering the way Sir Gavin had looked at Stefan and then laughed with Isobel de Montaine—and there had been something in the lady's eyes that made her feel afraid.

Chapter Five

It was pleasantly warm by the river with just enough breeze to prevent the sun becoming overpowering. The food Sir Basil's servants had provided was scarcely less festive than at the royal banquet the previous evening; the dishes were cold, but no less delicious for that.

Having eaten their fill, Constance and Elona were two of the first to be rowed down the river in Lord Fernhaven's barge. It was so relaxing on the water, listening to sweet music and the gentle splash of the oars. The young women were becoming fast friends and Constance did her best to persuade Elona to remain at court.

'Could you not persuade your kinswoman to allow you to remain at court?' Constance asked. 'You could stay with us as our guest and—who knows?—you might never leave us.'

The expression on Constance's face was mischievous, but also a little wistful; it was not hard to guess what was in her mind. She and her sisters wanted to find a young and pretty wife for their father. Elona liked Sir Basil and was aware that he found her attractive. It would not have been hard to agree to Constance's request had her heart not been given to another.

Not that she held much hope of future happiness as things stood between them. Elona knew that she did not have very long to make Stefan fall in love with her, for once they returned to Banewulf he would undoubtedly leave her there and return to his own manor, which she understood was in a more southerly part of the country. And then she might never see him again.

If she could but think of a way to delay their journey! But, remembering the bitterness in Stefan's voice when he had spoken of the Lady Isobel the previous night, Elona realised her self-imposed task might be impossible. If Stefan had been disappointed in love, it might be that he had no wish to marry anyone.

There were moments when he looked at her when she was certain that he desired her, others when she was just as sure that he felt nothing more than the common concern he would show to any lady.

'Why so sad, my lady?'

Elona smiled at Dickon as he came to stand beside her as she looked out over the water. The river seemed to sparkle in the sunshine, looking temptingly cool. 'I was thinking that we must soon be on our way and I shall miss the friends I have made here.'

'But Lady Alayne comes to court with her son from time to time,' Dickon said. 'She will surely bring you with her, and your husband, when you choose to marry, may decide to live here.'

'Perhaps…' Elona sighed. She could tell no one the true reason for her wish to linger here just a little longer.

She turned her head and her heart missed a beat as she saw that Stefan was watching her. That old, brooding look was back in his eyes and he seemed almost angry, but then as their eyes met she saw something else that made her heart catch. A slow, burning heat began deep down inside her and she felt a yearning need for something she only vaguely understood. Ladies were not supposed to be aware of desire. An unmarried girl should be pure and innocent of heart and mind, but how could she not be aware when her whole being seemed to demand union with his?

Her cheeks heated as he came towards her. What would he think of her unmaidenly thoughts? But she knew! He would think her wanton—a wicked, immodest wench—and turn from her in disgust.

'Are you not enjoying yourself, Elona?'

'Oh, yes,' she replied, feeling a little breathless. The nearness of him, the scent of him, cedar and leather and his own personal musk that she found so intoxicating, but she must not let him see how his nearness affected her. 'Too much, I fear. Constance begged me to stay on as her guest and—and I almost wish we could.'

'For myself, I would soon weary of the life,' Stefan confessed, a frown creasing his brow as his eyes dwelled on her face. 'But I suppose it might be arranged for you to return after you have visited your kinswoman. There is as yet no betrothal between you and Alain, though it is your father's wish.'

'My father merely wishes me married and safely beyond the Baron Danewold's reach.' There was a note of near panic in her voice. She turned away, hiding the tears that stung her eyes. He did not truly care for her! Had he done so, he could not have spoken so calmly of her marriage to another. 'I could find a husband at court as easily. Indeed, I know that…' She faltered and held back the words. What would it avail her to marry Sir Basil rather than Alain de Banewulf? Neither of them was the one she wanted. 'Oh, what does it matter? No one cares what I feel.'

'Why do you say that?' She moved away, but Stefan caught her wrist, detaining her. She felt his strong fingers curled about her wrist and knew that he could break it with one deft twist if he chose, but he was taking care not to hurt her. 'Are you so unhappy, Elona? Do you dislike the idea of marrying my half-brother so much?'

'Yes! But what does it matter how I feel? I am merely a woman. My hopes and wishes mean nothing.' She was close to tears, his touch having disturbed her. How could he ask such a question? Did he not understand? If he cared for her, he would know that she would be unhappy to marry anyone but him.

She broke away from him and this time he let her go, staring after her broodingly. The barge had returned to the river bank and the ladies were disembarking, others ready to take their place on board.

Elona walked away from the chattering, laughing crowd, wanting to be alone. She had thought she might be happy here, but suddenly she knew that without Stefan by her side she would feel alone wherever she was. Oh, how had it happened? She had begun by hating him, thinking him cold and harsh, but now she knew that it was but a mask and that beneath the ice lay the heat of passion. There was gentleness in him, though he kept it hidden as much as he could, almost as though it were a weakness to be ashamed of.

She turned as Dickon came up to her.

'My lord sent me to warn you not to stray too far from the others,' the youth said. 'These woods are dense, my lady. You could easily lose yourself in them.'

Elona had loved to walk in the woods surrounding her father's home, but she had known them so well and she knew that the warning was well given. Even so, the command irked her. Why must Stefan always be so watchful? Why could he not simply trust her to be sensible?

'Thank you.' She smiled at her young squire disarmingly. She would send him away and then do whatever she pleased! A walk in the woods would be pleasant. 'Would you fetch me a glass of cool water, please, Dickon? I am thirsty…' Her words died away as her gaze was drawn to Stefan once more. He was talking to Isobel de Montaine, arguing with her. He looked so angry! Now he was saying something, walking away from her. Elona's heart raced, pumping wildly as she saw the lady cry out something to Sir Gavin and sensed danger—danger for Stefan!

It all happened so swiftly that afterwards Elona could not recall what had begun the ugly incident. One moment Stefan seemed intent on coming to her, Elona, and the next Sir Gavin was calling out his name in a loud, strident voice that all could hear.

'You, Sir Stefan! Are you a knave or merely a coward that you insult a lady? Turn and face me, for I defend her honour.'

A terrible silence fell as Stefan halted. For one agonising moment that seemed to drag on forever, it seemed that Stefan would ignore him, and then he turned slowly to face the knight who had challenged him.

'You are a brave knight, sir, but you know not what you say. Since I bear you no grudge I shall let the matter go.'

'Nay, not if you would keep your honour, sir. You have insulted the lady. I say again, I defend her honour.'

Watching, Elona caught her breath, all thought of foolish defiance gone as she felt the fear turn her limbs to stone. She wanted to cry out, to stop what was happening, but she could not move nor yet speak. Sir Orlando was standing nearby. She saw him reach out to touch Stefan and urge caution, but it was already too late; she knew that as she heard their next words.

'Then you are a fool.' Stefan's icy, clipped tones drew a gasp from the onlookers. 'The lady hath no honour. It was lost long since, as you well know.'

'You will answer to me for that!' Sir Gavin challenged. 'You insult the woman I love and will fight me—a fight unto the death for one of us.'

'I refuse your challenge,' Stefan said. 'There is blood enough on the lady's hands…'

'What does he mean?' Elona looked anxiously at Dickon, her face pale with fright.

Dickon lowered his head to speak against her ear. 'It is whispered that she conspired to have her husband killed; though 'twas in a tourney and none can prove the blow was meant to kill him.'

Elona felt a spasm of nerves in her stomach as she watched the terrible scene unfold. How could Stefan refuse such a challenge? He would be branded a coward if he did not meet Sir Gavin in single combat.

'You are a cowardly knave. You no longer have the stomach for a fight, it seems. Has your blood turned to water?'

There was silence as Sir Gavin's jeers died away and the crowd waited with bated breath to hear what Stefan would answer now.

'You are a fool, sir,' he repeated at last and it was as if the words were forced out of him. 'Your death will be on her hands, not mine. Let all here bear witness that I did not wish to accept your challenge, but you leave me no choice. The fight takes place tomorrow in the presence of your chosen wit-

nesses and my own. Isobel de Montaine will not be present,
nor any other lady. That is my condition.'

Silence gave way to a round of applause and the ladies
cried out words of encouragement to Stefan as he strode away.
Elona would have run after him—he must not do this thing!—
but Dickon held her back.

'Let him go, my lady. You cannot change it. He had no
choice but to take up the gauntlet. Had he not done so, his reputation would have been tarnished.'

'But he may be killed!' Elona cried wildly. Her eyes were
wide, her face pale with anxiety. How could she bear it if Stefan were killed in such a cause?

Dickon shook his head, a wry smile on his mouth. 'Have
no fear. My lord will win and easily. I have seen Sir Gavin
fight and I know that he could not hope to win in such a fight.
Why do you think my lord did not enter the tourney? He did
not wish to fight mock battles. He has killed too many men
and had no desire to do so by accident. He is a fearsome warrior. Sir Gavin has only fought within the rules of a court tourney. He cannot know what he has taken on. My lord will win,
though he has no stomach for it.'

'Then Stefan should not fight. You heard what was said—
'tis to be a fight to the death. Stefan will surely take it hard if
he is forced to kill his opponent?'

'My lord will let Sir Gavin live if he can. Once he has the
victory, he may offer mercy if he chooses—and if the loser
accepts.'

Elona looked into the squire's face. 'And if Sir Gavin re-
fuses to accept mercy?'

'Then my lord will have no choice and must do as the law
and custom demands.'

'He should not fight,' Elona repeated. Something inside her was telling her that it was wrong. Stefan did not want to fight, especially over a woman he so clearly despised. She sensed that, whether he won or lost the fight, *she* would lose him. He would retreat into that icy silence she dreaded and this time she would not be able to reach him.

Stefan cursed himself for allowing the quarrel to happen. He ought to have guarded his tongue, given Isobel no chance to claim that he had insulted her, but her barbed words had made him lose his temper.

'You have become soft, Stefan,' Isobel had taunted, her eyes mocking him. 'Dancing like a tame bear after that milk-and-water wench. I thought you more of a man than to hanker after Elona de Barre—that passionless thing.'

'The lady is as pure and innocent as you are evil, Isobel. Pray refrain from using her name with your tainted breath. I want none of your spite, serpent.'

He had turned away from her, meaning to go to Elona and reassure her that she had nothing to fear. He was duty bound to take her to Banewulf, as he had promised, but he would not allow her to be forced into a marriage against her will. Rather than that…but all thoughts of another life had vanished with the day. He had been forced to accept Sir Gavin's challenge and that meant he must kill or be killed, for he did not imagine the knight would accept mercy from his hand.

Gavin Tremaine must be mad with love for Isobel to have challenged him! Surely he must know of Stefan's reputation? He had won every tourney he entered for years before the sport palled on him. It was the last battle he had fought for real that had soured him. The siege of a fortress that Duke Richard had ordered razed to the ground. The knight to be so punished, a man of ill repute who had aroused the Duke's anger.

Stefan had fought many such battles during his long career, for the nobles were a quarrelsome, fearsome breed, always falling out and fighting with one another, and Duke Richard had sought to subdue them to his will. Stefan had served him long and faithfully, but something about this last affair had turned his stomach.

'Sir Robert de Champagnier is to be brought back in chains to me,' the Duke had ordered in a thunderous voice. 'He will be an example to all who defy me.'

Stefan had known the punishment intended for the rebellious knight. He would have been paraded though the streets for the people to jeer and throw rubbish at and then shut in an oubliette and left to die a slow and harrowing death. It was a cruel death and one that made the strongest man weep.

Robert de Champagnier had known his fate too. When it was clear that his fortress could not stand against Stefan and the Duke's army, he had challenged Stefan to single combat. Stefan had granted him the privilege and killed him. His lifeless body had been chained and taken to the Duke, who had had it placed in a cage and hung above the city walls as a warning to others that would defy him. However, Stefan's disregard of his orders had displeased him, and it was shortly after that that Stefan had set out for the Holy Land.

He had no doubt that Duke Richard had meant to punish him by sending from the court, but in fact it had been a healing journey, and one that had revealed many things to Stefan.

He had not known that the death of Robert de Champagnier would haunt him! It was perhaps one too many on his soul, or more likely that he had admired the bravery of the man. The knight had, in his opinion, been more foolish than evil. Stefan had discovered later that his quarrel with Duke Richard had been a personal one, and he wished that he had been able to show mercy. His friends told him that the quick death he had delivered was merciful, but it still haunted him. It was one of the reasons he had left the Duke's service after his journey to the Holy Land; the other was Isobel de Montaine.

Now it seemed that he must kill again because of her. He had refused her bribes to murder her husband, but she had found other willing fools to do her bidding. Sir Gavin's blood would be upon her hands. Yet Stefan knew that he would carry the guilt on his soul.

He would spend the night in prayer. Ask that he might be forgiven for his sin before it was committed.

'Oh, I wish there was something we could do to prevent this fight,' Elona said to Constance and her father later that day. Stefan had gone off immediately after the incident, without speaking to her, and they had taken her to their home, because she was upset. Tears stung her eyes and she felt desperately unhappy, but several people had told her that nothing could be done to prevent it happening. 'It will prey on Stefan's mind if he is forced to…' Her words of protest died away as the tears came. 'Forgive me. I should not…'

'I do not like to see you in such distress,' Sir Basil said as she dabbed at her eyes with the end of her veil, which covered her lovely hair as it hung from a cap of silver. 'Pray do not weep, lady. I think I may be able to do something to help you.'

'What can you do, Father?' Constance looked at him in surprise. 'The challenge has been given and accepted—it cannot be stopped. Even the King could not prevent it happening.'

'The fight must take place,' Sir Basil agreed, but there was a twinkle in his eye as he looked at his daughter. 'No, no, I shall not tell you, daughter. But I think I know how to make sure that the end Elona fears is circumvented.'

'Tell us!' his daughter demanded, but he only shook his head and walked off, smiling to himself.

'What did he mean?' Elona looked at her friend, hope beginning to dawn in her eyes. 'Can Sir Basil really do something to help?'

'My father has certain powers at court,' Constance said. 'I have no idea what he means to do—but if he says he will do something, then you may be sure he will.'

'Yes, perhaps,' Elona said. 'I do hope he can prevent this terrible thing becoming worse—and now I thank you for your kindness, but I must go home.'

'Why not stay here with us tonight?'

Elona thanked her for her kindness, but refused the offer. She wanted to be at her home in case Stefan should come to see her, though she did not believe that he would. For the moment she was the last thing on his mind!

But he filled hers as he filled her heart and she knew that if he died life would be over for her. To live on when he was gone would be a pointless existence, for he had become everything to her—her friend, comforter and protector and she loved him.

Elona could not sleep that night, try as she might. Every time she closed her eyes her thoughts were so terrifying that she started up in fear. In the end she gave up all hope of resting and sat curled in a window embrasure wrapped in a cloak, watching as the dawn spread its rosy fingers over the dark streets of the city.

Now she could hear the sounds of people beginning to stir, but, instead of abating, her anxiety increased with every moment that passed. Would Stefan have fought with Sir Gavin yet—and, if so, what had happened? Was Sir Gavin dead? A worse thought still was that Stefan might have been killed. Everyone was so sure that it could not happen, but a cloud of agony and fear that it might shadowed Elona.

At last she could stand it no longer. Summoning her women to help her to dress, she was on the point of leaving the house when there was a sharp knocking at her door and then Constance was admitted.

Something had happened! Elona felt so faint that she caught at the nearest thing to steady herself, which happened to be a heavily carved oak coffer, her head spinning as she fought to compose herself.

'Tell me at once—is there news?'

'Yes,' Constance cried. 'I do not know whether it is good or bad, Elona—they have both been arrested. The lady Isobel de Montaine also.'

'Arrested?' Elona stared at her in stunned disbelief. 'When did it happen? Who ordered their arrest? And why?'

'They were arrested in the King's name,' Constance said, 'but I think my father interceded with him to order it. It happened only after Sir Stefan had vanquished his opponent, but before he could offer mercy or refuse it. As to the reason—it stands on a suspicion that one or both knights could have been involved in the murder of Isobel's husband.'

'But I was told that it could not be proven to be murder, because it was in the heat of battle,' Elona said. She did not know if her overriding feeling was one of relief or anxiety. Stefan had escaped one dire fate to be caught in another.

'Nor can it,' Constance said. 'My father knew that and it was a part of his plan. There will be an investigation, but Sir Stefan was in the Holy Land when the incident took place, and Sir Gavin was not the knight who delivered the death blow to Isobel de Montaine's husband in that tourney.'

'Then—what was the point of the arrests?'

'It was the only way Father could intercede,' Constance told her. 'He wanted Sir Stefan to prove his point, but to make sure that Sir Gavin was not killed uselessly. The only one likely to suffer from this is Isobel herself.'

'Why is that?' Elona was puzzled.

'An accusation of complicity in the murder of her husband does not have to be proven against her,' Constance explained. 'The knights can both prove their innocence—but she cannot. It is only her word against others and three people have come forward to accuse her.'

Elona's face turned pale. 'What will happen to her?'

'If the King is merciful, she will be sent to a nunnery and stripped of her wealth. It has happened to others before her. Her punishment would be far greater if it could be proven that she had incited others to kill her husband—but the knight that struck the fatal blow died soon after of a putrid fever…and there were some who wondered at his death even then.'

Elona frowned as Constance lifted her brows. 'What are you saying—that she might have caused him to die? Poison…' She looked at the other girl in horror. 'If that is true, her punishment is hardly severe enough.' The likely punishment for such a crime would in a woman's case often be that she would be burned as a witch.

'As I said, nothing can be proven—and so his Majesty will

show mercy. She will be sent to the nunnery before the day is out. The trial of the knights will take longer.'

A shiver ran through Elona. She believed that Isobel de Montaine was not a good woman, and it was possible that she had conspired to have her husband killed, yet her punishment would be the same if she were innocent. She had been accused and had no way of proving her innocence and therefore she would be punished.

Elona could not help feeling sorry for her despite knowing that she probably deserved whatever was meted out to her—but it did seem unfair that the knights would be given a fair hearing and would prove their innocence while Isobel could not.

'Do not feel sorry for her,' Constance said as she saw Elona's look. 'She was not a chaste woman; had her husband not been a soft fool, he would have sent her to the nuns long since. It is our duty to be chaste and guard our husbands' honour, Elona. Isobel hath lain with many men and it is time that she was punished for her immodesty, if nothing else.'

Elona made no reply. A woman could not be immodest without the involvement of a man, and yet it was she who must bear the shame and the disgrace. Yet such was the world into which they were born, and the rules of conduct were clear. Some men even locked their wives into chastity belts before they went away, often to the crusades or foreign wars. Women were, after all, the possession of their fathers or husbands.

'I cannot help feeling a little sorry for her,' Elona said. 'Though I know that she probably does not deserve it.'

She could not help either the feeling that she had in part caused the other woman's downfall. Everyone had suspected Isobel de Montaine of plotting her husband's death, but nothing had been done about it—until Elona had begged Constance's father to help Stefan. It was a clever plan, for it had achieved what everyone wanted, punishing only the woman who had instigated the whole sorry business. Yet it was a severe punishment for a woman like Isobel.

'When do you think Sir Stefan will be released?'

'Perhaps not for a day or two,' Constance said. 'There must be an inquiry and judgement must be passed—but do not worry, Elona. My father will preside over the proceedings and he intends that the knights shall shake hands and go free once Isobel is safely out of the way.'

'Yes, I see. We have much to thank your father for, Constance.'

'My father admires Sir Stefan—and he likes you. Had your heart been free, I think he might have tried to win it for himself.'

'Had my…?' Elona gave her a wry look. 'Are my feelings so plain to you?'

'To me and my father, yes,' the other girl replied with a smile. 'Because we are both fond of you, Elona. But I doubt that anyone else realises the truth—unless it is Dickon.'

'Yes, I am sure that Dickon knows,' Elona said. A little shudder of relief went through her. 'I have been so very worried.'

'Well, you need worry no more. You are to come home with me, and Sir Stefan may come to look for you there. I want to make the most of your time with us. And it will not do for you to stay here and brood alone.'

Elona would have preferred to remain where she was, but she could not refuse Constance's request after the kindness shown to her by her good friends. Without Sir Basil's help, Stefan might have had to kill a man he would prefer to let live—and the least she could do was to go home with Constance as requested.

* * *

It was three days before the judicial court was convened and the judgement finally passed, three days that might have been months or years as far as Elona was concerned. She could neither rest nor sleep, for her mind was in a turmoil. Even though she knew that Stefan would eventually be released, she was still on thorns until it happened and she saw him again.

One thing that she had discovered, from the knights and ladies she met as she attended the King's court with Constance, was that most believed Isobel had received her just deserts. The lady had been disliked by the other ladies and despised by many of the knights who believed her guilty of conspiring in her husband's death. Proud and cruel, she had discarded too many lovers, made too many enemies, and there were none to speak out for her.

Elona could not but be glad that Isobel was no longer at court, though she could not quite rid herself of her own involvement in that lady's fate. Undoubtedly, she had played a part in the drama.

However, there was nothing she could do but accept what had happened and wait in patience for Stefan to come to her. On the morning of the third day, Sir Basil told her to have her women prepare her things.

'It will be one of the conditions of Sir Stefan's pardon that he leave the court immediately and does not return for three months,' he said. 'Sir Gavin will be banished for a year. He is to be sent to Duke Richard's court and may within a few weeks be on his way to the Holy Land to join the knights at a garrison there. It is the King's judgement—to make sure that the two knights are not tempted to pursue their quarrel on another occasion.'

'It seems hardly fair that Sir Stefan should be punished for a quarrel that was none of his making.'

'I believe you will find that he does not consider it a punishment. He had intended to leave almost at once and I do not believe he wishes to return for a much longer time than his banishment entails. I think it is his intention to live at his manor in peace.'

'Oh…' Elona absorbed this in silence. It was clear that her time at court was at an end. She did not mind that so very much, but Stefan would deliver her to Banewulf and then…she might never see him again. What a fool she was to have given her heart to a man who had no use for it. 'Thank you for telling me, sir. I must make sure that we are ready to leave.'

Elona took a tearful farewell of her friends, for they were to attend the court and she must wait here for Sir Stefan to come for her.

'Perhaps we shall meet again one day?'

'Perhaps,' Constance said. 'I think my father seeks a match for me with Sir Robin before Christmas. It may be that we shall go on a pilgrimage to the Holy Land after our wedding. There is talk of more fighting and Robin will want to be a part of that if it comes.'

'Will you go with him?'

'Oh, yes,' Constance said. 'I love him, and he loves me. I know that some knights leave their wives to guard their manor while they take up the Cross, but Robin would never expect that of me. If he goes, I shall go with him.'

'Then I wish you a safe passage—and happiness,' Elona replied. 'But if you are married to the man you love, you cannot want for more.'

She wished that she might be as happy, but she could not see any hope for herself.

As the day wore on and Stefan did not come, her nervousness increased. Had something gone wrong? Had Stefan and Sir Gavin fought again?'

It was almost dusk when Elona finally received a message that she was to join Stefan's retinue in the morning outside the city walls. He had sent three of his men to escort her, besides her squire.

There was no mention of his trial, nor yet the outcome. The message had been brief and to the point, giving her no insight to his feelings.

Elona sensed that he was angry—but surely not with her? What had she done to deserve such a curt message? Why had he not come himself to set her mind at rest? She had been on thorns all day, and now this! It brought her to the edge of tears, and yet she was angry too. How could he dismiss her so lightly? Did he not understand what she had suffered for his sake?

She had spent another restless night and was ready long before first light, feeling glad when they were at last on their way. Her nerves were stretched and her heart was beating too fast when they finally reached Stefan's camp, which had been packed into carts and on stout ponies, and was ready to depart. She saw him mounted and surrounded by his knights, and she knew that he had noticed her join them, but he did not smile or raise his hand in salute. His only reaction to her arrival was to give the order to move off.

Elona's heart sank. What chance had she now of reaching him? He was the cold stranger she had so disliked when he came to her father's house. She knew that his stern features could relax into a smile, and that his smile could turn her insides to water, but now he had a barrier in place between them.

Did he blame her for what had happened? How could he? Yes, she had asked if the fight could be stopped, but she had not known what would happen. She had never dreamed that he would be arrested on a false charge.

Was he angry because Isobel had been punished? He was certainly angry about something! Yet he had seemed to despise the other woman…but something had happened to make him become this icy stranger once more.

Close to tears, Elona kept her distance. She would not beg for his love, despite the ache building inside her.

Stefan rode without looking in Elona's direction, his mood one of bitter anger. He felt that his honour had been besmirched by the accusation that he had conspired with Isobel to cause her husband's death. It was unjust and demeaning and it pricked him like a thorn in his side.

It mattered not that he had been released from custody, his name cleared of the suspicion. The taste of his brief stay in a small dark room that was only a little better than a dungeon was too recent, too bitter to be swallowed and forgotten. Sir Basil had seemed to think it a clever plan, almost a jest, and he had been hard put to it not to strike the fool. Especially when he had prated on about upsetting the Lady Elona!

How dared he take it upon himself to interfere? Stefan had needed no help from him or anyone else, and his pride was touched by the suggestion that the fight might have gone the other way. He had been in control the whole time and was on the point of offering mercy, which might or might not have been accepted… Sir Gavin was a fool, but he had fought well and it had been Stefan's intention to spare him whether he willed it or no. He would have managed it somehow, even had he had to knock him unconscious to do it. As it happened, the other knight was barely conscious by the end of the fight and no one would have known whether he had refused mercy or not.

To be arrested when he had just fought and beaten a knight of Sir Gavin's calibre—and Stefan admitted that it had been more difficult than he had imagined—was infuriating.

Such was his anger that he did not trust himself to speak to Elona. Their journey would take at least three days and his temper would have cooled long before then. It would be wiser to keep his distance for the moment.

There were things that needed to be said before they reached Banewulf, but for the time being they could wait.

Two days had passed and hardly a word had been spoken between them! Elona knew that she was almost as much to blame as Stefan for she had reacted to his angry silence with a proud haughtiness of her own, refusing him a smile when he had seemed to want to talk to her the previous evening. Now they were only a few hours' journey from Banewulf and once again one of the wagons had broken down and was in need of repair.

'I shall see that my men have their orders and then we will ride on with a small party ahead of the others,' Stefan told Elona.

'As you wish,' she replied coldly, for if he could retreat behind a barrier of silence so could she. 'I dare say you wish to be rid of me as soon as possible.'

'Do not be ridiculous!' Stefan said with a sigh of exasperation. Why was she looking at him so accusingly? He was torn between a desire to shake her and another, stronger, to take her into his arms and devour her with hungry kisses—and that he had promised himself he would not do. He had vowed to deliver her safely to Banewulf and that he would do if it killed him! 'I shall not be long, and then we shall talk before we ride.' Her only reply was a shrug of her shoulders, which made him want to shake her. 'Do not wander into the woods. They are dense and I have no time to set up a search party for you if you get lost!'

He walked off, obviously past patience with her, and for Elona that was the last straw. She would not be treated like a child, nor would she be told what she could or could not do. She would show him that she was not a foolish child and could find her way in any woods!

She walked away from the clearing where they had stopped to make repairs and take some refreshment, following what was clearly a path used by woodsmen and villagers.

It was cooler beneath the trees and pleasant, the sun filtering through the canopy and playing on the fern-covered path before her. In the trees she caught sight of a squirrel, his red tufted ears alert as if he listened for sounds, his eyes bright. Suddenly he started to leap through the trees, such daring feats of skill and balance that Elona laughed in delight and ran to follow and keep him in her sights.

Oh, the woods had a magical feel, the sound of birdsong all around her and the scent of the wildflowers that flourished in any patch of open ground where the sunlight filtered through. She had a feeling of well being, of happiness, as if she had been released from a shadow that had hung over her these past days, and realised how foolish she had been to sulk because Stefan was angry.

Now she began to see that she was as much to blame for the coldness between them. Why should he not be angry? He had been accused of a heinous crime and, though acquitted, it must have stung his pride. She knew that, for he was a true knight and would feel that any slur was a stain upon his honour. She ought to have realised how he felt and waited patiently for him to recover his spirits. Sulking would gain her nothing. She would talk to him, tell him that she had come to care for him, hear what he would say to her.

Turning, Elona began to retrace her steps towards the camp, and then stopped as she realised she had strayed from the well-trodden path as she ran after the squirrel. She turned in a circle, looking for her way and felt pleased as she saw it. She had not strayed so very far after all. She could hear the sound of voices…men's voices close by…and horses. She would soon be back with Stefan… But she could see the men now. They stood directly ahead of her, between her and the path she must follow—and they were not Stefan's men!

No! It could not be. She had strayed only a short distance from the camp. These men could not have known she was here—but they had and there was something about them that made her suddenly afraid.

An icy trickle ran down Elona's spine. Those men looked uncomfortably like…but, no, it could not be! Yet she knew from the colours of black and purple of the livery they wore that they were Baron Danewold's men.

Chapter Six

Elona was frightened as she realised that she had fallen into a trap. She had forgotten about Danewold! Her pleasure at being at court and then the shock of Sir Gavin's challenge and Stefan's arrest, her feelings for him—all these had combined to drive any thought of the Baron's pursuit from her mind. Besides, she had thought she was safe here in England and so close to Banewulf.

Was it possible that Danewold's men had been shadowing them all this time, waiting their opportunity? They must have been! Had Stefan guessed that the Baron's men would continue to shadow them? Of course he had. All at once she understood why she had been warned so many times not to stray into woods or too far from her friends. What a heedless, vain, foolish woman she was to ignore those warnings!

Elona looked behind her. Should she try to flee that way and risk becoming lost? It was surely better than allowing herself to be caught tamely by the Baron's men. Yet if she could just dodge past them and reach help… Even as she hesitated, a horseman came riding out of the trees from behind her.

His purpose was clear. Elona gave a little yelp of fear,

turned and ran in the direction she had been walking when she followed the squirrel, hoping to avoid her pursuers by plunging deeper into the wood. But the horseman was almost upon her and flung himself down from his horse, pursuing her into the part of the wood where the trees grew more densely.

She ran as fast as she could, her breath coming in tortured gasps as the fear swept over her, but he was faster. He was so close that she could hear the rasp of his breathing, and then he was upon her, bringing her down to the ground, subduing her as she fought against him, pummelling at him with her fists, kicking and biting. But it was all in vain. He was so much stronger and she knew she could not escape him try as she might.

'You're a little hellcat,' the soldier muttered furiously as her nails raked his face, drawing blood. 'Think yourself lucky that my master wants you in one piece or I would teach you a lesson you'd not forget in a hurry.'

Elona opened her mouth to scream, but his large, none-too-clean hand was clamped over it, cutting off the sound. She bit him and he swore, drew back his hand and hit her across the face. The force of the blow made her head snap back and the blackness descended over her as he carried her over his shoulder and back towards his horse.

'You caught her, then,' one of the other men said, coming up to him. 'Damn it, Boris, you've near killed the poor wench!'

'She fights like a hellcat,' the first man said. 'I had to subdue her.'

'She's lost her senses for the moment. I hope for your sake that you haven't damaged her permanently. If you've lost him a chance of her lands, Danewold will hang you from the nearest tree, Boris.'

'I slapped her, that's all.' Boris glowered at him. 'She'll come round in a few minutes.'

'You'd better take good care of her. I wouldn't be in your shoes if she dies.'

'Help me with her, Jedro, and I'll pay you five silver pennies,' Boris said, looking nervous now. 'I swear I never meant to hurt the stupid wench.'

'We'll look after her together; if she lives. we'll share the gold Danewold promised. If she dies…'

'If she dies, we'd better leave her and run for our lives,' Boris said. 'You don't think she will—do you?'

'You'd best leave the care of her to me,' the crafty Jedro said, already sure that it was only a matter of time before she began to stir. 'Go and tell the others that she fell and hurt herself. I'll see if I can bring her round, and then I'll follow.'

Boris hesitated. He was not known for his wits and had acted unthinkingly when Elona bit him, and yet he suspected that his companion might try to cheat him of his share of the reward.

He moved closer to Jedro, his eyes glittering with menace. 'I caught her, remember that. Cheat me and you won't live to spend the gold!'

'Don't be a fool,' Jedro muttered. 'Go and tell the others we've got her. I'll see if I can bring her round and then I'll join you.'

Boris had laid Elona on the ground. He glanced down at her pale face, then went off, his dull brain beginning to see a way through the maze. He would tell the others that he and Jedro had caught her together, but that it was Jedro who had hit her. The plan seemed a good one to him and he smiled as he left his companion to tend the girl.

Jedro took a drinking horn from the belt at his hips, holding it to Elona's mouth and tipping a little of the contents down her throat. It was a potent wine and would bring her round if her wits were not scattered from that brute's blow.

Elona choked and her eyelids fluttered. She gave a cry as she opened them and looked up at the man bending over her. He had a dark, wrinkled face with a scar at his left eyebrow, but it was not the man who had threatened her earlier.

'Who are you?' she asked, shrinking back. 'What are you doing to me?'

'I am going to look after you,' he told her. 'Be careful, lady, for if we are heard I shall not be allowed to help you.'

'Baron Danewold…you are one of his men?'

'For my sins,' he acknowledged. 'I was bound to him at birth and have no choice but to serve him, lady. However, I would not have you mistreated and I shall guard you well until you are in my master's care.'

'Help me to escape and I shall pay you well. My father would take you into his service…' She faltered as she saw the expression in his eyes. 'What is it? Tell me at once, I pray you.'

'I do not like to tell you such news, lady.'

'What news?'

'Your father—the Lord John de Barre—he was taken ill two days after you left your home and…died soon after.'

'My father dead…'

Elona was stunned by his news. She stared at him, feeling close to despair. Her father had sent her away so that she had not been with him at the end, and now she would never see him again. Grief overwhelmed her. Her eyes filled with tears, trickling unheeded down her cheeks. Now she was truly alone, for there was no one to care for her.

'Do not weep, lady,' Jedro said. 'I did not wish to tell you, but it was best that you knew. My master is determined to have you and your lands, and it was to that purpose that he remained in France—but we are to take you to his English stronghold to await his coming.'

'Help me, please,' Elona begged. 'My father's lands belong to me now and I will arrange to make you rich if you help me.'

Jedro looked at her, clearly considering her words, but then voices were heard and three other men came through the trees.

'Can she walk?' one of them demanded. 'If not, I'll put her over my shoulder.'

'I can walk,' Elona said proudly. She rose with Jedro's help, clutching on to his arm as her head swam for a moment. 'Remember,' she whispered to him as they followed the others towards the clearing where the horses were being held. 'Help me to escape and get to Banewulf and I shall reward you richly.'

Jedro nodded at her, his crafty mind at work once more.

'Trust me, lady,' he told her. 'Make no trouble and when it is time I shall do what I can.'

Elona inclined her head. She was not sure that he was trustworthy, but for the moment she had no choice but to do as she was told and hope…but would Stefan come after her? Why should he bother? She had certainly given him no smiles of late. Why should he not simply abandon her to her fate? And yet somehow she did not believe that. Stefan would consider it his duty to find her and fetch her back.

She closed her eyes. Her jaw hurt where the other brute had hit her and she felt unwell, her chest tight with misery. Her beloved father was dead and she was Baron Danewold's prisoner.

Elona felt the despair wash over her in a great wave. Oh, why, why had she not listened to Stefan and stayed safe within the camp? She had been so foolish, so wilful, and now she was punished.

'Why could the foolish wench not stay safe within the camp?' Stefan demanded angrily of her squire. 'And why were you not watching over her, Dickon?'

'Forgive me, my lord. I turned my back only for a few moments and she had gone. If anything has happened to her, it will be my fault.'

'No, no.' Stefan sighed as he saw the youth's look of guilt. 'You must not blame yourself. We shall search for her; it will be but one more delay. This journey seems as if it was meant to be nothing but delay—with all these accidents anyone would think someone did not want us to reach Banewulf…'

Stefan knew well enough whose fault it was that Elona had disobeyed him and strayed into the woods. He had been harsh to her and her pride had reacted to his scolding. He had let his temper rule him too long, but he had been suffering from indecision and was afraid of speaking to Elona lest his feelings show through. He knew that she was special, meant something special to him, made him feel special in a way no other woman had or could again.

The challenge and then his arrest, his own feelings of guilt because of the death of Robert de Champagnier, his uncertainty, had combined to blacken his mood. Elona was the woman he would have to wife if he were free to take her—but she was intended to be Alain's bride.

Therein was the sting. How could he steal his brother's bride? How could he betray the trust his stepmother had placed in him by asking him to bring Elona to Banewulf—and yet how could he stand aside and see her wed another?

When he looked at her, he felt desire course through him such as he had never experienced for any other woman. And there were other feelings, stronger, deeper than he had experienced before for a woman, feelings he did not entirely understand. Was it possible that this tenderness he felt when he saw Elona's uncertainty, the hurt shadowing her lovely eyes, was the emotion people called love? He had not believed in romantic love, but now he had begun to change his mind.

It was this that had caused his black mood to linger longer than it ought, preventing him from speaking to Elona, telling her what was in his heart. He had no right to press his suit—and yet, now that she was lost, he knew that he would not be able to bear it if he never saw her again.

Once again he cursed the wasted hours they had spent searching the forest, and himself for speaking so harshly to her that she had deliberately defied him. If the worst happened, he would always blame himself.

Elona felt so weary she wished she could sleep for a week. They had been travelling for days, riding hard, she behind her self-appointed protector, forced to hold on to him for fear of falling as her weariness grew by the hour.

'Shall we never be there?' she asked as at last they stopped for rest and food. 'How much further must we go? I am too tired to go on.'

'Tomorrow we shall reach my master's stronghold,' Jedro told her. 'We are making camp now. You will be able to sleep for a while.'

Elona was too weary to do more than nod her head. Perhaps she would sleep that night, though for most nights on her journey she had lain awake, tossing restlessly on the blanket she had been given, the ground hard beneath her. These men travelled light and there was no pavilion to give her comfort and protect her from the elements, and the nights were cold, especially as they travelled further to the north.

Each day she had hoped for rescue, but it had not come. Her captors had hardly stopped in their haste to get her to their master, who had promised to pay them handsomely in gold for their trouble. Stefan's men had moved far more slowly so that the cumbersome baggage wagons were never too far behind. She understood that that was for her sake. Alone, without the comfort of the ladies to consider, they could obviously travel much faster. Perhaps they would catch up with her captors before they reached Danewold's stronghold.

How long would it have taken Stefan to discover that she was not simply lost in the woods? Would he have found the piece of torn veiling she had managed to leave for him? Would he know that Danewold's men had captured her—and would he come after her?

That was the question that haunted her. Would Stefan put himself to the trouble of pursuing Danewold's men?

Surely if he wanted to recover her, he would have made his move long before this? As each day passed without the pursuit she hoped for, Elona's hopes began to fade. Perhaps, after all, Stefan did not consider it worth his while to rescue her?

She supposed in a way that she was lucky that Jedro seemed to have taken her under his wing. Though a sly creature, he was better than most of the rough soldiers who formed her guard. She was not afraid of Jedro, though she did not trust him. He had told her it was impossible for her to escape and that it would be better to try and ransom herself from Baron Danewold.

'For if you ran away we should pursue you, lady,' Jedro told her. 'And then others might take it upon themselves to be your jailer—and I cannot answer for what might happen then.'

Elona had suppressed a shudder. From the evil leer in some of the men's eyes as they looked at her, she knew that it was only fear of their lord's anger that kept them from having their way with her—that, and the fact that Jedro had taken it upon himself to be her guardian. She was most afraid of Boris, who had hit her so hard that she was knocked senseless, though she did her best to hide it, staring at him coldly whenever they met.

However, he had kept his distance during their journey. She thought that Boris seemed almost to fear the crafty Jedro, though he was the smaller man and not as powerful. Indeed, all the men seemed to give him respect, and she suspected that the easy manner he showed to her was perhaps a mask to cover a different nature.

She knew that she walked a knife-edge, for these were not cultured knights who lived by a code of honour, and, if challenged, their baser natures might hold sway. Somehow she must live through this nightmare until all hope was gone.

Elona's skin was beginning to itch; she had been given only enough water to drink and none at all for washing. Nor could she have washed her body, had the water been given her, for she was never alone. Even when they rested for a few hours at night, someone stood watch over her.

Her physical discomfort was as nothing to the turmoil of her mind. Besides the constant grief for her father, the hurt of knowing that she would never see him again, was the realisation of her own folly in disobeying Stefan.

He was constantly in her thoughts; her hopes of seeing him kept alive by her determination not to give in to the fear that would otherwise overwhelm her. She was well aware of the fate that awaited her at Baron Danewold's stronghold, for she was her father's only heir and his lands were now hers. The Baron was not the only man who would seize her and her lands for himself if he could; others would also see her as a rich prize, and it was clear that she must marry or be for ever vulnerable, prey to any lawless warlord who chanced upon her.

Elona wept silent, bitter tears as she lay upon the hard ground that night. They had been upon the road so many days and yet Stefan's men had not caught up with them. Surely they must have done so if he had intended to pursue them? If he did not care enough to follow her…but she would not give in! She would rather die than be wife to a man like Baron Danewold.

'You must ride for Banewulf,' Stefan had told Dickon once it was clear what had happened to Elona. A piece of torn veiling had been discovered and there were signs of men and horses having been in the woods. 'Tell my father that Danewold's men have stolen Elona and that we are setting out in pursuit immediately.'

He had hoped at first that he might catch up to them before too many hours had passed, but Elona's captors had had several hours' start on them, hours that Stefan bitterly regretted having wasted. At first he had believed she had merely got lost in the woods, not thinking that Danewold's men would have continued to follow them all this time.

He cursed himself for the lost hours, for no matter how hard he pushed himself and his men, those they pursued were always ahead, seeming to know the wild countryside through which they travelled far better than he or his own people could.

He believed that they would be heading for Danewold's stronghold and his fear was that he would not catch up with them in time, a fear that gnawed at his stomach like a hungry rat, giving him no peace. The news had reached him at court of John de Barre's death, but he had not told Elona; he did not wish to spoil her pleasure in the entertainment offered her there. Time enough for that when they reached Banewulf.

He was afraid for Elona, knowing as he did that Danewold would consider himself safe from retribution. The Baron must believe that, with her father dead, he had nothing to fear.

By heaven! If that rogue laid a hand on her, he would die for it. A red mist of rage possessed Stefan as he rode. Danewold would think himself secure in his northern stronghold, but he had reckoned without Stefan, and, if Dickon had reached Banewulf safely, the men garrisoned there. Combined, they would make a considerable force that few could stand against.

If Elona had been harmed—or dishonoured, perish the thought! It was too painful to contemplate. The thought of her innocence being taken from her by that vile rogue was unbearable. If that had happened, Stefan would show no mercy. He would strike down every last one of the devils who had stolen her if it cost him his life.

For what would his life be to him if harm had come to her?

Stefan faced the fact of his love at last. Elona meant more to him that he could ever have dreamed. Her loveliness, her innocence, her spirit were all qualities he prized in her. And there had been times when she looked at him, when she clung to him, as if needing his strength, when he had believed she felt something for him.

The agony of loss was strong in him as he pushed himself and his men even harder. They could not be far behind now. If their luck held, they would catch up with Danewold's men that night.

Suddenly his horse stumbled, throwing Stefan forward. Such was the speed at which he had been travelling that neither he nor his mount had had time to realise that the ground gave way suddenly to a steep incline. He fought to retain his balance, but could not hold on and was thrown over the horse's head, striking his own against the ground as he fell.

They were riding into Baron Danewold's stronghold. Elona shivered in the chill wind that whipped her long hair about her face, but as much from fear as from the cold. She had hoped, longed, for rescue, but nothing had happened to stop her being brought to this place and now it was too late. She sensed that it would take a small army to breach the defences of these stout walls—and who would bother to send an army to rescue her? If Stefan had not cared enough to follow her, no one else would take the trouble to save her.

She was but one woman, insignificant and of no political importance. Had her father or brother lived…but she had no one to care what became of her. Clearly Stefan had not thought it worthwhile to pursue her. Why should he? He had forbidden her to leave the camp and she had disobeyed him. He was probably relieved to be rid of her, thinking her a wilful child and not worth his trouble.

Her thoughts had grown gloomier as the days and hours passed and the crushing sense of loss, both of her father and of the man she loved, had weighed heavily upon her. But she would not give in tamely, she decided. No matter what the

Baron threatened—what he did to her—she would not let him break her spirit. She would fight him to the last, and at the end she would die rather than submit.

Her head lifted proudly as Jedro reached up to help her dismount. She gave him a look of cold disdain for he had lied to her, promising to help her escape, but in truth he had guarded her too closely for her to have a chance of escaping on her own. She realised now why the other men showed him respect; he was as sly as a serpent and possibly just as dangerous.

'Do not despair, lady,' he said softly to her as she would have turned away. 'It was my duty to bring you here, but perhaps all is not yet lost.'

'You have the tongue of a serpent,' she said and moved away. The fear was gripping at her insides, churning and eating at her as she saw the Baron with his steward. He had seen her and his triumph was evident in his evil leer.

'So you are here at last, lady,' he said as he came towards her. 'I have anticipated your coming and am eager for our wedding.'

'You had no right to bring me here against my will,' Elona cried, her eyes flashing. Temper flared in her, temporarily banishing the fear. 'I have no wish to marry you, nor shall I. You cannot make me.'

'Come, Elona,' he said, his narrow-set eyes boring in on her angrily. 'You surely do not believe that you can resist me? Your father flung my offer in my face. I was not good enough for his daughter—but now he is dead and you are here, my prisoner. Who is there to stop me doing as I will with you? I think that, once I have had you in my bed, you will be glad enough to take your vows.'

Elona stared at him, unable to think for a moment, but then

inspiration came to her and she raised her head, looking into his face mockingly.

'I am your prisoner,' she said, 'that I cannot deny, but if you imagine that I am friendless you are wrong. I am betrothed to Stefan de Banewulf and he will not allow what you have done to me to go unpunished…'

'You lie!' Danewold's ugly face became uglier with temper, his nostrils flaring. 'It was to his brother you were to be promised.'

'That was before Stefan discovered that he loved me,' Elona replied. 'We were betrothed at court and the contract we signed bears the King's seal. If you violate that, you could be called to account by his Majesty—'

'Damn you, wench, you lie!' The Baron stepped closer as if he would strike her, but she lifted her head proudly and something in her eyes stayed his hand. He stroked his beard, studying her face. 'Yes, you lie. I would have heard of this if it were true.'

'You will see,' Elona said, her manner much calmer than she felt inside. 'Stefan will come after me. He will bring others to besiege your keep and raze it to the ground, if need be. Harm me and you will pay the price with your head.'

Danewold's eyes flickered with uncertainty. He was furious that she should dare to speak out against him. No other woman had ever dared to answer him back, and he would not stand for it from her—and yet, there was a chance that she was telling the truth.

'Take her to her chamber and keep her close,' he said to one of the men about him. 'By the stink of her she needs a bath. I like my women to smell clean.'

The insult was meant to sting, but Elona was glad of the

respite. Thank goodness his men had not let her take time to clean herself! Elona swallowed the insult, following the servant who beckoned her into the keep, taking her through the great hall, which was cold and dark and comfortless, to a winding stair at the far end.

'Your chamber is above in the tower,' the servant told her. 'You will find women there to do your bidding, lady. I go to order hot water for your comfort.'

'Thank you,' Elona said. 'What may I call you?'

'Friedrich, my lady. I serve my master—but I apologise for your poor welcome here.'

Elona inclined her head, but did not answer. His words were soft enough, but she would trust no one in this place; even the women who would serve her must be treated warily.

They were waiting for her within the chamber she had been given, a small round room with barely enough space for her bed. Surely the Baron did not expect her to live here? The walls seemed to press in on her and she felt that she could not breathe. If this were truly to be her home she would find some way to escape, even if it meant ending her life.

Two women came towards her as she entered, their faces schooled to smiles of welcome, though she could see they were uncertain how to behave towards her. They did not know whether she was their mistress or their master's hostage.

'I am the Lady Elona de Barre,' she announced, raising her head with a flash of pride. She was a lady of rank and would be treated as such. 'Your names are?'

'I am Roberta, my lady.'

'And I Philippa.'

'I need water to wash and a change of clothing,' Elona said, determined to assert her authority at once. 'And I am hungry, for I have been given nothing but bread, water and a hard cheese that I could not eat these past few days.'

'I shall fetch food,' Philippa said at once. 'Roberta will bring you clothes, my lady. I fear we have only a plain tunic to offer you for the moment, but at least it will be clean.'

'I shall have your own clothes washed,' Roberta assured her as the other woman departed. 'When do you expect your goods to arrive, my lady?'

'I do not expect it,' Elona said tartly. 'I am here against my will and shall not remain long.'

Even as she finished speaking there was a knock at the door and, when Roberta answered it, a servant entered bearing a wooden tub. Others followed him into the room, carrying jugs filled with water, which they poured into the tub, before leaving as swiftly as they had come.

Once they had gone, Elona bid Roberta bar the door before helping her to disrobe. She slipped into the water, closing her eyes as she felt the ease of aching limbs in its relaxing heat.

Roberta brought her scented soap and then departed. She smoothed the soft substance over her arms and body, relishing the feel of the water on her aching limbs.

The serving wench had gone through a curtained alcove into a small space where clothes were stored and did not return until Elona called to her to bring her drying cloths.

She was wrapped in a large cloth as she stepped out of the bath and gently dried before being helped into a clean tunic, which she tied with her own girdle of gold threads.

It was one of the girdles that Stefan had bought for her, Elona realized, and the thought brought tears to her eyes. She tried to hold them back, but the memory of those happy days at court flooded into her mind, making her feel what she had lost all the more keenly.

'Ah, no, do not weep, my lady,' Roberta said. 'He is a brute and tears will not help you. If you wish to avoid his attentions, you must use your wits.'

'Use my wits?' Elona looked at her sharply. 'What do you mean?'

'My master is not known for the cleverness of his mind,' Roberta said, a scornful twist about her mouth. She was a plain girl, slender but with a square, flat face and snubbed nose. 'I am fortunate that he does not notice me—but there are others here who have wept bitter tears because of his bestiality.'

'I have heard that he is cruel,' Elona said, hesitant still, yet inclined to trust this girl despite her resolve not to. 'But what can I do if he is determined? It is my wealth, my father's lands, he wants, not my person.'

'You are beautiful,' Roberta said, 'and he will take pleasure in humbling you if he can, but, as I said, he is sometimes slow witted, though he thinks himself clever. You must find a way to keep him at bay until help can come to you.'

If help came… Elona was not sure that it would, though she had told Baron Danewold that Stefan and his men would come after her. Pray God that he did!

'I am betrothed to Stefan de Banewulf,' she said, deciding to keep up the pretence. 'He will come and he will demand satisfaction of the Baron if he harms me.' Pray God that he did come!

Roberta nodded, looking thoughtful. 'If the betrothal was conducted legally, it would be a bar to your marriage—but it cannot prevent *him* taking you to his bed. Once he has despoiled you, your betrothed may seek to have your contract set aside. My master's steward will tell him this… You must think of another reason to hold him off, lady. Otherwise he will send for you and—'

'Supposing I was carrying my betrothed's child?'

Roberta looked shocked at the idea. It was something that no chaste lady should ever allow to happen and she was a moral girl. To behave so wantonly was a sin.

'My lady…'

Elona smiled and shook her head. 'No, no, do not look like that. It is not so. I have never lain with a man, but supposing I could convince the Baron that it was true. A man would take revenge against someone who dared to lay hold of the woman who carried his child, would he not? And a knight as brave and true as Sir Stefan de Banewulf would be certain to take revenge on the man who had despoiled his lady, would he not?'

Roberta smiled and nodded her agreement. 'This is true, my lady—but you must give the Baron proof of your condition…'

'How can I do that?'

'Trust in me,' Roberta said. 'And tell no one. Philippa may be trusted to serve you well, but she is hopeful of marrying my master's steward and might not keep your secrets, my lady.'

'But why should you help me?' Elona looked at her intently. 'You do not know me and you might be punished if it were discovered that you had interfered with your master's plans. Why should you risk punishment for my sake?'

'My cousin was but twelve when my master forced her to his bed,' Roberta told her and her eyes flashed with anger. 'The things he did to her shamed her so that she took her own life by jumping into the moat the next morning and drowned there. I hate him and I would not see you suffer as she did.'

Elona nodded, seeing the truth in her eyes. Jedro had betrayed her, but perhaps this woman would help her. She had little choice, for there was not much time. Once the evening wore on and the men began to drink, the Baron would send for her.

'Then I shall trust you—tell me what I should do…'

Elona felt better when she had eaten. Her stomach had protested at the rich food, but she had eaten her fill, for it was a part of her plan with Roberta.

It was evening now and she had been left in peace for most of the time, alone with her thoughts, which were so gloomy that she found it difficult not to give way to despair. The plan she had worked out with Roberta was cunning and might serve to hold the Baron at bay for a few days—but unless someone came to rescue her, in the end he would discover that she was lying.

Lying on the hard couch, which was all that had been provided for her, Elona closed her eyes against the tears. She would not think of her ultimate fate if no rescue came. She thought instead about Stefan, about the way he had looked at her, smiled at her, and of how she had felt inside. How she wished that he had taken her to his bed. If she were truly carrying his child, how happy she would be!

Feelings of loss and need swept over her. She loved Stefan so much and she might never see him again. If that were the case, then she might be driven to the terrible sin of taking her own life—just as Roberta's cousin had—but she would fight the Baron to the last in the hope that someone might come for her.

Surely Lady Alayne's husband would not allow his wife's

kinswoman to be forced into marriage against her will? The thought that perhaps Sir Ralph might come himself raised Elona's spirits once more. Perhaps after all she was not as alone as she had feared.

Her courage lasted until it was nearly dark and then the Baron sent for her to come to him. Her heart raced and she looked at Roberta fearfully, knowing what likely fate awaited her.

'What shall I do?'

'Take this now.' Roberta pushed the small earthenware flask into hand. 'It will take some minutes to work, but when it does it will be horrible.'

Elona hesitated, then took it and swallowed the contents hurriedly before Philippa could return from the inner chamber where the clothes were kept and the two women slept on straw pallets.

What did it matter if the potion poisoned her? Elona thought recklessly as she tasted the bitter liquid and gagged on it. Better that she should die than live to be that man's thing, used and abused as he willed. Besides, she was inclined to believe that Roberta was truly on her side, not like the crafty Jedro who had promised much and delivered nothing.

'Do not worry, the effects are temporary,' Roberta assured her as she gave her a wan smile and went out.

Walking down the twisting stone stairs to the huge, shadowy hall below, Elona was aware that a large gathering of men was present. Clearly the Baron followed the old custom of dining with his men and did not have a private chamber. Perhaps he slept on the floor with his men too, she thought, lifting her head as she caught the stink of unwashed bodies and other odours that wafted about the hall. The only light came from torches flaring from iron sconces on the wall, which gave off a pungent odour. Dogs were hunting in the filthy straw that covered the floor, looking for discarded bones and scraps of food that were dropped when the men became drunken and careless.

One of the dogs growled at her as she passed, her skirt brushing against its mangy body. She ignored it, refusing to flinch as it bared yellow fangs at her before one of the men kicked it out of the way. No wonder the poor brute was so fierce if that was its usual lot, she thought, and lifted her head proudly.

The Baron lived in a way her father would have thought beneath him, and her body recoiled at the thought of being forced to live with these people. Much better that she should take her own life!

'Come here and sit by me, lady,' the Baron's voice boomed at her from the table at the far end. 'I would have your company for a while before I seek the comforts of my bed.'

Laughing greeted this announcement and it was clear that the assembled soldiers knew what he meant by *comforts*. Elona felt her cheeks heat, but she could also feel the queasiness beginning in her stomach. Roberta's potion was working.

'I have eaten,' Elona replied as she went to stand next to the Baron. 'I beg you to excuse me, sir, for I do not feel well.'

'What ails you?' he growled. 'You look well enough to me. And you smell better too.'

'I wish I could say the same of your hall, sir. I vow 'tis a disgrace.'

The Baron glared at her, then roared with laughter. 'I like a bit of spirit in a woman—it makes her more fun to tame. Make no mistake, Elona, I shall tame you. You'll beg for your scraps at my hand before I'm finished with you.'

'Your threats do not frighten me, sir,' Elona replied, discovering that it was true all of a sudden. Her courage returned. He was nothing but a dull-witted bully, as Roberta had told her. 'If you lay a finger on me, your life will be forfeit.'

'You are a lying wench, but even if your tale be true it does not matter. Your lord will not want you once he knows that I have stolen what should be rightfully his.' Another burst of laughter greeted this sally and Elona raised her head. How she hated to be the butt of this man's coarse jesting!

'But there is more than the contract between us,' Elona said in a clear voice that could be heard by all those close by. 'Stefan de Banewulf is the father of the child I carry in my womb. Harm me or that child and he will surely kill you.'

'Are you a whore, then?' Baron Danewold's ruddy cheeks blenched. He was clearly stunned by her revelation and the manner of it. She had spoken as though she were proud of her wanton behaviour. 'I thought you chaste, lady.'

'I have no lover but the man I am to wed soon.'

His eyes narrowed to malicious slits. 'You lie…' he began, but even as he blustered, torn between striking her and carrying her to his couch to test the truth of her words, she convulsed suddenly, clutching at her belly. 'Damn it, woman…'

Elona's body shook with the force of her sickness as it rose up her throat in a great tide, spilling over, splattering on to the Baron's tunic and surcote and over the board, his trencher and even on to his leather boots. And it smelled vile. She had never smelt anything as disgusting in her life. And it kept coming. Three times she vomited before she managed to stagger away, the sound of the Baron's cursing following her as she walked slowly from the hall and up the stairs to her chamber.

She felt so ill. Her head was going round and round and

her stomach felt as if she had been kicked several times. She was dying. She was sure she was dying! Yet the look on the Baron's face as she had spewed her vomit over him had been worth it, Elona thought, her triumph sustaining her. If she did not feel so ill, she would laugh until she cried. He had been so furious, so outraged that she should vomit all over him— and so much vomit! There had seemed no end to it, and its sour taste was in her mouth.

'My lady…' Roberta was hurrying to greet and support her back to her chamber. 'You are feeling ill? I feared it might be so. I gave you a strong dose of the potion, for I wanted to be sure it worked at just the right moment. It did, didn't it?'

'Yes…' Elona groaned and clutched at her stomach again as she felt the griping pain. 'Yes, it worked perfectly. Am I dying, Roberta? It feels as if I am like to die.'

'No, my lady, you will feel better soon.'

Philippa had come out to see what the matter was and gave a cry of dismay as she saw that Elona was clearly ill. 'Oh, my lady,' she cried. 'Has that brute harmed you?'

'No. I was already feeling sick before I went down,' Elona said. 'I'm afraid the Baron is not pleased with me. I vomited all over him—and the table where he sat—and it did not smell pleasant. I vow it was the most awful stench I have ever encountered.'

'You…' Philippa laughed, amused by the thought. 'It serves him right. Oh, my lady, I wish I had been there to see his face.'

Elona gave her a weak smile. 'It was almost worth it just for that,' she said. 'Please help me, I feel so weak. I must lie down.'

'You are faint,' Roberta said. 'You must sleep now and it will pass. I will make you a tisane to ease your stomach.' She smiled as Elona pulled a wry face. 'Trust me, my lady, it will help you feel much better.'

As Elona lay down on her hard cot, she felt the aching in her stomach and wondered if she would ever feel better again, and yet she would not have changed what had just happened for the world. For what might have happened had she not vomited did not bear thinking of!

Oh, please God, let Stefan come for her, for if he did not she would ask Roberta for a potion that would make certain she could never be the Baron's wife.

'How long have I lain here unconscious?' Stefan asked as he gazed up into the face of the man who tended him. 'Elona! We have lost too much time.'

'Nay, my lord, there is no sense in pushing yourself before you are rested,' the soldier told him. ''Tis but a few hours since your horse threw you and went lame. I sent a man on ahead and he saw the lady being taken into the castle. He has returned to tell us the lie of the land and gone back to keep a watch.'

Stefan sat up. His head was spinning and it ached like hell, but at least no bones were broken.

'We must go on,' he said. 'I dare not leave her there at that rogue's mercy an hour longer than need be.'

'We have received word that your father and his men will be with us by the morning. Would it not be better to wait, my lord? The greater the show of force we have, the more likely that Danewold will surrender.'

Stefan saw the sense of the man's argument. Besides, it was already dark, and if the Baron's intent was to despoil Elona and thus force her into giving consent for the wedding, it might already be too late.

Something inside him cried out a protest. He wanted to cover the short distance between them, scale the walls and kill the Baron with his bare hands, but he knew that it would avail him nothing. The fall from his horse had delayed them too long.

Elona was Danewold's prisoner now and only God could help her at this moment. He rose to his feet, needing the assistance of the soldier's hand for one second until the dizziness had passed, then he walked away. He would keep a vigil and he would pray that no evil would befall her, though his mind was sorely troubled.

Elona felt better when she woke, the sickness having left just an ache in her stomach, which eased when she ate the coarse bread and honey her women brought her to break her fast.

'I hope I shall not have to take that vile stuff again this evening,' she said to Roberta when they were alone. 'If it made me as sick as I was last even, I should surely die.'

'It would make you ill in truth if you swallowed it too often,' Roberta agreed. 'We must pray that my master does not feel amorous for a few days. They say that he is in a foul mood and that two of his servants have been whipped for no reason this morning.'

'He is an evil man,' Elona said and shuddered. 'I am sorry that your people suffer, Roberta. I did not mean to cause trouble for others.'

'They are used to it,' she said with a grimace. 'All of us who serve the Baron know that his moods can be violent. Some have tried to leave him, but he is a vengeful man.'

'He should be punished.'

'I wish it might happen,' Roberta said. 'But while he stays

in his stronghold and sends others to do his foul work, there is little chance of it.'

Elona wanted to offer her comfort, a chance to leave the castle in her service, but how could she when she did not know if she would leave this place alive?

'I shall get up now,' she told Roberta. 'But if I am sent for, say that I am still too ill to leave my chamber…'

How long could she play this waiting game? How long would it be before Stefan came for her?

Surely he would? She must believe it or she would be lost.

'Thank God that you have come,' Stefan greeted his father warmly as they both looked up to the castle that stood on a rise beyond the dense woods surrounding it on three sides. To the rear was a steep ravine, which made it impossible to reach from behind, and there was a moat all around the stout walls of the keep. 'It would take a month to breach those walls, but my hope is that Danewold will realise he is beaten when he sees our combined forces and give in without too much of a struggle.'

'When I give him the news that Elona's lands have been taken into protective custody by Duke Richard's men, it may give him pause for thought,' Ralph told his son. 'The messenger reached us but an hour before Dickon told us what had happened. Had Danewold known what he risked, I dare say he would have thought twice before abducting her.'

'It cannot help but sway the balance in our favour,' Stefan agreed grimly, but his thoughts were far from eased. Elona had spent several nights upon the road with the men who had stolen her and one within the walls of Danewold's stronghold. Pray God that nothing had happened to her! 'Then we are agreed, Father. We take our men forward and make a show of force, then send in our demands for Elona's release.'

'Yes, that would seem the best plan,' Ralph nodded, a thoughtful expression in his eyes. He could not fail to notice his son's agitation and wonder at it. True, the girl had been under Stefan's protection and he would feel it reflected badly on him that this had happened, but there was more here than met the eye. Something deeper, stronger—hidden. 'If we must fight, we shall for as long as it takes, and for that I rely on you. It is many years since I did more than drive off a few marauders from our lands and they were but poor creatures, badly armed and ill trained.'

Stefan nodded. He knew that his father still trained often with his men to keep himself fit, but neither he nor they were battle hardened. If it came to a fight, it would be his own men that must lead the way, but sometimes a show of force was enough. Besides, the Baron would realise that forcing Elona to become his bride would avail him nothing as far as her lands were concerned. If the deed were done already, he would be punished for it, Stefan vowed. If she was a wife, she would be a widow ere long—but that would not restore all that she had lost, nor heal his own grief at her distress.

'You are no more than a few hours behind her,' Ralph said, somehow feeling Stefan's agitation without understanding it. 'He will not have had time to wed her yet. There are laws, which must be observed.'

'That man does not regard convention,' Stefan growled. 'What does he care for the law unless he is forced to bend the knee?'

'We must pray that he had at least the grace to allow her some rest,' Ralph said. What ailed Stefan? Anyone would think he was in love with the girl! Yet how could that be? He had known Elona was intended for his half-brother's bride. Surely he would not...? There Ralph's thoughts were suspended, for one of his men had come up to him with some news and he turned away to greet him.

Stefan strode away to deploy his own men. He hoped that Danewold would be thrown into confusion by the news he brought of Duke Richard's stewardship of the de Barre lands. Elona's father had done well to protect her and his manor by making the Duke ruler of the lands in the event of his death. Whether the Duke would be happy to hand them back when she married was another matter, but one that did not concern Stefan. Anyone who cared for Elona would not care a toss for her fortune.

'What is this?' Baron Danewold roared his anger at the man who had brought him the news that at least a hundred armed men were massed before his gate. 'Who dares to attack me?'

'It is the combined forces of Sir Stefan and Sir Ralph de Banewulf,' his steward told him, his knees shaking as he saw the rage in his master's face. He would probably be whipped for daring to bring such news. 'They are a formidable force, sir, much stronger in numbers than we are, and I do not think we can hope to drive them off.'

'Damn them!' The Baron cursed several times. He had not bargained for this, thinking that, as there was no true betrothal, Sir Ralph would not bother himself for a distant kinswoman of his wife's. It seemed that he had underestimated the man and his son. Supposing the wench's story were true and she was betrothed to Sir Stefan...carrying his child. Her vomit had turned his stomach sour and he had not yet recov-

ered. He had been forced to bathe and discard his tunic—his
second best that he had put on in honour of what was supposed
to be a night of triumph. 'Give me their demands, then—or
read them to me if you will.'

His reading skills were not as good as he would like,
though he tried to keep this a secret for fear that his steward
would cheat him if he realised how difficult he found it to de-
cipher letters. He must be clear about what these men had to
say, for though he craved the lands Elona de Barre would
bring him, there were other ways to make sure of them.

'They demand that you deliver the lady up to them unharmed,' the steward said. 'They say that, if she has not been
touched in any way, you will be allowed to keep your stronghold and go unpunished—apart from a fine of one hundred
golden marks.'

'One hundred golden marks!' The Baron swore furiously.
'Be damned to them. I'll see them all dead first.'

'There is more,' the steward cautioned, though he trembled
at the thought of his master's fury. 'It seems that John de Barre
made Duke Richard custodian of his lands and it is decreed
that if the girl is forced to a marriage she dislikes or dies…the
lands become the property of the Duke.'

'The Devil take him!' Danewold raged as he realised that
he was cheated of his prize. He might choose to fight Sir Stefan, though it was doubtful if he could win, but to go against
the King's son, a man who would be the future King of England—that was more than even he dared, for he knew his fate
if he tried. 'Curse the wench. She is not worth it—a dammed
whore by her own confession. She should be whipped at the
cart's tail!'

'Sir Ralph demands that you meet with him and his son

outside the walls of your keep to discuss the terms of your surrender.'

Danewold's face flushed ruby red with fury and he was tempted to tell his steward to send back a message that he would see them in hell before he would surrender, but then he thought of the consequences of such action. Perhaps he could find a way to escape the fine—and, if not, he would have his revenge another way. A crafty smile touched his mouth. The lady was a self-confessed whore and he would see that Sir Ralph knew it.

Oh, yes, he would wipe the smile from their faces!

'Send word that I shall meet alone with Sir Ralph outside the walls,' he told his steward. 'I am not agreeing to the fine, but I will parley with him and discuss the merits of his demand.'

'Yes, my lord.'

Danewold's steward wondered what had pleased his master. Something must have, for he had seen that evil smile before. The Baron was planning something—of that much he was certain.

Chapter Seven

'But why does he want to speak to you alone?' Stefan asked. His hands curled at his sides in frustration at this demand. He had wanted the chance to get Danewold at his mercy. 'Do not let him persuade you to mercy, Father. If he has harmed her, I shall not stay my hand. I swear he shall die if he has laid so much as a finger on her!'

'You wrong me, Stefan,' Ralph told him with a frown. 'I am not a soft fool nor yet a hothead. What is it that you fear? What does the girl mean to you?'

'I was entrusted with the care of her,' Stefan said, his eyes staring at a point somewhere above his father's head. He could not speak of his feelings for Elona—not until he had settled things between them. 'This is a slur upon my reputation.'

Ralph was not convinced, but understood that his eldest son was in a difficult position. He knew that Alayne had intended the girl as a possible bride for their son—but nothing was settled. She would not insist upon it if there was something between Stefan and Elona. Besides, he was not sure that Alain was ready for marriage as yet. He had sensed restlessness in the young man of late and wondered if he was troubled by thoughts of a marriage that would bind him too soon.

'Very well, if that is your only reason.' There was no point in pushing too hard at this time. First they must settle this business with Danewold. 'I shall bring Elona back with me—but I shall make sure that she is untouched before I give him pardon.'

Stefan inclined his head. He did not like it that he was to be left behind. Damn it! He should be there when Elona was brought out—he should be there to comfort her, to teach that vile brute a lesson he would never forget. His spirit rebelled at waiting tamely for her to be brought to him when he longed to strike out at his enemy.

And yet he knew that she was vulnerable. Until the walls were breached, she would be at the mercy of Danewold and his men. Better then to make peace if he could rather than risk more harm to her.

But supposing Danewold had… Stefan crushed the thought that threatened to overwhelm him. It did not matter. He would still wed her even if—but the thought of that brute touching her, forcing her, turned his guts and he knew it would haunt him, as it must her. She might be forever scarred by it, shamed so deeply that she would never recover. Pray God she did not ask to be sent to a nunnery! That way he would lose her as surely as if she were dead.

'Do what you must,' he told his father, tight-lipped. 'Only bring her back safe.'

No matter what was promised, he would punish the Baron if Elona had been harmed!

'I am glad you agreed to my terms,' Danewold said, eyeing Sir Ralph uncertainly. The son had a fearsome reputation, but there was little known about the father, who had lived peaceably on his manor for years. 'I am sure we can reach some agreement.'

'Our terms are that you hand over the lady at once and unharmed,' Sir Ralph said, fixing him with a hard stare. In his heart he would have liked to see the man whipped and brought before the King's justice, but it would be better to avoid a long siege and much loss of life if it could be managed. Besides, the longer the dispute went on, the more the lady would suffer. 'I have managed to restrain my son thus far—but should you refuse, I dare not think of the consequences. He will subdue you and your men no matter how long it takes and you will pay the price with your life.'

Danewold felt a queasiness in his stomach. It seemed that Sir Ralph was himself no easy mark and this interview might prove more difficult than he had hoped.

'The lady has not been harmed by me or my men, that much I promise you,' he said. 'My men were under orders not to touch her and would have paid with their lives had they dared. I have scarcely seen her. She has been unwell since she arrived and kept much to her chamber.'

'Unwell?' Ralph's gaze hardened as he looked at the other man. 'What do you mean, unwell? Explain yourself, sir.'

'Her trouble is none of my making,' Danewold said. ''Tis the trouble that comes to a woman when she lies with her lover. She vomited at table last even and told me herself that she carries your son's bastard in her belly. She says that she is betrothed to him, but I think she lies. She is most like a whore and the child may be anyone's—'

'Be careful what you say, sir,' Ralph warned and his mouth

was white-edged with anger. 'You malign the good name of my son, Alain, who has never yet seen her.'

'I meant the elder—the one who brought her to these shores. She swears that he is the father of her bastard and that they were betrothed at court. And she seems to be with child, for she has the vomiting that plagues women in their first months of carrying.'

Ralph's eyes narrowed. Surely it was a lie! Stefan would not so far forget his honour as to deflower a maiden—and one promised, though not yet betrothed, to his brother?

'I would see the lady,' Ralph said. 'Talk to her alone.'

'You are welcome to her,' Danewold said, his mouth curling sourly back from teeth that were blackened with neglect. 'Take the whore and good riddance—but you'll get no gold marks from me. You can burn the damned keep around us and I'll see it burn before I pay.' He raised a hand and signalled to one of his men and a woman was brought out of the stronghold, riding on a white palfrey. A serving woman riding on a mule accompanied her. 'There she is—take the whore for all I care.'

Ralph controlled his temper with difficulty. There was still time for Danewold to change his mind and order the girl stopped; he must let the Baron's remarks go for the moment. Elona's safety was the most important thing at this time.

He noticed that she rode well, her head high, cheeks pale, but her eyes were proud and her expression determined. She was certainly very lovely, he realised, the kind of woman that many a man would lose his head over.

As her palfrey drew abreast of him, he dismounted and went up to her, taking hold of the reins and gazing up at her. Close to, she looked as if she might have been unwell of late, her eyes shadowed and red as if she had wept many tears.

'Are you hurt, Elona?' he asked softly in a voice that only she could hear. 'Have they done aught to harm you?'

'The only harm was in bringing me here in the first place,' Elona said. 'It was against my will and…I was threatened, but nothing happened, perhaps because I was unwell.'

'The Baron claims that you told him you are carrying a child—Sir Stefan's child. Is that true, Elona?' His eyes narrowed as she hesitated, glancing towards the Baron nervously. 'You are safe now. You may tell me the truth. I wish only to help you, in whatever way I can. Are you carrying my son's child? Has he promised to wed you?'

'He…' Elona was about to tell him the truth and then she stopped. If she admitted it had been a lie to stop the Baron ravishing her, she would be taken to Banewulf and compelled to marry Alain. At the start of her journey it had not mattered so very much, but now she saw clearly that she could never marry any other than the man she loved with all her heart. If she told the truth, she might never see Stefan again. And she might not be believed. The realisation that people would always suspect her of losing her honour was shaming.

If Alain de Banewulf did not want her after what had happened, there was a possibility that Elona would be forced into a marriage with anyone who would still have her—and if her reputation was lost she could not hope for a good marriage. She had branded herself a whore and, even if she now denied it, some would believe it still. And if she did not tell the truth…what then?

She believed that Sir Ralph was a man of honour. He would think of his duty towards her. He would do what was right by her, she was certain of his mind, and suddenly she knew what she was going to do. It was a terrible, terrible thing, but something inside her compelled her to speak as she did, 'Yes, I am carrying his child—and he did promise to wed me, though we are not yet betrothed.'

Ralph's expression became stern, his mouth drawing into a grim line of disapproval. At that moment he looked so much like an older version of Stefan that Elona shivered. All of a sudden she realised the enormity of what she had done! To lie to the Baron was one thing, but to lie to Sir Ralph was quite another.

Stefan would never forgive her for her wicked lies! She wanted to take them back but could not find the courage or the words and stared helplessly at the man gazing up at her.

'Do not fear, Elona,' Ralph said in a soft voice that belied his looks. 'You shall be wed to my unworthy son before the day is out. Unless you would prefer to go to a nunnery and spend your life in prayer?' Elona shook her head dumbly, unable to speak, and he nodded. 'I must apologise to you for Stefan's behaviour—and for the disgraceful way you have been treated. I must finish my business with the Baron now. This scandal must be kept quiet for your sake, lady. Go with my men and they will see you safely back to our camp.'

Elona could not answer. Her heart was pounding as she let one of the de Banewulf men take the reins of her palfrey and lead her away, feeling that the world had come crashing down about her ears. It was a wicked, wicked thing she had done, and she was sure that she would be justly punished for it. Either God would strike her down or…more likely Stefan would hate her.

She did not dare look back at the two men, who were now both on their feet and talking earnestly, nor could she see anything ahead of her for her eyes were blinded with tears.

She did not even look back to see if Roberta was following or had returned to the castle. Oh, why had she done such a terrible thing?

Stefan paced restlessly, his hands clenched at his sides as he fought against the urge to ride after his father and demand to be a part of the conference that was even now taking place outside the Baron's stronghold. Why was it taking so much time? His father had been gone more than two hours. Why had he not gone with them? What could possibly be taking so long? He was on the point of riding to find out when he heard voices and the sound of hooves and harness jingling, and then he saw them. His father, the men he had taken to the parlay—and Elona!

She looked so pale, so distraught, that he wished Danewold were there so that he could run his sword into the devil's heart and destroy him. What had he done to her?

'Elona!' he cried and strode towards her, his heart bursting with grief at her pain and from love of her. It did not matter what the Baron had done, curse him. He, Stefan de Banewulf, loved her and he would make things right for her again somehow. Even if all he could offer was the protection of his name. 'Elona…' He moved towards her as someone helped her down from the palfrey, intending to greet her, to tell her that he loved her more than his life, but before he could get near her two of his father's men barred his way. 'I command you, let me through…'

'Stefan, forgive me…' She tried to speak, wanting to explain, to take back her lies, but she was not allowed to reach Stefan. Sir Ralph's men had mounted a guard around her, as if to protect her. 'Forgive me…' She smothered a sob as she looked at Sir Ralph and saw his anger. What had she done?

'Stay where you are, Stefan,' Sir Ralph commanded and his face was as cold as ice. 'I would have words with you first.'

'In a moment. I must speak with Elona!'

'You will have time enough for that later,' his father replied, giving him such a cold look that Stefan was shocked. What could have brought that look to his eyes? He feared the worst and wanted to explain that it did not matter. He loved Elona enough to wed her even if she had been dishonoured. 'Come with me. What I have to say is private.'

Stefan glanced at Elona, but she would not meet his eyes. She must be in terror of what his father was going to tell him. He believed he understood her shame and distress.

'Stefan, I must tell you…' she cried. 'Forgive me, I beg you.'

'It does not matter,' he told her, but he was not allowed to get near her. 'We shall talk later. Nothing matters but that you are safe, Elona.'

'I must speak with you…'

Her request was ignored and she was steered away from him forcibly. Yet as she looked back she felt his eyes upon her and longed with all her heart to confess her wickedness. But she was not to be given the chance!

Stefan tried to break through to her, but there were five men now, guarding her from him, it seemed. What did they think he meant to do to her? Did they think that he would kill her if he learned the truth? Men had been known to kill a wife who had been taken by another and dishonoured, but he cared only for her feelings, her pain. She gave a little sob and turned away.

Frustrated and angry, Stefan followed his father to a part of the camp where they could be alone. Ralph's eyes were cold as he looked at him and Stefan was chilled. Why was he looking at him like that?

'What has happened to her? Has that brute harmed her? Tell me at once!'

'Why did you lie to me, Stefan?'

'What do you mean?'

'You told me she meant nothing more than a sacred trust. That was a lie. Do not try to defend yourself. What you have done is beyond forgiveness.'

'I do not understand you.' Stefan felt the bitterness rise in his throat. Of what was he being accused? He had recently been accused of one heinous crime and now it seemed he was being blamed for something more. 'What are you saying? Come, speak out, Father. I would know of what I stand accused?'

'Elona has told me the truth,' Ralph said, his lip curling in scorn. 'Your behaviour sickens and shames me, Stefan. I had thought you were a man of honour.'

Stefan felt the coldness sweep over him. Of what did he stand accused? Did his father believe that he had conspired to kill the Lord de Montaine despite his name having been cleared of all complicity?

'I know that I should never have allowed her to walk alone in that wood…' His gaze narrowed. 'But that is not what you mean, is it? Please speak plainly, sir. I would know of what I stand accused.'

'As if you did not know well enough! Or perhaps Elona has not dared to tell you that she is carrying your child?' Ralph's expression was so condemning that Stefan recoiled from it. 'She was your sacred trust. How could you so betray it? I know that she is beautiful, but could you not control your lust long enough to tell us that you wanted her for yourself? I hope that you do want to marry her, Stefan—for I have sent for a priest and it will be done before nightfall. I have promised her this and I shall keep my word. You defy me at your peril. I am still your father and, unless you wish me to disown you, you will wed her.'

'Be damned to you!' Stefan cried, beside himself with fury at his father's high-handed manner. How could he believe that *he* would behave in such a way? 'If you imagine that I care for Banewulf—'

'Have a care, Stefan. I still have influence with the King, and I can have you arrested if you defy me. Where is your honour? Where is your compassion? Would you have Elona bear the shame alone? Do you not know what will happen to her if you reject her now? No one will wed her, even for her lands—and 'tis not certain they can be recovered now that Duke Richard holds them. She will be soiled goods when she gives birth to your child. No man will want her to wife.'

'Then let her go to a nunnery where she belongs!'

Stefan said the words as anger ripped through him, but then felt the agony pierce him. No, he would not have her shut away from the world to do endless penance for her sins. Rather than that…his gorge rose to choke him as he thought of her in another man's arms. It must have been her squire, Will de Grenville, of course. He had prevented her eloping with the young man, and now she had decided to blame him for her predicament.

His pride wanted to deny her, to denounce her as the whore she surely was, but his heart would not let him. There was a part of him that hurt so badly he felt that he might be dying, bleeding inside, drop by drop, so that he felt his life slipping away. Yet his mind was angry, his pride wounded, protesting. It was useless to proclaim his innocence, for he would not be believed. Sir Ralph believed Elona—and he had never cared for his eldest son. He had sent Stefan away when he was but five and yet Alain had been kept at home. The old wound twisted inside him, making him bitter and tearing at him.

No, he would not deny that he had fathered Elona's child since she had claimed it was so. He would not see her shamed before the world, though she deserved it. He would wed her since his father was determined on it, but then…he would leave her at Banewulf and go away.

If he stayed with her, if he took her to his home, in his present mood he might do her some harm.

Elona glanced at her bridegroom's face and shivered inwardly. She had never seen Stefan look so angry. He must hate her now! She had told such terrible lies to his father, and now he thought her a wanton and beyond all consideration.

Her mind repeated the words that begged for forgiveness over and over again, but she could not say them aloud. It was too late. Stefan was angry and bitter. He would never forgive her for besmirching his honour.

He had not looked at her once since the priest began the ceremony that would bind them together for the rest of their lives. Nor had he looked at her as they signed the priest's register as man and wife. Sir Ralph had insisted on the hasty ceremony, refusing to wait until they reached Banewulf, but now he was ignoring them both as he joined his men at their feasting. She sensed that there was anger between them and it made her feel guilty. How she wished that she had told Sir Ralph the truth!

However, it seemed that, despite the atmosphere between the two, the wedding was being celebrated by both Sir Ralph's and Stefan's men, none of whom were aware of the forced nature of the marriage. There was much laughter and a few sly glances as Elona left the company and sought the privacy of her own pavilion.

She was married now and nothing could change that. Stefan had given his vows in a strong clear voice before witnesses, though she knew they had been given grudgingly and in anger.

How had Sir Ralph managed to force his son's hand? Had he threatened to disown him or was there some other power he held over Stefan? She could not know, but it played on her mind and she felt the guilt strike deep at the harm she had caused.

How could Elona have told such terrible lies to his father? It angered Stefan to know that Sir Ralph believed such tales, that he had acted hastily and without giving his son a chance to give his side of the story. Not that he would have dreamed of doing so! Let those who were so distrusting believe ill of him. It mattered not.

Yet the bitterness stirred inside him, a feeling of betrayal by his father that he had believed long conquered rising up in his throat like gall. Even bitterer was the knowledge that Elona had needed to lie to protect herself, which meant that she was fearful because she carried her lover's child.

As his father had pointed out in his righteous anger, she was in a perilous situation, her honour lost with her maidenhead, all chance of a good marriage gone. Except that she was now his wife.

Only a few hours ago he had longed to make her his own; now he was barred from taking her to his bed by the anger that consumed him. His feelings were so inflamed that he dare not touch her for fear that he might do her harm.

How could she betray him with that mewling squire? His pride had received too many blows of late and he was suffering from a bruised ego. Not usually a vain or pompous man, his feelings were at odds with each other, for beneath his anger lay the truth. He was feeling so wretched because he loved a woman who had preferred the kisses of another man.

Only as a child cast out from his home had he felt such grief, and much of that had come from bewilderment, from the shock of finally being told by a nursemaid that it was he who had killed his mother. The pain he felt now surpassed what he had experienced then, combining as it did with a shaming, all-consuming jealousy.

He wanted to tear her from limb to limb, to sink his sword deep into Will de Grenville's breast and watch his lifeblood drain away. He wanted to inflict pain, to hurt others as he had been hurt, to take his revenge in a blind rage. *No!* That must never be! The red mist of fury cleared slowly from his brain as he realised where his terrible thoughts were leading him, remembered too why he had given into his father's demands when he might, if he had wished, have refused to marry her and ridden off with his men, leaving her to suffer the consequences of her recklessness and his father to think ill of him. But Sir Ralph must always have despised and hated him. The realisation was like a douche of cold water, clearing his mind.

Grown to manhood now, Stefan knew that women too often died as a result of childbearing, and that in all truth the child could not be blamed. He had believed himself free of the past, his festering hurts washed clean in the searing heat of battle. Indeed, he had been able to seek out his family again, to seek a relationship with his father—and had, it seemed, been rejected as unworthy.

He would not beg for Sir Ralph's good opinion. If it could not be given freely, it was not worth the taking. Nor would he stay at Banewulf to see the reproachful glances of his step-mother and Alain. He would take his men and go once Elona was with her family.

Elona was sitting on the stool provided for her comfort when the flap of the pavilion was pulled back and Stefan entered. Her heart fluttered nervously as she waited to hear what he would say to her. The grim line of his mouth told her that he was very angry, but her heart raced in the hope that he had come to claim her as his bride.

She rose to her feet to meet him, her face pale, her lovely hair flowing about her shoulders and down her back as she waited for the onslaught that was sure to come.

His first words, cold and cutting, destroyed her hopes of any chance of reconciliation. 'You should have told me the truth. I would not then have prevented you from going with your lover. Instead you chose to lie—it would seem that your nature is to deceive, Elona.'

'I did not mean to be so wicked…'

'Spare me your lies, woman!'

Elona shivered, afraid to speak out. How she wished that she might speak, might explain her reasons for deceiving his father, but she knew that he would not believe her. She could see the hatred in his eyes, searing her with his contempt. She wanted to tell him the truth, to confess that she had lied because she loved him, because she feared that she would lose him if she did nothing, but it was hopeless.

'I…forgive me,' she whispered and then faltered, the words in her mind impossible to say. She felt so ashamed of what she had done and wished desperately that she could take back her lies. 'I have done you a great wrong.'

'You lied to my father and shamed me,' Stefan said coldly. 'Your safe conduct was a trust given me by the Lady Alayne and you have shown me to be wanting. You have defamed my honour.'

'I am sorry. I should not have done so but…I was afraid of…'

She had been afraid of losing him and his anger was confirming that her fear had come to pass. She had forced him into a marriage he did not want and now he hated her. How foolish she had been to think she could gain her heart's wish by falsehood.

'I am well aware why you were afraid,' Stefan said and the icy tones whipped over her like an east wind in winter. 'To bear a child out of wedlock would leave you nowhere to go but a nunnery—'tis where you belong for your sins. By right I should send you there to do lifelong penance—'

'No, I beg you!' Elona cried, moving swiftly towards him. 'I lied, but please do not punish me so.' Her eyes were wide with distress. His threat was no idle one for even the powerful Queen Eleanor had been punished thus when she'd pushed King Henry's patience too far. 'Stefan, I…forgive me.' A sob broke from her, her lovely eyes sheened with tears as she sought for the words that would tell him why she had lied and failed. How could she defend herself against the indefensible?

'No, I shall not do that,' Stefan said, touched by her tears despite himself. The temptation to take her into his arms and carry her to the bed was overwhelming. His loins burned for her, the need to lie with her so strong that it took all his willpower to control it. 'You deserve some punishment, Elona, but I have not yet decided what it shall be. I am too angry to be near you at this time. I shall see you safely delivered to Bane-wulf and then return to my own manor.'

'But you will take me with you?' she cried and clutched at his arm. 'I am your wife, Stefan!'

'Not by my choice,' he said, whipping her with a cruel look. 'True, you have trapped me into this marriage, but you will not dictate the terms of it, Elona. As my wife you are bound to obey me and I will be obeyed. You will stay at Banewulf until I decide what to do with you.'

'Please…I beg you. I…'

She meant to tell him of her love, but in that instant he caught her to him, his mouth crushing hers in a cruel hard kiss that bruised her lips. It was a kiss meant to punish, to destroy, not to nurture or love, but Elona clung to him despite the anger she felt in him, her whole body ready to surrender if he would but take her. She would bear even this if it bound him to her. She felt the strong shudder go through him and the burn of his erection against her thigh, and knew that his lust was aroused. He wanted her despite his anger.

'Take me, love me,' she cried. 'Do as you will with me, but do not send me from you.'

Stefan flung her from him so savagely that she stumbled and almost fell to the floor of the pavilion, which was merely earth covered by a thick carpet. 'I want none of your wiles, harlot,' he cried, his anger fuelled by the knowledge that he was close to casting pride aside and taking her to him as his wife despite all. The desire burned so fiercely in him that he was breathing hard, as if he had been running, his voice rasping as he denied her. 'You will learn a proper maidenly modesty before I will consider giving you a place in my home. I shall keep no wanton as my wife.'

'Stefan…' she wept as she pressed the back of her hand against her bruised lips, holding back the sobs that shook her body. 'Please do not look at me so. Forgive me. I love you…' The words were out at last but their effect was to make his lips curl in scorn, his eyes darken with disgust.

'So do all wantons cry,' he replied. 'I have heard it from other cheating women. Do not imagine that your lies will be believed, Elona. Perhaps when you have learned proper humility, when you truly repent of your ways, then—' He realised what he was saying and broke off, unsure whether he was more angry with himself or her. It would be wrong to offer hope when he did not know whether he could ever forgive her. Then, without another word, he turned and walked out of the large tent, leaving her staring after him in dismay.

Sinking to her knees, Elona covered her face with her hands as the sobs of despair broke from her. Such cruel, cruel words. Stefan hated her, despised her, believed her wanton and false, and she had lost him.

'Do not break your heart, my lady,' Bethany said, coming to kneel on the ground beside her and put her arms about her. 'He is wicked to say such things to you and so I shall tell him. You are as chaste as the moon and undeserving of his unkindness.'

'No, you must not,' Elona cried and clutched at her friend in fright. 'Please do not, Bethany. He would not believe you. He would think you lied for my sake. He does not believe that I love him…'

Bethany rocked her in her arms, her face stony. No matter what her mistress said now, there would come a time when she would change her mind, and then Bethany would take great pleasure in telling Sir Stefan what a fool he had been to treat Elona so harshly!

Elona travelled the last few leagues in silence as they neared the manor of Banewulf. She had not seen Stefan since they started out and she believed that he rode ahead of the main body, obviously preferring his own company.

'You must not fear your reception at Banewulf,' Sir Ralph said, bringing his horse to walk beside hers. Her white, strained face had moved him and he wondered what had taken place between her and Stefan that first night. It had clearly not been a happy night for either of them. Stefan had been in a foul mood throughout their journey, speaking to no one, and Elona was obviously distraught. 'Lady Alayne will not blame you for what has happened, nor indeed will our son. I am certain that my wife will welcome you to her home as warmly as if nothing had happened.'

'I thank you for your kind words, sir.'

Elona tried to smile, but could not quite manage it. She believed that her heart was broken and she did not know how she would manage to live through the months and years before Stefan sent for her.

Surely he would send for her in time? What would she do if he turned his face against her? When no child was forthcoming, she would be branded a liar. She might as well get herself to a nunnery, she thought miserably. Without Stefan there was no hope of happiness for her.

She saw him briefly as the main party rode into the walled courtyard of the attractive manor house. It was, she thought, much the same size as her father's house, but looked as if it had been much improved in recent times. There were more windows than she was used to and the house was designed for comfort rather than as the fortress her father's had been. True, there were stout walls surrounding the courtyard and an iron portcullis guarding the moat, but once inside the defences it was pleasant and she caught a glimpse of a garden with pretty, shady walks where the lady of the house might take her ease.

She had hoped that Stefan might come to help her from her horse as he had sometimes in the past, but instead it was Dickon who helped her dismount. She looked for her husband, but saw that he was talking to some of his men, and then she lost sight of him as a lady came to greet her. Looking at her in some trepidation, Elona was struck by the serenity of her manner and her beauty. Although covered by a cap, strands of hair the colour of spun gold escaped to curl about a face of such sweetness that Elona was immediately drawn to her, losing her fear of rejection as the lady opened her arms to embrace her.

'My dearest child,' Lady Alayne cried and embraced her as a small sob escaped Elona. 'There is no need for tears. You have been through a terrible time, but you are safe now, my dear. We shall look after you at Banewulf until such time as Stefan has prepared his house for your coming.'

'Prepared…' Elona faltered, gazing at her uncertainly.

'Of course,' Alayne replied. 'He has only recently returned from his travels and has not had time to put the house to rights. He has explained to me that, although it is a good property, it is sorely in need of the comforts that a lady has the right to expect. As I imagine he has told you, he will go on ahead to set everything to rights and then we shall arrange for you to go to him.'

'I see…' Elona swallowed nervously, her throat tight. 'I would not mind that so very much.'

'You would prefer to go with him, of course.' Alayne looked understanding. 'I would feel the same in your place, Elona, but men see things very differently. He cares for you a great deal and has only your comfort in mind. Besides, he is set on the plan and I think Stefan is not a man to be persuaded against his will.' There was a twinkle in her eyes. 'He is much like his father and I have learned not to try when the cause is lost.'

'No, I know that he is not…' Elona faltered. 'I mean…he is stern sometimes…but at others he can be kind.'

Alayne touched her pale cheek. 'Do not distress yourself. Stefan has told me that you have been through a terrible time these past few weeks. He believes that it would not be right to force his needs as a husband on you until you have had time to recover from your ordeal. Such consideration is not always met with in a husband, my love, and I think he is very wise to give you a little time to grieve for your father and to recover your spirits. Besides, I shall be glad to have you with me for a time. I have been looking forward to seeing you and we shall all welcome you here as one of our family.'

How foolish she had been to dread her reception here! It could not have been kinder, Elona thought, though given her choice she would have gone with Stefan. But he did not want her and she could not force him to take her with him.

'Come, I shall take you inside,' Alayne was saying. 'You must be weary and will need to rest before we sup.'

'Thank you,' Elona said, casting a wistful glance at Stefan. He had his back to her and she believed that he was making plans to depart almost immediately. Would he leave without even saying goodbye to her? Elona's heart was heavy at the thought. How could she bear it if he went without so much as a word to her?

She was drawn away, taken into the house and up a stone stairway that led to an upper landing where several rooms were situated. Her father's house had been built in the old way, with a great hall and a great chamber above, her own solar in a tower away from the main keep. However, this house was of another design entirely and she saw that the passages led to various rooms that all opened on to the narrow landings.

'How different this is,' she observed. 'It is much more comfortable and warmer than my father's house—and much nicer than Baron Danewold's castle.' A shiver ran through her as she recalled the awful little room where she had been kept a prisoner. 'That was horrible…'

'Do not think about that time,' Alayne told her and pressed her hand. 'It is over now and no one will speak of it again. You are safe with us, I promise you. Here is your room, Elona. I shall leave you to rest for a while—and then you shall meet the rest of my family. They are eager to meet you, but I thought it best to let you settle in a little first.'

'You are so kind. I do not deserve it…'

'Of course you deserve our kindness,' Alayne replied. 'You have done nothing of which you have cause to be ashamed. The Baron abducted you and the rest is nothing.'

Was it possible that no one had told Lady Alayne of her shame? Elona had thought that she must have been told, but now she realised that perhaps it was not so. Both Sir Ralph and Stefan must have conspired to keep it private, for her sake, she sensed, so that she would not be exposed to more shame. Her eyes filled with tears as she hung her head, overwhelmed by their forbearance.

She did not deserve it!

'You will feel better soon,' Alayne said and went away,

more than ever sure that Stefan had been right to put his wife's needs before his own.

Elona barely glanced around the chamber, but she realised immediately that it was furnished for comfort and contained many items that would make her stay here pleasant. There were stools and chests, and velvet hangings to hide the bareness of stone walls and bring warmth to the room. Also a great bed with silk curtains and covers…if only she could share it with Stefan that night!

The door opened behind her and she turned, expecting to see one of her women, but instead Stefan stood looming on the threshold, a brooding expression in his eyes as he stared at her. She trembled, wondering what to expect. He would be within his rights as a husband to beat her—and he looked angry enough to do it.

'Lady Alayne knows nothing of what has happened between us,' he said, echoing Elona's thoughts. 'She believes that we fell in love on the journey from France, that it is a true marriage—and that I go on ahead to make ready for your coming.'

'You seek to hide my shame,' Elona said. 'But what will she think when you do not send for me?'

'I have not yet decided what to do with you.' His eyes seemed to harden for a moment, sending shivers down her spine. 'It may be that I can find a use for you in my household, Elona. For the moment I am too angry. I might do you harm if you were near, but one day I may be able to find forgiveness in my heart. If that day comes I shall send—until then I expect you to behave modestly and not shame me further.'

He thought so ill of her! Her chest felt as if it were being crushed with the grief his words roused in her. It was so unfair that she should have lost his respect, for she had told her lies to save her honour—and yet she had lied to his father, that could not be denied. The knowledge of her guilt shamed her so that she could not meet his accusing gaze.

'Yes, Stefan.' Her cheeks were pale, her eyes filled with unshed tears, but her head was high. She knew that she deserved this of him, though at any other time she would have flown into a temper at such words. 'I shall do nothing to shame you. I give you my word.'

Why did she not fly into a temper with him? Stefan did not like to see her thus, though she deserved it. 'I cannot answer for my actions if I should hear otherwise.'

'You may believe that I shall behave with all modesty, my lord.' Her face was pale, her hands clasped in front of her as though she held them to keep from trembling.

'Very well.' Stefan felt the ache nagging at his insides, his anger warring with the deeper need to hold her in his arms, to feel her soft lips beneath his and the satin of her flesh pressed close to him. Another moment of this and he would lose control and ravish her, perhaps hurt her with the ferocity of his feelings. It must not be! He would not give way to the beast inside him! For then he would be shamed. 'I am leaving now and I but came to say goodbye.'

Elona's heart was surely breaking. 'Must you leave so soon?' she asked, fighting her tears. 'Could you not stay a few days? If we could but talk…'

'Elona….' Stefan hesitated, and for a moment she thought that he would weaken, then he shook his head, more for his own thoughts than her pleading, she suspected. 'It is for the best. You do not know the beast that lives inside a man, Elona. You have roused that beast in me and I dare not let it roam free. Give me time to think and then perhaps we may meet again.'

'Fare you well, husband,' Elona said, the remnants of her pride returning as she lifted her head and met his gaze. 'I shall think of you and I shall pray for your forgiveness, though I know I have wronged you and I do not blame you for your anger.'

She was so meek! It was unlike her. He felt the prick of suspicion and knew that he dare not relent towards her. If she planned to slip away to her lover and he discovered it he didn't know what he'd do.

'It is not easy to forgive, lady.'

'No, but I do beg that you will find it in your heart in time, for I am sincere in my regret.'

Stefan inclined his head, but said nothing more as he went out. Elona stared after him, feeling as if her heart was being torn to shreds. She longed to run after him, to beg him to take her with him, to love her, make her his wife, treat her as he would. She did not care what he did to her, as long as he did not ignore her.

But she could say none of the things in her heart, because he did not wish to hear them. She could only wait and pray— pray that he would send for her one day, and that he would learn to forgive her.

'I love you so,' she whispered. 'May God forgive me for what I have done. I love you so much that if you never send for me I shall want only to die…'

Chapter Eight

⁓⁓⁓⁓⁓

'You are so beautiful,' Marguerite said, smiling at Elona shyly.
'I am not surprised that Sir Stefan stole you from my brother.'

Elona had been told that the Lady Alayne's daughter had been
named for a friend she had been fond of, though her son had, of
course, been named for her. The girl was young yet but bidding
to be a great beauty, and her nature was gentle and sweet.

'No, no, it was not like that,' Elona protested, her cheeks
colouring. She liked Marguerite and they had spent many com-
panionable hours together these past few weeks. Lady Alayne's
shy daughter had shown her about the manor, telling her where
to find certain berries and herbs that grew in the gardens or in
the meadows about the village, and introducing her to the people who worked at Banewulf. It was like a small town in itself,
with craftsmen of all kinds at work in the courtyards, which
were sheltered by the stout walls against both the sometimes-
harsh winds and attack from raiding parties. 'We…fell in love.'

'That is so exciting,' Marguerite said, her pretty face glowing. 'Just like the songs the troubadours sing when they come

to entertain us on feast days. Besides, Alain did not want to be married. He told me so.'

'Alain told you that he had no wish to marry?' Elona's attention was caught. She had found Marguerite's brother charming, so different from Stefan with his merry smiles and ready jests. But he was seldom in her company, merely greeting her with a soft word in passing, and she had assumed that the reason he had avoided her was because he thought himself cheated of his bride. 'When was that?'

'Oh, months ago.' Marguerite shrugged her shoulders carelessly. 'He wants to go abroad and fight wars. It is so foolish when he could stay here with us and be safe.'

'Alain wants to fight?'

'If there were a worthy cause, he would go tomorrow,' Marguerite said and pulled a face. 'His head is full of dreams. He wants to win honours for himself as Stefan did, but I think that he will find he does not like war.'

'Why do you say that? I have heard he has won several tourneys.'

'Mock battles,' Marguerite replied scornfully and tossed her head. 'My brother cannot bear to see a bird with a broken wing. He will risk being bitten to free an injured fox from a trap. How could he kill anyone?'

'Ah, I see.' Elona understood and smiled. Although she had seen little of Alain de Banewulf, she had thought him gentle and kind, a much softer man than Stefan. 'But a man cannot always stay safe in his father's house, Marguerite.'

'That is what Alain says. I dare say he will go, though I am not sure what will become of him.'

'Perhaps he will fall in love and bring his bride home.'

'Perhaps…' Marguerite looked at her curiously. 'When are you going to join Stefan? Surely the house is ready by now?'

'When—when he sends word,' Elona said, her cheeks heating beneath the girl's clear gaze. How could she answer when the truth was so terrible, so shaming?

Three weeks had passed since she'd arrived at Banewulf, three whole weeks during which she had shed too many tears. There was a bitter ache inside her, a sharp regret for what she had done, and the punishment she must bear because of it. She would never cease to wish that she had not told such wicked lies, for though life was good here at Banewulf and she had been made welcome, her heart was sore.

When would she see Stefan again? Would he ever forgive her?

Stefan looked moodily at the work the stone mason had just completed on the east wing, the wing he had planned for his wife's apartments. It was very fine, but it gave him little satisfaction. He had set the work in motion before he went to Banewulf and now it was finished. The furnishings he had ordered when in London had arrived that morning on a score of wagons, and all that needed doing was for the goods to be unpacked and carted upstairs for the rooms to be ready.

For what? There was now no hope of the simple, uncomplicated life he had envisaged when he had, half in jest, asked Lady Alayne to find him a bride. Love had not entered into his plans, especially the consuming, jealous burning that filled him now, keeping him wakeful and souring his thoughts.

Damn Elona! She tortured him day and night, for he could not be free of her.

There was not one night when he had not thought of her. Often he paced the floor of his chamber as the memory of her pale face lingered in his mind, making him feel guilty for speaking to her so harshly. He had seemed to see a terrible hurt in her lovely eyes, and her manner had been so subdued. Had he done that to her—or was it Danewold's men?

How had she managed to get beneath his skin, so that the thought of her never gave him peace? He could see her at every turn, smell the scent of her perfume, which was like no other, feel her pliant body close to his as his cried out with need.

What was he to do about her? Stefan could not answer. His first white-hot anger had cooled a little, but he was afraid it might return the moment he gazed on her lovely face. Especially as her waist began to thicken and her womb swell with another man's child. Therein lay the rub, for he knew his jealousy would prick at him like poison thorns and he could not answer for his temper.

He would rather die than harm her, and he was shamed that his jealousy rode him like a devil. He ought to be able to find the strength to face her with equanimity, to forgive her, take her into his household as his chatelaine and in time…the mother of his own children.

What would people think of him for leaving his wife at his father's house? The world would believe that she carried his child and that he deliberately neglected her. Folk must either think him a rogue or her a wanton. In time they would begin to reflect that there must be a reason for Stefan to turn his back on her, and they would point the finger of blame at Elona. She would then be heaped with the shame he had married her to prevent. It was no good. He must find a way of forgiving her, of accepting that she had given herself to another man and blame him for the bastard she carried in her womb.

If he could not he ought to have refused the marriage, defied his father and left her to her shame. He knew that he must send for her eventually, but not yet. The hurt was too raw, too deep, and he knew not what might happen if he saw her.

He must bury his lust in work! There were tasks enough, for the manor had been sadly neglected until he purchased it from the King, the last owner having died without issue—as he might if he could not bring himself to forgive Elona.

Yes, he would send for her, but not until he had conquered this need for her, this longing that was like to drive him mad.

Six weeks and there had been no word from Stefan! Elona's heart felt as if it were breaking. Her life was empty despite the kindness of her hostess and Marguerite. Perhaps it might be better to put an end to it? She had only to take the sharp knife she used for her embroidery threads and draw it over her wrists. She had considered it more than once, and yet something inside her clung to life and to hope.

Tears sheened her eyes as she sat on the little wooden bench in the gardens. Autumn was almost upon them, the summer days fleeing despite the aching need inside her that made each one seem an age. How could she bear to live, knowing that she might never see Stefan again—and that it was by her own fault that she had been brought to this?

Suddenly, her grief overcame her and she bent her head, a sob of despair escaping her. She was so alone without him, needed him so desperately.

'Ah, do not weep, lady,' a soft voice said beside her. 'It grieves me to see you so sad.'

'Sir…' Elona glanced up at the face of the young man who was gazing at her so kindly. 'I am a foolish woman, Alain. You must forgive me.'

'You need no forgiveness,' Alain said and sat down on the bench next to her. 'Do you weep for my brother—because he leaves you here so long alone?'

'How did you know?' Elona was surprised. Yet she ought not to have been, for he was truly one of the gentlest, most sensitive people she had ever met.

'I have seen it in your eyes,' Alain told her with a smile. 'You love him. Very much, I think?'

'Yes—but he does not love me…' Elona gasped for she had not meant to say so much. 'I mean…he is angry with me.'

'I have sensed some mystery,' Alain said. 'I know Stefan to be a man of strict honour and I do not think he would have wed you so suddenly without cause.' He paused as her cheeks flamed and he realised he had hit upon the truth. 'But perhaps you would rather I went away and did not ask such questions?'

'I…no,' Elona said chokily. 'I have been too ashamed to tell anyone the truth.'

'You speak of shame. What can you have done that is so very wicked?'

'I have lied,' Elona said, her head lifting as she faced her sin and pride was restored. She would speak out and take her punishment. 'I told Baron Danewold that I was with child because I thought it might stop him…forcing me to his bed… and it did. I took a potion that made me vomit all over him and convinced him that I was carrying a child.'

'I would have liked to see his face,' Alain told her with a merry smile. 'It was perhaps the only way you could have prevented him from seducing you. I have heard that he is a man of ill temper.' He looked thoughtful. 'I take it that you told him and my father that Stefan was the father of your child?'

'Yes, and it was a wicked lie,' Elona said, her cheeks pale, hands trembling as she clasped them in her lap. 'He would never have betrayed the trust your mother placed in him. That is why he is so angry with me, because I defamed him, cast a slur on his honour.'

Alain was silent for a moment. He was not certain that Stefan's anger came entirely from that cause. Perhaps he above all other men knew the softer side of the nature that Stefan believed entirely hidden. 'You are not with child, I think? Nor have you lain with a man?' he asked and Elona's cheeks flamed as she shook her head. 'So you lied to my father and I believe I can guess why.' A smile of rare sweetness touched his mouth, his eyes warm and understanding. 'You had fallen in love with Stefan and did not wish to be forced into marriage with me?'

'I love him so much,' Elona replied brokenly. 'Now that I have met you, I know that I should not have been forced to wed you, Alain, but…it was the reason I lied.'

To her surprise he threw back his head and laughed merrily. 'It seems that we have both been playing a deep game, Elona. I sent one of my men with my brother to delay his journey here. I believe you had certain little accidents on the journey?'

'We thought that was Baron Danewold's men!' She stared at him and then smiled as she appreciated the jest. 'Marguerite said that you did not wish to marry.'

'I am not ready to take a wife,' Alain admitted with a rueful look. 'You are lovely and it would be no hardship to wed you and stay here, but if I did that I should never be a true knight like my brother. I must win my honours and will not have them handed to me on a golden platter because of who I am.'

'Your sister said that you look for a cause?'

'It is in my mind to go to Duke Richard's court,' Alain

said. 'I would have gone sooner, but my mother held me here with soft words. I feared to grieve her—and then I could not leave before you arrived, for it would have been discourteous.'

Elona smiled and touched his hand. 'You are a most gentle knight. I vow a truer knight could not be found, sir, though you have not been knighted. And I thank you for your kindness.'

'And what will you do about Stefan?'

Her eyes widened in surprise. 'What can I do? He is my husband and he bids me stay here until he sends. I must obey him.'

'Must you?' Alain's brows rose. 'My brother is a fool to think ill of you, lady. Anyone can see that you are as innocent as you are lovely. Shall I tell him that? I could tell him what a fool he is if you will allow me.'

'He would be angry…' She looked at him steadily, a faint flicker of hope in her mind. 'What should I do? How can I win him?'

'You are his wife. Your rightful place is with him. In your stead I would go to him with all your goods and chattels. He can hardly bar you from the gates. Once he has admitted you, you will find a way to make him see the truth. And if you do not, then I shall challenge him…that's if I'm still in England.'

'Go to him?' Elona gasped at the boldness of his plan. 'Without waiting for him to send for me?'

'Why not?' Alain's merry smile lifted her spirits. 'I vow the man is behaving like a fool and I dare swear it is jealousy that rides him—because if he believes you are with child and knows it is not his, he must think you have lain with another.'

'Lain with another?' Elona felt the dizzy relief sweep over her. 'You think it is because he believes I have known another man that he keeps from me? But if he is so jealous, might that not mean…?' Her words trailed off, for she did not dare to hope so much.

'I know my brother,' Alain said. 'Had he despised you as you imagine he would not have tamely allowed our father to push him into wedding you. He would have refused and ridden away. The very fact that he married you must mean that he cares for you—enough to protect your reputation, and I believe far more.'

'If that were true…' Elona's heart soared on the hope he had given her and she jumped up, her face alight with new eagerness. 'I cannot thank you enough for all you have done for me, sir!'

'And I shall do more,' Alain said, a hint of mischief in his blue eyes. 'A letter shall come for you tomorrow and you shall tell my mother that Stefan sends for you. I shall offer to escort you. My brother shall not deny you entry if I am with you, lady.'

'How good you are,' she cried and laughed, clapping her hands at the plan. 'I was so foolish to fear coming here.'

'I cannot vouch for Stefan's actions when he has been forced to admit you,' Alain told her with a wry look. 'I believe he hath a temper and you may bear the brunt of his anger—but you must be patient. Show him in every way that you can that you are prepared to be a good wife. Let him see that there is no child, and, when he is ready to listen, tell him the truth.'

'I have tried, but he would not listen.'

'Because he was in the white heat of anger,' Alain replied. 'It will have cooled by this time. I dare say he has begun to regret leaving you here. When he sees you, all his feelings for you will come flooding back and he cannot fail to want and love you.'

'I have been such a fool,' Elona admitted. 'I should have sent him a letter before this, confessing my fault, but I was too shamed to think of it.'

'Do not fear,' Alain said and gave her the sweet smile that was so like his mother's. 'Stefan is not such a fool that he could turn his back on you when you are there in his house every day. If he loves you, it will irk him to keep a distance from you. You must find a way to show him how much you love him. It may take time, but in the end you will win him back to you.'

Elona looked at him shyly. 'I thank you from the bottom of my heart. I could not have confessed my shame to your mother or to Sir Ralph.'

'My father is very like Stefan,' Alain said and chuckled. 'They both seem to be growling bears, but underneath you will find there is a heart as true as any man's.'

'Yes, I know it,' Elona said. 'And now I shall go to my chamber and tell my women to prepare my things.'

'No, not until after you get the letter,' Alain said, that wicked gleam in his eyes. 'My mother will question it else and we must not let her suspect anything.'

'Yes, you are right. I am too hasty.'

But now that she had something to do, something to fight for, she was full of energy and resolve. Alain was right. She had been foolish rather than wicked and had been overcome by her shame. It was wrong of her to lie, but if Stefan loved her…if he loved her he would forgive her one day.

'I am sorry that you must go and leave us.'

Elona smiled and embraced the younger girl. 'I dare say you will visit us one day,' she said. 'Besides, it will not be long before you are wed yourself and mayhap I shall be invited to your wedding.' A delicate blush touched the young girl's cheek. 'I believe there is someone you like very much?'

'Oh, no—at least, he would not be interested in me. He came here but once with Stefan and has never returned.'

But you will marry one day. I am sure of it.'

'Of course you will be invited when that happens,' Marguerite said and hugged her. 'I shall miss you, Elona. You have been the sister I have longed for and never had. But you must go to Stefan. I know that is where you want to be, and I am sure that he must be impatient for your coming.'

Elona smiled but made no reply. She was filled with trepidation as she took her farewell of Sir Ralph and Lady Alayne, thanking them for their kindness to her.

'It was a pleasure to have you here,' Alayne told her and kissed her warmly. 'We shall always be pleased to see you and Stefan at Banewulf, Elona. You will tell him that I said that, won't you? I have sometimes feared that he felt himself cast out when his father sent him from home at such a young age. It is the custom to send sons away for their training, but must often be hard for the child.'

'Yes, I shall tell him,' Elona said, but in truth she did not know when. Would Stefan even speak to her—would he admit her? What would she do if he turned her away?

'God speed, lady,' Sir Ralph said. 'I am sending ten of my best men with you and Alain. I do not believe you are in any danger, but I would not have harm come to you from my neglect.'

'I thank you for your care of me—and I ask you to forgive me, sir.'

'For what?' His brows rose and he was so like Stefan that

her heart jerked. 'You are a lovely woman, Elona, and I believe no lasting harm has been done.'

Elona nodded, but could not meet his eyes. She had wanted to confess her sin to him, but Alain had advised against it.

'My father would not approve of what you did,' he told her. 'It is better that he does not know for the time being. When you have made your peace with Stefan will be time enough for the truth, I think.'

Elona could only take his advice, though she knew that Sir Ralph must suspect something, for it must be obvious to him that she was not carrying Stefan's child. Indeed, her grief had caused her to lose weight and she was more slender than she had been before she came to Banewulf.

'You are ready, lady?' Alain came to help her mount her palfrey.

She gave him her hand, her heart racing wildly. She was far from ready for Stefan's reaction when she arrived at his manor, hardly daring to think how he would look or what he might say to her. Indeed, she knew that she would never have dared to set out on this venture without Alain's help and reassurance.

Their journey took them three days. They rode at a steady pace, finding time to talk and enjoy the pleasant countryside about them. He was, Elona thought, a wholly charming companion, but there was no danger that she would fall in love with him. Alain's smile brought her cheer, but it did not cause her knees to tremble or her body to ache with longing as the merest glance from Stefan always had.

When the large manor house came into view, Elona drew rein, her breath catching in her throat as they looked up to it, as it sat broodingly on a rise, its grey stone walls imposing and severe. The fortifications had been strengthened recently, as though Stefan felt that the peace England had enjoyed during much of King Henry's reign, despite the rebellions of his sons, might not always hold good. Yet the dwelling had also been improved, with new windows added to bring light and sunshine to what might otherwise have been a dark interior.

'Supposing he will not admit me?' she said to Alain as he brought his horse to a standstill beside hers. 'Where shall I go? I could not return to Banewulf.'

'Fear not, Elona. My brother will not send you away.' Alain smiled at her encouragingly. 'Do not forget that you are the Lady de Barre as well as Stefan's wife, and you have the right to be treated with respect if nothing more.'

Elona's head went up. She must have the courage to carry out this bold plan, though her knees felt suddenly turned to water and her mouth was dry.

As the column of men, women, and wagons wound slowly up towards the manor of Sanscombe, she could see activity about the gates and wondered if they would be closed against her. However, nothing happened and their entire party was allowed in unchallenged.

Alain helped her dismount as a man she had never seen before came to greet them. He was in his middle years, clearly a steward and just as clearly bewildered by seeing his lord's wife in their courtyard.

'Sir—my lady, I fear I was unprepared for your coming. My lord did not tell me he expected you.'

'My brother must have had other matters on his mind,' Alain said, covering Elona's confusion with his easy charm. 'Where is he? I would have words with him.'

'My lord and some of his men went hunting this morning,'

the steward said. 'Forgive me, sir. My wits are scattered. I am Piers, Baron Sanscombe's steward. I shall have rooms made ready for you at once.' He turned to Elona with a bow. 'Your apartments have been ready for some time, my lady, though a fire would have been lit had I known you were expected.'

'It may be done when your people have time, Piers,' she said and smiled at him. 'If you could have someone show me the direction, please? I would rest for a little—before my lord returns.'

Her heart had stopped racing. The meeting that she had dreaded had been postponed. Stefan had not been here to deny her entrance, as she'd feared—but what would he say when he returned?

'My wife is here?' Stefan managed to keep his tone level as he looked at the steward. Why had his heart leapt with joy? Was he fool enough to love her still, after her self-confessed wanton behaviour? 'And my brother? He escorted her here himself?'

'Yes, sir. I am sorry that I was not better prepared for their arrival. If you told me of it, I had forgotten.'

'No, no, it was not your fault,' Stefan said, his face expressionless as he fought against the warring emotions raging through him. The immediate joy had faded swiftly to be replaced by doubt and rage. Elona here? How dare she defy him! He would send her packing immediately!

And yet in truth he had been thinking of sending for her this past month or more. Stefan had begun to realise that it was foolish to keep her at arm's length. She was, after all, his wife and he could never take another without casting her off. How could he do that when it would shame her? Surely he was man enough to accept what was past and look to the future?

'I had not realised that she would be here so soon.' He nod-ded dismissal to Piers, pacing the room as he tried to calm himself for the inevitable interview with Elona. She was here now and he must learn to live with the knowledge of her sin, the fact that she was bearing another man's child. He must learn to control his feelings! To accept that what had been done could not be undone.

'Ah, brother. I am glad to see you returned safely from the hunt.'

Stefan swung round as his half-brother came into the room. 'Alain,' he said, some of his anger defusing as he saw the oth-er's merry smile. He had never held a grudge against Alain, blaming his father alone for his banishment from Banewulf. 'So you have brought my wife to me. I must thank you, though I should have come to fetch her myself in time.'

'She was pining,' Alain replied with a careless shrug. 'She truly loves you, Stefan. You should have brought her with you instead of leaving her at Banewulf. She would not have minded a little discomfort to be with you.'

Stefan's eyes narrowed, his hackles rising like a dog de-fending its food. Elona was his, even if he had not claimed her. 'Did she tell you that?'

'Yes…' It was on the tip of Alain's tongue to reveal all, but something held him back. If Stefan loved his wife, he would discover the truth for himself, and if he did not—then Elona must bear the consequences. He did not have the right to in-terfere between husband and wife. 'I admire her a great deal, Stefan. She is as brave as she is lovely.'

Stefan's eyes narrowed. Had his brother come here to pick a quarrel with him? 'No doubt you think me a knave for steal-ing her from you?'

'Indeed not,' Alain cried and laughed. 'It was for this reason that I brought her to you myself, Stefan, so that we might clear any misunderstanding between us. I admire her and love her as a brother should, but I have no wish to marry—Elona or any other woman. I am not yet ready to marry. I have other plans.'

'You wish to prove yourself, I think?'

Alain nodded. 'I must gain my knighthood. I have stayed at home for my mother's sake, but I shall go very soon now.'

'Then perhaps you might care to hear news that reached me yesterday? Duke Richard has decided that Saladin must be stopped and he intends to march against him. He is even now rallying men to fight with him in the Holy Land.'

'Take up the Cross!' Alain's eyes lit with excitement. He was as devout as any young man of his era, but it was the thought of battle, of winning glory and earning his knighthood that appealed to him; to join a great crusade was exactly what he had yearned for. 'I vow 'tis a worthy cause. Even my mother will not deny that—nor that I must offer the Duke my sword. Think you he will accept it?'

'I am sure he will be pleased to accept your service, brother. I have had my share of fighting and shall not go, but you will stand in my stead and win honour for yourself and our family.'

'It is my heart's desire. I cannot bide at home forever, even to please my mother.'

'She will understand and give her blessing,' Stefan assured him. 'But you will stay with us for a few days?'

'For one night,' Alain told him. 'You have no need of me here, brother.'

'You are always welcome in my home,' Stefan said with a smile. 'I have never held a grudge against you, Alain.'

With the insight that was a part of his nature, Alain had known and understood that Stefan felt his father had rejected him as a child, but between them there had never been anything less than friendship.

'I envied you, living and training with our kinsman's men, learning to be a knight. When you were winning your spurs in battles with Duke Richard and I just a boy, I wished I could follow in your footsteps. The travelling minstrels sung stories of great heroes of the past, but you were my hero, brother. I wanted to be you.'

Stefan smiled, for he could not doubt the other's sincerity.

'I believe you will surpass me, Alain. You have it in you to be a great knight, a man of mercy and right.'

'If I can do as well as my brother, I shall be satisfied.'

'Then I shall wish you God speed. I can offer you no advice, for a man must find his own way in life and you have chosen yours.'

'Then we part as friends—no shadows between us?'

'We are friends. May God keep you safe until we meet again on English soil.'

'And may God give you peace and happiness,' Alain said. 'But I keep you talking and you will wish to greet your wife.'

'My wife…' Stefan's mouth hardened. 'I shall go to her shortly. But first I have a gift for you…' He crossed to one of the huge oak chests ranged against the walls at the end of the large chamber and lifted the heavy lid, taking from it a sword of shining metal, the hilt chased with gold and silver, the sheath a work of great art. 'I won this in a great tourney in Aquitaine. Take it with my good wishes, Alain. It was too light for me, but I believe it is about your weight.'

Alain took the sword, marvelling at its balance and the way

the handle seemed to fit his hand so perfectly. It was not only a thing of beauty, its blade sharper than any he had yet seen, it felt right, and he knew it to be valuable.

'This is a precious gift, Stefan.'

'Worthy of the knight you will become,' Stefan said and clasped his shoulder. 'The knight from whom I won the sword claimed that it had magical powers and that he had it from a magician in the east, but I do not believe in such nonsense. Yet in the hands of the right man I dare swear it could do marvellous things, and I believe you are that man.'

'I do not know how to thank you.' A slightly awkward expression came to his eyes. 'I have a confession that I must make to you, concerning…'

'The little accidents on our journey?' Stefan's brows rose, a hint of mockery in his eyes. 'Always they were the thorn that pricked me, but nothing terrible happened because of them—no man was killed, no beast injured. At first I wondered if Danewold had a spy in the camp. I even suspected my own men, and then I began to wonder. Now that you have told me you had no wish to marry, I think I need look no further for the culprit.'

'It was a boy's prank,' Alain admitted. 'I worried lest Graylin should do something that resulted in injury and wished I had not sent him with you. 'Tis time I had more to occupy my time than foolishness.'

'I agree that you should leave your home and seek life,' Stefan said. 'Though you may not find it as sweet as you expect—but now, come and drink a cup of ale with me. I dare say Elona has plenty to do settling into her new apartments. And I shall see her at supper. Let us talk, Alain, for it may be many years before we meet again.'

Indeed, it might be that they would never meet in this life, for there were many perils on the way to the Holy Land and too many men died in battle or its aftermath.

Elona was aware that her husband had returned to the manor and steeled herself against his anger. She was sure that he would come to her in a rage, mayhap to send her away before her women had time to unpack her chests.

Yet her apartments were comfortable, furnished with all the basic necessities she needed. There was a bed of huge proportions, its ends carved and gilded in a manner she had never seen before, but thought must come from some exotic land to the east. One wall of the chamber had a window that looked down at the courtyard below, and beneath it was ranged a large oak chest banded with iron clasps and studs. Other chests stood about the room, giving her space to store her gowns and possessions, and there were two stools and a chair with X-shaped supports, which was also carved and gilded on the back and arms. A frame for her needlework stood by the window, also a trestle and board. Here she would sit to write her accounts, Elona thought, and then flushed as she wondered if Stefan would trust her to keep his household accounts. Mayhap he would choose to leave that to his steward.

The walls were hung with tapestries of rich hues that gave the room warmth and light, and there was a separate room where her clothes could be laid on wooden shelves.

Her women had a room beyond that she would use as her privy and there was a further room at the opposite side of hers that she had been told led to her husband's bedchamber. She had not so far dared to look inside.

She had been busy directing her women to unpack her

own goods, and now had all her things about her, small personal treasures that had belonged to her mother. With the sewing box her brother had given her as a gift one Christmastide, her Bible, and various combs, brushes, scent flasks and ornaments, the chamber had taken on a permanence that made her feel as if she truly belonged there.

But for how long? she wondered uneasily. Would her women be ordered to pack her things as soon as Stefan had had time to consider?

Now that all was in order, she had changed into a fresh tunic and kirtle with a surcote of blue wool, because the chill of autumn had settled with the evening. She waited nervously for Stefan's arrival, certain that he would burst into her chamber and demand an explanation for her unannounced arrival.

When the summons came it was from Piers, who told her that Baron Sanscombe awaited her in the hall, where a meal was being served.

'Forgive the tardy invitation, my lady. It was expected that you would come down when you were ready.'

'I was not sure…at what hour you supped.'

She had not thought she would be expected to join her husband and his men at supper in the hall. Indeed, she had expected to be banished and her stomach was a spasm of nerves as she followed Piers from her chamber, along the gallery and down the wide, important staircase. How different this house was from those she had known before she left her home. Banewulf too was more of a home than a fortress, which she knew from Lady Alayne was because there had been peace in England since King Henry II came to the throne.

'Before that there was always unrest,' Alayne had told her. 'But whatever history may say of this king, he has done that much for his people. There have been rebellions by his sons, but thus far the nobles have lived peaceably with one another—for most of the time.'

Elona knew that noblemen grew greedy for wealth and lands, quarrelling with their neighbours over the merest trifle as an excuse to fight and steal their property. Her father had constantly been fighting petty battles with his close neighbours, and she marvelled that the English King had managed to keep stability in his kingdom for so long.

The hall was not as large as some she had seen, but it was large enough for the gathering of perhaps sixty men who sat at the boards that had been set on long trestles. They were drinking ale and wine from cups of pewter or horn, but as she entered they rose as one and saluted her.

'To the lady of Sanscombe, welcome.'

The cheering brought a lump to her throat. She had not expected this and the tears were close as she made her way to the high table where Stefan, Alain, a round-cheeked priest and the steward stood to greet her. Her heart was hammering as she made her curtsy to her husband. Now, now if he so chose, he could shame her so deeply that she would never dare to defy him again.

'My lord…'

'My lady,' Stefan said, his dark grey eyes dwelling on her face. He had noticed the slenderness of her figure as she walked so proudly down the full length of the hall, the heavy train of her gown trailing behind her. He noticed that it was the gown she had worn to the tourney, the one he had bought for her, and wondered if that was why she had chosen it. Oh, unworthy soul that he was to rejoice in the loss of a child! Yet the relief was so overwhelming that his throat ached from it.

'We had not thought to send for you sooner. Please take your seat by my side if you will.'

'Thank you, my lord,' Elona whispered, daring at last to meet his eyes. She could see that they held a serious, thoughtful expression, but no sign of the icy anger of their last meeting. Had he forgiven her? But no, he was merely showing mercy. She knew that he was renowned for the mercy he had shown his enemies, how could he be less forgiving to her?

She took her place at his left side, the right occupied by his brother, who was their guest and entitled to the place of honour. A servant came forward with a dish of fowl swimming in a rich sauce, another brought bread, another cold meat and cheese on a silver platter.

She accepted a little of the cold meats, refusing the richer dish and taking a chunk of the fresh bread, which crumbled in her fingers as she ate. She was conscious of Stefan sitting next to her, of the slight scent of leather and horses, of cedar wood and his own musk that she found so attractive. At court some of the men had used perfumes to mask the body odours beneath their rich robes, but she knew that Stefan bathed regularly, either in a handy stream when travelling or in the tub his men provided, and needed no such arts to cover the stench of stale sweat.

Wine had been poured for her into a silver cup. She sipped it and discovered that it tasted sweeter than she was used to and looked at Stefan in surprise and pleasure.

'Honey wine,' he told her. 'Have you not tasted it before, lady?'

'No, never,' she said and took another sip. 'My father's taste was for something much different. I found it sour and often drank only water at table. This is much more pleasant to the tongue.'

'I had it brought here…for those who prefer it,' Stefan said. 'But be careful, Elona, it is a potent brew. Too much and you will lose your senses and your dignity.'

'I have never drunk more than one cup of wine at table, my lord.' Her head went up, pride making her eyes glitter. Was he reminding her that he expected her to behave with a proper modesty?

Stefan was surprised at the way his heart gladdened to see such pride in her eyes. He had thought it crushed entirely and regretted the part he had played in her humiliation. She had lain with her squire and that could never be changed; it was a stain upon her honour, but not such a terrible sin. He could have understood and forgiven it in another, but in the woman he loved—the woman he had thought returned his love—the knowledge had sent him reeling to a pit of despair.

'I am merely warning you,' he said now, denying the urge to smile at her, to tell her that he was pleased to see her despite the jealousy that still lingered at the back of his mind. But it had abated now that his first shock had cooled, and he believed he could keep it at the back of his mind. He was after all a grown man, not a sullen child. 'I would not want you to be taken unawares by its potency.'

'I thank you for your concern, my lord,' Elona said and defiantly took another sip, but then, remembering that she relied on his tolerance, she put it down and summoned the servant carrying the water jug. 'Some water, if you please.'

'We are all pleased to see you here, lady,' the priest said to her, claiming her attention. 'I am Father Fernando and I serve Sir Stefan as his chaplain here. I am always at your service should you need me.'

'Thank you, sir,' Elona said and smiled at him. 'Do you

read the Latin? I can read and write in my own language, and in English, for my stepmother taught me, and I know how to keep accounts, but I confess I cannot read the Latin.'

'Would you wish to do so, my lady?' The priest was a little surprised, for few ladies bothered to learn more than how to write their name, though some could keep accounts.

'Oh, yes,' Elona replied. 'For then I could read the Bible. I have a copy that belonged to my stepmother, but I can only look at the illustrations, which are very fine and coloured in gold and crimson and blue—but I would like to be able to read from it sometimes.'

'It would be my pleasure to teach you,' the priest said, his plump cheeks dimpling. 'Your husband is a man of learning, as I am sure you know. He too has a beautiful Bible and also a very precious Book of Hours that he allows me to use. There are many scripts that he has collected on his travels and had bound into volumes with tooled leather; I think he might let you look at them if you wished.'

'Oh…' Elona could not help feeling surprised, for she had not realised that Stefan had such a collection of rare and valuable things. 'Yes, I should—if my husband would allow it.'

'If I would allow what, Elona?'

'Your lady was expressing a wish to learn the Latin, my lord,' Father Fernando told him. 'I mentioned that you have a collection of rare scripts that have been bound and that you might allow Lady Elona to look at them.'

'Are you truly interested?' Stefan smiled oddly as she inclined her head. 'Then of course you may look, my lady. It shall be my pleasure to show them to you myself. I have other treasures collected from my travels that you might care to see also.'

'Like the bed and chair in my bedchamber?' Elona asked. 'I have never seen anything like them before.'

'Yes, like them,' Stefan agreed. 'The chair came from Rome, I believe, and the bed from the land of Mesopotamia, I am told, though how true that may be I do not know. I bought treasures home with me from my travels to the Holy Land, some of which were supposed to have belonged to Alexander the Great—though again I do not know how true the tale is, for some of these travelling merchants are rogues and would lie through their teeth.'

Elona wondered at his knowledge, for she had heard only vaguely of the great king who had conquered an empire, and knew nothing of the lands of which Stefan spoke. She nodded, ashamed of her ignorance, though in truth it was not a lack of interest on her part; her father had not considered it necessary that she should receive more than a rudimentary education, and it was only through the kindness of her stepmother that she had learned her letters and her numbers. Her stepmother had known little history herself, and they had never talked of such things.

'I have scripts that relate the history of many lands and many great men,' Stefan told her, guessing what lay behind her silence. 'One of the things I plan to do now that I have come home is to translate some of these into English. If you are interested, I shall show you some that I have begun to work on.'

Oh, how she longed for a friendship between them, the kind of relationship that she had witnessed at court. If she could only be as easy with him as she had been with Constance and her father! If he would but relent towards her, consent to let her stay here as his wife…

'Yes…please,' Elona said, her heart catching as he almost

smiled at her. She had not expected such consideration from him and felt a rush of tears as the longing to see that look of desire in his eyes almost overwhelmed her. He had desired her once. If only he would look at her that way again! 'It would please me—if it were no trouble to you, my lord. I wish to be a good wife to you now that I am here. You must tell me what my duties are—what you expect of me.'

'Must I, Elona?' His eyes dwelled on her face for a moment, making her tremble inwardly. Her breath caught in her throat, her stomach clenching with nerves. How strangely he looked at her. She felt as if he were a wolf and she his prey, as if he were considering whether to devour her now or savour the thought of a meal later. 'Our case is a little different, I think. You must give me time to decide what I require of you. I have not quite made up my mind.'

Elona dropped her gaze, her cheeks hot as she felt his eyes on her. So, he was prepared to tolerate her here for the moment, but he could yet change his mind and decide that she would be better in a nunnery.

Chapter Nine

Elona's fear of being sent away was beginning to fade a little. She had been at Sanscombe for three weeks now, and though she had seen no sign of her husband wishing to claim his rights of her, she had been aware of a gradual change. He treated her with courtesy, the polite, meaningless consideration he would show to any lady of gentle birth.

The morning after his brother departed for Banewulf, he had sought her out, telling her that she must feel free to order his household as its chatelaine.

'You ask what your duties are, Elona. I think they must be that of any true lady. You will watch that the household servants do their work properly, consult with my steward about what stores are in need of replenishment, and give the sewing wenches their instruction. You may look over the household accounts if you choose, though Piers is trustworthy, and inspect the kitchen from time to time. And, if you hear of deserving cases amongst the poor of the village, you may take alms to them. Otherwise, your time is your own.'

Elona smiled inwardly. If the duties of a chatelaine were

truly hers, she would find much to occupy her here and was glad of it. Already her women had told her of linen needing mending, of fruit needing to be preserved and a sad want of many cures and simples that any good housewife knew how to prepare from herbs and flowers that grew in the woods and meadows.

'I thank you for your consideration, my lord.'

'I suspect that my household stands in need of you and your women, Elona,' Stefan said, a flicker of humour about his mouth. He was well aware that there was much to be put right, which was the reason he had considered taking a wife in the first place. 'The kitchen wenches are fit for nothing but rough work and the cooks might do better with some instruction from a mistress.'

'I noticed that the meal lacked variety last night. We must see what is in the stores to improve it.'

'You may tell Piers to order anything you consider necessary.' Stefan hesitated. 'I…believe you have experienced a loss, Elona. I am sorry if you suffer because of it.'

'I grieved for my father, but I have put that behind me,' she replied, her eyes downcast, knowing that it was not her father's death of which he spoke. She longed to tell him that there had never been a child to lose, but was afraid of rousing his anger. He was furious that she had lied to his father, but excused her in his own mind on the grounds that she had been afraid of being shamed before the world. How much worse would his anger be if he knew that she had lied without cause? He would surely be justified in turning her from his house and sending her forth to beg her bread with the lepers who sometimes clustered about the monastery. No, she dare not tell him, for she was sure he would never forgive her. At the moment there was a kind of peace between them, and she could not bear to rouse his fury once more. 'If you will excuse me, my lord, I have much to do.'

She walked away from him, her thoughts in chaos. Why had she not told him at once that she had lied to protect her honour from Baron Danewold? She should have made Stefan listen to her explanation, that she had been vulnerable and frightened, that she had seized upon the only thing that she had believed would protect her from the evil man who had captured her. The answer was, of course, that there was no excuse for what she had done afterwards. She had lied to Sir Ralph, because she had known that he would demand that Stefan marry her. And she had wanted that so desperately that she had been prepared to risk everything.

Her husband was justified in his anger against her. Something deep inside her sensed that the breach between them could not be easily healed. Stefan was not ready to forgive her yet. He had already made great concessions to her and she must not ask for too much too soon.

Watching her walk away, Stefan was afraid that he had hurt her with his clumsy attempt to console her. Women were often deeply affected by a miscarriage, though she was young enough to bear more children…his children.

Had she loved Will de Grenville very much? Stefan was convinced it must be so, because she would not otherwise have given herself so completely. Elona was not a wanton, despite the accusations he had hurled at her. Therefore she must have loved deeply.

Yet she had surrendered to his kisses so sweetly, melting into his body so readily that they could easily have become one. He could not believe it had been pretence on her part, for he had known other women and was sure Elona's response had been instinctive. How could she have been willing to give herself to him if she loved Will de Grenville?

It was a mystery. Unless she had been forced? In his anger, Stefan had truly not considered this explanation and now he wondered if he had hit upon the truth. If she had not surrendered willingly, the case was altered. It did not explain why she had accused Stefan of fathering her child, but it did make the knowledge easier to bear.

Stefan smiled wryly at his thoughts. What weak, vain creatures men were! It should not matter in either case, but it seemed that he might have found a way to soothe his injured pride, to accept what could not be helped.

Perhaps it did ease the burning jealousy, though the thought of her being forced to yield, of her being hurt by some rough fellow—perhaps one of those who had captured her—roused him to sudden fury. If he knew for sure who had violated her, he would kill the man. There should be no mercy given to such a monster!

Stefan was struck by guilt as he realised that he too had treated Elona harshly, ignoring her pleas for forgiveness, refusing to listen, her vows of love denied. He blamed others for hurting her and yet did so himself, such was the contradiction of love. A jealous man was a cruel man, and Stefan was shamed by his own behaviour, but as yet he could not find the strength to banish his jealousy altogether.

He was not yet ready to take her back into his heart or his bed, though there had been moments during the night when he burned for her, when temptation had nearly driven him to her. No, he could not yet forget, but he had reached a stage where he thought it might be possible to forgive.

Unaware of Stefan's own confusion, Elona strove to be all

that he could want in a wife. She began with the food stores and found them lacking in spices and preserves. Until she and her women had arrived, it had been a house of men, for the few kitchen wenches knew nothing of such things; born to serve, their lives consisted of work that lasted from dusk to dawn. Something that Elona would change in time. Her stepmother had taught her charity and she would see to it that all their servants were treated fairly, given time to dance and sing as well as work. Stefan had no time for such things, but it was her duty to care for all their people and she would do so with a good heart.

There was always a supply of fresh meat, for the forest covering one-third of Stefan's demesne teamed with game and they had a stewpond in which fat carp swam ready for the days when meat was forbidden by the church. However, nothing had been preserved in salt for winter, when the game was not so plentiful. She had already set the process in train and intended to have as many preserves on the shelves of her stillroom before the ice and snow set in as she could manage.

The village was a short ride to the east, and when Elona visited, accompanied by Dickon and Piers, she discovered that her husband had begun improvements here. In place of the shameful hovels that had housed the village folk, he had begun to build small cottages of stone faced with wattle and daub and washed with lime to keep out insects. He had built a wooden *ghildus,* a hall where the people could drink ale and dance when their work was done, and hold their feasts on special days.

It seemed that she was not the only one to consider their people's welfare! Stefan's generosity had made him popular and when his wife rode into the village on her palfrey she was greeted by smiling faces and cries of good wishes.

Elona asked if there was sickness in the village and was told that they were all well, apart from one old man who could not walk and was near to death, and a widow who grieved for her husband and would not speak to anyone.

The old man was clearly dying, but from age, not sickness, and Elona could do nothing for him but give his daughter food and money to care for him. The widow's name was Mary the Wise, and discovering that her father had been an apothecary and that she knew a little of his art, Elona invited her to come and live at the manor.

'You can help me in my stillroom,' she said. 'For though there is no sickness now, we must be prepared for the future.'

'You are kind, my lady, and if I can be of use to you I would be glad to come,' Mary answered. 'Though my skills did not save my poor husband.'

'They tell me he died because of a terrible accident at his work?'

'The blade of a scythe cut deep into his leg. I bound it for him and applied salves, but he took a fever and died of it and I could do nothing to save him.'

'Only God has the power to give or take life. We can sometimes ease the suffering of those in pain, but it is not for us to question God's will. Yet I am sorry for the loss you suffered. You have no children?'

'We were married for but six months and God did not see fit to bless us.' Mary's eyes were sheened with tears. 'I have wondered what my sin may be that I have been so cursed.'

'You are unfortunate and this was not God's curse,' Elona told her kindly, though she knew many would say it was so. 'You have been unhappy because you are alone, but you shall not be so in future. You are intelligent and I have need of your service.'

'I can write my name and keep simple accounts, my lady. But I am best known for my cooking.'

'Then you are just what we need,' Elona told her with a smile. 'You may take charge of the kitchens as well as helping in the stillroom. Come to the house tomorrow morning and Bethany will show you what to do.'

'God bless you, my lady. I was near desperate, for I did not know how I should live this winter.'

'I am glad to take you into my household,' Elona told her. 'I have need of more ladies about me, especially those with your skills, Mary. I shall be pleased to have your services.'

'And I right pleased to give them.'

Elona told Stefan what she had done at supper that evening.

'I hope you do not mind that I told her to come here, my lord?'

'Why should I?' He raised his brows, a hint of mockery in his eyes. 'Did I not tell you to order my household as you would? I have not spoken, but I have noticed the changes. It seems that I must be grateful that you chose to join me here. It was the household of a rough soldier, as I am sure you have realised.'

He was teasing her. The first time he had done so for many weeks. Elona's cheeks heated and she looked down at her trencher. The food served was much better than when she had first arrived.

'I would have come sooner had you sent for me, my lord.'

'Perhaps I should have done,' he said, and something in his voice made her raise her head. 'Perhaps I have been a fool, Elona?'

Her heart raced as she saw that hot glow in his eyes. It was so long since he had looked at her that way!

'I was the fool, my lord. I should never have lied to Sir Ralph.'

'No, you should not,' Stefan said and the glow faded.

Elona lowered her gaze, her spirits sinking. For a moment she had thought that the old Stefan had returned, but it was hopeless. He would never forgive her.

'I thought that perhaps you might like to see some of those manuscripts I told you of?' Stefan suggested. She had thought he had forgotten and was slow to answer in her surprise. 'But perhaps you would prefer to retire to your chamber?'

'Oh, no, my lord. I should truly like to see them—if it is no trouble to you?'

'Have you eaten your fill?'

'Yes, my lord.' Elona's heart was hammering wildly as he rose to his feet and offered her his hand. She felt that all eyes were upon them as he led her from the hall, and wondered if the men knew that he did not visit her bed.

'I have many manuscripts in my chambers,' Stefan told her as he led her towards the staircase leading to the gallery above. 'Some are histories of England and of other lands, as I mentioned previously, but others are stories. I have a volume of stories about King Arthur that I think you will like. It has coloured illustrations at the beginning of each tale and is a joy to touch and use.'

'It must be very valuable,' Elona said. 'Where did you find such a work, my lord?'

'I have gathered scripts from my travels,' he replied. 'I have work by Geoffrey of Monmouth on the Kings of Britain, which was penned in the years after 1130. But the stories came from all kinds of people and were written down at my bidding to be bound in vellum. I thought it would be good to preserve some of them for the future or else they may be forgotten.'

Elona listened respectfully as they walked together from the hall. She had known Stefan was a brave, true knight, but she had not realised the extent of his knowledge. She had called him a mannerless oaf, but it was not so, she saw now. He was actually a man of learning, wit and charm.

When they reached the chamber that housed the treasures Stefan had spoken of, she saw that he had ordered deep wooden shelves to be fastened to each of the walls. They were stacked with scrolls or bound scripts, which had beautifully tooled leather covers. Elona had never seen more than two books in one place, for her father had not been a great scholar. Pierre had studied for a few years, but even he possessed only his Bible and a journal in which the details of their family history had been laboriously compiled by various scribes.

Stefan showed her a copy of the *History of the Kings of Britain,* which had been written by Geoffrey of Monmouth. There was also a description of the country of Ireland from the hand of Gerald the Welshman.

'This is something that may interest you,' Stefan said, handing her a tiny book. 'It is a collection of poems, many of them anonymous. Most of the scripts here would be of no interest to you, for they are dull works—like this on the laws of England. But here is the book I promised you. It is filled with romantic tales about King Arthur and his knights. I believe you will find that to your taste. Father Fernando may use that for your lessons, if you wish.'

'You are generous, my lord. I thank you for allowing me this privilege.' Her hand touched his as he held the book out to her and she trembled. She felt a little breathless as she looked into his face and saw the glow in his eyes. He had not looked at her like that for so long. 'Oh, it is beautiful—the binding and the script is all so carefully done. It is a very precious thing…are you sure I may look at it?'

'You are my wife,' he said. 'All that I own is at your disposal.'

'I do not deserve your kindness.' There was a break in her voice, for something in his manner told her that he was close to forgiving her. Her heart was beating so fast that she felt as if he must hear it.

'Do you not?' Stefan's eyes dwelt on her for a moment. Then his hand reached out towards her, and he trailed one finger down her cheek. The lightest of touches and yet it sent a torrent of sensation coursing through her body. It was all she could do to keep herself from falling into his arms. 'I was very angry with you, Elona, and might have done you harm. I have thought long and hard, and I understand why you lied to Danewold about your condition, but not why you also lied to my father. You must have known that we would help you no matter what.'

Elona's breath expelled, her breast rising and falling beneath the heavy silk of her tunic as she looked into his eyes and saw something that gave her hope. He was no longer angry with her and surely…surely that was desire she read in his eyes? She swallowed hard, knowing that what she said now might determine her future.

She must tell him the truth and bear the consequences! 'I was in great distress. I acted hastily for the most selfish of reasons and I have regretted my lies a thousand times.'

He knew her reasons. 'Was it Will de Grenville—or one of Danewold's men? Did you go to him willingly, Elona? Tell me truthfully, for I shall know if you lie.'

Elona's heart was racing. He looked as if he wanted to take

her in his arms and she longed for it so desperately, her whole body crying out for his.

'It was…' Elona began, but before she could tell him that it was all a lie, that she had never lain with any man, they heard the sound of running feet.

The door burst open and Piers entered, breathing hard. He halted as he saw them so close together, and sensed that he had interrupted more than a discussion about learned scripts.

'Forgive me, my lord.'

'I trust you have good reason for entering in such haste?' Stefan frowned, for he knew that Elona had been on the verge of telling him the truth, and it was suddenly terrible important that he should know. 'Speak out, man! What is so urgent?'

'There is a raiding party in the village. They are killing men and ravishing the women, and the villagers need your help.'

Stefan cursed aloud. These things happened but he had not expected an attack, for he was on good terms with his neighbours.

'Forgive me, Elona, I must go. We shall talk of this another time.' His attention now was all for his steward. 'Tell me, is it known who attacks us?'

'We are not sure, but we think it may be some of Baron Danewold's men.'

Elona did not hear Stefan's answer, for he had left the room and was striding away, clearly in haste. It was terrible news and she knew that he had had no choice but to answer the call from his people, but she felt a wave of despair that the summons should come at such a moment. Another few seconds and she would have found the courage to tell her husband the truth.

Yet perhaps all was not lost. He had shown her his precious books and told her she might use them for her lessons. And, just for one moment, he had looked at her with desire.

If only they had not been interrupted. Even now she might have been in his arms, losing herself in his kiss, thrilling to the nearness of his body. Now a shadow lay over her for, with fighting in the village, anything might happen.

But she would not allow herself to think such gloomy thoughts. Stefan and his men would soon see off the raiding party and then he would come back to her and she could tell him what was in her heart.

Elona left the books he had said she might use on the table, for she did not like to remove them from his special room without permission. He had begun to thaw towards her and she wanted nothing to come between them.

Despite the faint anxiety at the back of her mind, she was smiling as she went to her own chamber. Stefan was too wise to leave the manor unprotected, and he would take only as many men as necessary to drive off the party of raiders. It would not be long before he was back with her and this time she would tell him the truth and hope that he would believe her.

There was a cloud of black smoke over the village as Stefan and his men approached. Several houses had been set on fire, as had the *ghildhus* he had been building for the villagers.

'My lord!' A man came running to his horse. 'You are too late. They have gone.' Tears had streaked his soot-blackened face. 'They killed my wife because she fought them and took my son. He is but ten years old and I fear for him.'

'Your name is?'

'Ulrich, my lord.'

'Fear not, Ulrich. Go back to the village and bury your wife. If your son lives, we shall bring him back to you.'

The man stepped back and Stefan urged his horse forward. His face was grim as he rode through the village and witnessed the devastation caused. Those responsible must be made to pay for this night's work. Their fate must leave none in doubt of what happened to those that dared to attack his people.

'It will not be easy to follow them in the dark,' one of his men said to him. 'Should we return to the house and give chase in the morning?'

'We go after them now,' Stefan said and his mouth was a hard, thin line. 'We follow them until we catch them and punish them, whether it takes us a day or a year. Send one of the villagers to the house to tell them that we may be gone for some days…'

The soldier nodded, knowing that look of old. His lord was known for his mercy, but after what had been done here there would be none for the raiders!

'But where is Sir Stefan?' Elona asked the next morning of his steward. 'Why has he not returned? He is not injured— or dead?' Her heart pounded with sudden fear.

'My lord sent word that they were determined to pursue the raiders,' Piers told her. 'I fear that much damage was done last night and Sir Stefan will not rest until the perpetrators of this outrage are caught and punished.'

'Yes, I see.' Elona felt upset. She had believed that there was peace between Stefan and his neighbours, just as there was at Banewulf. 'Do they know for sure who the raiders were?'

'We are not certain, but we believe it may have been some of Baron Danewold's men.'

'Surely he would not dare to attack my husband's village?'

Yet even as she spoke, Elona was recalling the fury in the Baron's face when she had vomited over him. He would have been even more furious at being forced to pay a fine, and this might be his way of taking revenge on Stefan. He had not dared to attack the house, for he knew it was well guarded and the portcullis lowered every night, but the villagers were vulnerable. They must have been sleeping in their beds when the attack began.

Elona shivered as she thought about the horror of being woken by screaming and shouting, the sight of houses being burned to the ground and people slaughtered.

'I must go to the village,' she told Piers. 'They will need help and I must do what I can to ease their suffering.'

Piers looked at her doubtfully. 'Sir Stefan would wish you to be safe inside the walls, lady. Supposing some of the raiders were left behind?'

'I do not think it,' Elona said, a stubborn look in her eyes. 'They must know that Stefan will seek revenge. I believe they will be long gone, for my lord will show little mercy to such rogues.'

'Then you must take several men with you to guard you, my lady. I should not be easy in my mind if you went unprotected.'

'I shall take Dickon, Bethany, Roberta and Mary the Wise, and one soldier to accompany us,' Elona said. 'I have no fear that we shall be attacked and a show of force might frighten our people.'

'As you wish, my lady.' Piers could do nothing to prevent her, though he feared for his life if anything should happen to her. 'I shall have a basket of salves prepared for you—and anything else you may need.'

'We may need all kinds of things from our stores,' Elona told him. 'But for this first time, we shall take only salves and cures that may help with burns and wounds. When I return, I shall tell you what else is needed.'

She left him to stare after her and wonder what his lord would say if he returned in her absence.

Stefan did not return while Elona was at the village, nor yet the following day, but she did not have time to worry for his sake, because she and her women were too busy helping those that had been injured and bereaved by the raiding party.

Some of the men had burns to their hands and arms where they had fought the fires that were destroying their homes. Some of the women had been ravished and beaten; those who fought hardest had scars to show for their pains and one woman was dead.

'What beasts they were,' Elona told her women when she was moved to tears by the sight of a young child with a wound to his head where one of the raiders had ridden him down. 'I truly hope that my lord will catch and punish them.'

Her anger was such that she shed no tears for herself. Her happiness could wait for Stefan's return; some of these people would never know happiness again.

She did what she could for the sick, ordered that meat and grain from the store at Sanscombe be brought to them, asked Piers to set the work of rebuilding the houses in train, and at the end of the third day went home weary and heartsore that she could do so little.

Elona had never felt so weary as when she allowed Julia to disrobe her. Her women had taken turns to help her in the village, but Julia had not been with her that day, and she was smiling as she poured warm water into the tub for her mistress to bathe.

Elona wondered what the girl could find to smile about at such a time, but said nothing as she climbed into the water and closed her eyes. It felt good to let the scented water enfold her and she sighed with content as someone began to rub soap into her shoulders.

'That feels good,' she said. 'I think I shall sleep for a month.'

'And so you should, my lamb,' a voice she knew well said and she sent the water flying as she turned to look at the face of the old woman she loved so well. 'There's no need to soak me, girl!' Melise scolded, giving her a toothless smile.

'Melise! When did you arrive?' Elona was overjoyed by the sight of her. 'Oh, it is so good to see you. I need you so much…' There was a faint sob in her voice. 'I've missed you so…'

'And so I should think,' Melise said, though her old eyes were bright with tears. 'After I have travelled so far to be with you, it would go hard if you were to send me back.'

'Send you back?' Elona laughed and shook her head. 'You must know that I should never do that, Melise. I love you and need you to soothe me when I am tired or ill.'

'As you always did,' her nurse crooned, well satisfied by her welcome. 'I thought we should never get here. We arrived at Banewulf some weeks ago to be told you were not there and I had to rest before I could come to you. It's just as well I got here when I did, for you have been doing too much, you foolish child. Why could you not leave the nursing to others?'

'Because the people were in such need, Melise,' Elona said. 'Besides, you would have told me I was failing in my duty if I had neglected them.'

'I should have told you to share your labours,' Melise replied with a shake of her head. 'But I shall not scold you, my love. I am here now and I shall look after you.'

Elona smiled as she sank back into the tub, letting the water ease her. It was so good to have her nurse with her again, but for the moment she was too weary to do anything but sleep.

Stefan's eyes felt gritty with tiredness, but there was a smile of grim satisfaction about his mouth. They had pursued the raiders for two days, but on the morning of the third they had caught them just as they were breaking camp.

What had followed was something that even battle-hardened soldiers might wish to forget, for many of his men had had friends, lovers or family in the village and he had not restrained them. Those raiders that were left alive had been sent in chains to the King for justice, which would mean their deaths. It would also mean punishment for the evil master who had sent them. Danewold would be called to account, his lands confiscated and the least he could expect was banishment.

It had had to be done if the villagers were to live in safety, and Stefan had not shirked his duty, but he was weary of conflict and bloodshed and wanted peace. Peace so that he could be with Elona and raise a family.

The plight of the villager whose wife had died had touched something in Stefan. One reason for his satisfaction was that the boy had been recovered, frightened and bruised, but otherwise unharmed; he would be restored to his father on their return to the village.

Stefan had thought constantly of how he would have felt if the raiders had killed Elona while trying to ravish her, and he knew that his grief would have been beyond bearing. It was senseless to carry a grudge for something that had happened in the past, and he would do so no longer. On his return, he would tell her that he cared for her and that he wanted her to be his wife in truth.

Yes, he would make an end to the conflict between them, Stefan thought. It was, after all, of his making, for she had done everything she could to make amends and he would be a fool to let his jealousy over a past lover sour his relationship with her.

Some of the weariness sloughed off him as he told his men to prepare for the journey home. He could not wait to be with her again, to hold her in his arms and kiss her. But this time there would be no barriers between them, nothing to stop him taking her to his bed and making love to her as he had longed to do for so many months.

She would be his at last, his wife, his love, and, if she did not yet love him, he would teach her to know him and hope that it was enough.

'I have to thank you for bringing Melise to me,' Elona said to Will de Grenville when she saw him the following day. She had been busy and this was her first chance to speak with him. 'It was kind of you to go to so much trouble, for I know you have had many months on the road when you might have been at the Duke's court.'

Will looked at her, his eyes searching her face. She looked tired—but was she happy? Had she been forced to marry a man she had sworn she hated?

'I was happy to serve you,' he said. 'I knew that it had made you unhappy to leave your nurse behind and I wanted to make you happy.'

'And you have,' Elona told him, smiling at his eagerness. She was fond of him, for he had been her friend and she had needed him in the months after her brother's death. 'I shall always be grateful to you, Will. And I hope we shall continue to be friends?'

'You know I am ever at your command.' Will hesitated, knowing that he must be careful. To suggest that she run away with him would be a dangerous business, for Sir Stefan was a man of fearsome reputation and his revenge would be terrible. Yet Will would risk it if she were to ask it of him. 'I have thought of asking your husband if he would accept my service, Elona. I would be near at hand if you should need me and…'

Elona was silent for a moment. It would be churlish to refuse when he had done so much for her, and yet she would have preferred that he leave before Stefan returned. The problems between her and Stefan were not fully resolved and she knew that he might believe Will to have been her lover.

'I am not sure…' she began, but before she could say more Piers came hurrying into the hall, his manner one of excitement as he came towards her. Elona's heart leaped as she saw the expression on his face. 'You have news for me?'

'Good news, my lady,' Piers told her. 'My lord is returned to the village in triumph. He has recovered the boy that was stolen and the raiders are either dead or sent in chains to the King for trial and punishment.'

'And was it Baron Danewold's men?'

'Yes, my lady. My lord has laid charges before the King and the Baron will be tried and punished in front of his peers—and that means the Crown will confiscate his lands and he will be banished from England for a period of years.'

'God be praised,' Elona cried, her face lighting up. 'My husband is well—and his men?'

'Two were injured, but none killed. Sir Stefan is unhurt.'

'Then all is well,' Elona said her eyes glowing with relief and happiness. 'I thank you for the news, good steward.' She turned to the man standing next to her, 'And you also, Will, for bringing Melise to me. And now, if you will excuse me, I must go, for I would be ready when my lord returns.'

She hurried from the hall, running up the stairs to her own chamber, her heart singing as she contemplated her husband's return. He would be weary and hungry; she must have a bath prepared for him, and a meal that he could savour in private. She would have the bath brought to her chamber and she would tend him herself.

If he felt as she did…but she was too impatient. He would want to rest after he had bathed and dined. She must not expect him to think of her the moment he returned.

How glad she was that he would soon be here! She had refused to give way to anxiety these past days, trusting in her husband's skill and prowess as a great warrior to bring him safely home.

She must not be impatient for his attention, for he would have many things on his mind, and Piers must have much to tell him concerning what had been done in the village.

She would use the time to prepare herself, dressing in one of the new gowns Bethany had sewn for her. The green one that matched the emeralds he had given her when they were at court, a gift she had always known in her heart must have come from him.

He had cared something for her then; surely he still did—if only he could find it in his heart to forgive her wicked lies.

Stefan listened impatiently to his steward's account of the damage to life and property. He had seen at first hand what was needed, and heard what had already been done before he left the village.

'Where is my lady?' he asked. 'Excuse me, Piers, but this may keep until the morrow. I need to rest and eat—and then we shall discuss what must be done to set all to rights.'

'But, my lord…' Piers sighed as his master strode away. He had not yet told him that Elona's nurse had arrived or of the young man who had accompanied her.

Stefan ran up the twisting stair to Elona's chamber. He was on fire with the urge to see her, to tell her of his love and need, to hold her in his arms. And this time he would bar the door so that none might enter and disturb them!

Elona was standing by a tub of scented water when he entered, testing it with her hand. He paused to look at her before she was aware of him, thinking how beautiful she was and how much he desired and loved her.

'Elona…'

'My lord?' She turned and saw him, the colour washing out of her cheeks as though she was overcome by emotion. 'My lord, you are safely home.' She thanked God for it, her heart filling with joy at the sight of him standing there, so vital and full of life and strength.

'You were about to bathe?' His eyes moved over her, for she looked as though she had recently changed into a fresh gown. It was a simple tunic that he had never seen before, fashioned of some fine material that clung lovingly to her slender figure.

'The water is for you, my lord,' Elona said. 'I thought you would be weary and in need of refreshment. There is food and wine—and water to relax in while you tell me of your triumph.'

'The water is for me?' Stefan's eyes held a hint of the humour she had not seen in many a day. 'And who is to be my handmaiden?'

'It will be my pleasure to wash your back, my lord,' she said, a faint flush in her cheeks, '—and any other part of your body that you desire.'

'I believe you make me an offer I cannot refuse, Elona,' Stefan said and felt the burning in his loins intensify. How often he had dreamed of a moment such as this! She was so beautiful and he wanted her so badly. 'Where are your women?'

'I have sent them elsewhere,' she told him. 'We are quite alone.'

'In that case…' He turned back to the door, turning the heavy iron key in the lock and then coming back to where she stood, a smile on his lips. 'I expect my handmaiden to help me disrobe, Elona. Do you think you can manage that task?'

'I shall do my best to please you, my lord, but perhaps you will need to help me, for 'tis the first time I have performed such a task.'

Had her lover taken her in haste or with force? The thought flashed into Stefan's mind, but he crushed it ruthlessly. All that was in the past and he would not allow his jealousy to spoil this homecoming.

'Shall we see if you can manage my belt for a start?' His smile was teasing as she struggled with the heavy silver buckle that held his sword belt tight to his body, managing to free it in the end. 'And now the jerkin—you will find that easier, I think, for it has eyelets and thongs.' He watched her as her fingers worked at the fastenings; freeing them, she hesitated before easing it over his head. Next came his shirt, which was a plain loose garment and easily disposed of. Her hands lingered a moment on his naked chest, causing a growl of pleasure to issue from his throat. 'And now the hose, Elona…'

She looked at him uncertainly and he grinned, easing forward so that she could loosen the ties at his waist so that the flaps fell away and the hose began to slip down over his muscled thighs. He was wearing nothing more and he laughed as he saw the flush come to her cheeks. It was clear that she was not used to seeing a naked man, and one who was already fully aroused, and that pleased him, for she was no wanton, even if she had known another man.

To save her blushes, he kicked the discarded hose away and lowered himself into the water. Elona took up a pot of soft soap and began to soothe it into his shoulders and back. Her hands moved rhythmically, stroking and kneading as she rubbed the soap into his flesh. He purred with pleasure as she worked, enjoying the sensations her touch aroused in him. He wanted to lie with her, but it was good to ease the strains of the past few days, and to anticipate what would come later.

As her hands moved further round, beginning to stroke his chest and down over his flat, hard navel, he felt the urgency quicken so that it was almost beyond his strength to control the need he felt to sweep her up and carry her to the bed.

'Be careful,' he warned as she went lower still. 'I can only take so much, Elona, and then…'

'What will you do, my lord?' she teased, her confidence growing as she saw the heat in his eyes and knew that his desire matched her own. 'Will you teach me to be a wife? Will you show me all the things I should know to please you?'

'Perhaps…' He frowned slightly, not certain that he wanted her to continue in this vein. There was a touch of the wanton about her now, and though it pleased him, it also stirred his jealousy. Had she been thus with her lover? 'Enough for now, Elona. I would eat. What have you there in that dish?'

Elona got up and went to fetch a dish of tasty morsels that she had ordered for him. He selected a date stuffed with a paste made of marchpane and walnuts and bit into it, swallowing it with relish and then two more.

'They were good. Have we a new cook? I did not think our stores held such delicacies as this.'

'They were prepared for you by Melise,' Elona told him. 'I had ordered the ingredients from London and they arrived here a few hours ago. I thought that you might find them tempting.'

'Melise?' Stefan's eyes narrowed as he looked at her. 'She is your nurse—the woman you could not bear to leave behind?'

'Yes, my lord. You sent Will de Grenville to fetch her for me and she arrived yesterday. She was here when I came back from the village.'

'And what of him?' Stefan's air of content fell away, his eyes suddenly as cold as ice. 'Is he also here?'

'Yes…' Elona faltered as she saw the anger in his eyes. He could not think…? Pray God that he did not believe ill of her. She had tried so hard to please him and now…now he was getting out of the bath and she knew that he was furious. 'He brought Melise here and…'

'Did you show your gratitude, Elona?' Stefan growled. 'Was this how you entertained your lover last night? Perhaps this feast was meant for him, but I returned too soon?'

'No, my lord. How can you think so ill of me?' Elona cried, the tears very close. 'Have I not proved my love for you?'

'By playing the whore?' Stefan shook her hand off his arm as she tried to reach him. 'No modest woman would do what you have, Elona! I thought that we might deal well together, but—'

'I love you, Stefan,' she said desperately. 'I wanted to be your wife and so I lied when your father asked me for the truth. I knew that he would demand that you marry me…'

'To cover your shame?'

'There was no child…'

'Do you say that you have never lain with a man?'

'I swear it. On my honour.'

'A whore's honour. We shall soon see the truth of this!'

Elona gave a squeal of fright as he grabbed hold of her wrist and began to drag her towards the bed, throwing her on to it as he glared down at her. He was angry but the evidence of his desire, his need, was there for her to witness.

'Take me if you will, my lord. I am yours. I want to be yours—but take me in love, for I love you.'

'I'll have no more of your lies.'

Stefan was there beside her on the bed, reaching for her. He ripped away her gown, staring greedily at her breasts, before his mouth covered the nipples, sucking at them and nibbling with his teeth. He was not hurting her, but his actions were rough and demanding instead of the tenderness of which she had dreamed.

'Love me,' she begged. 'Do not despise me, my lord. I have paid for my mistake.'

'You are mine to do with as I will,' he muttered and ripped her gown further to reveal the flatness of her belly and the dark curls clustered about her mound of Venus. 'Whores deserve no better.'

'I beg you…' she whispered. 'Do not take me in anger…'

Stefan's only answer was a groan and she realised that her

behaviour earlier, when she had deliberately tried to arouse him, had worked too well and he was beyond the point of no return. He was angry, but he wanted her, wanted her so desperately that he could not stop himself if he'd tried—and in truth she wanted him, even if his loving was merely lust.

His body was covering hers, his hand parting her thighs, his fingers seeking out the moist centre of her womanhood, and as he touched her she cried out, for the pleasure outweighed the pain. He thought her wanton, a whore, but he still wanted her, he still desired her—and she wanted him. She wanted to feel him inside her, filling her. She wanted to belong to him even if it was only this once. If he afterwards rejected her, she would at least have had this of him.

'Love me, Stefan,' she whispered as he thrust himself deep into her. Her body stiffened as she felt the tearing pain of his entry, and she cried out, but then she pressed herself closer to him. The pain was nothing compared to the easing of such want inside her. She was his whether he denied it or not, and at last he would know that she had not given herself to another man. 'I love only you, always you,' she murmured, her back arching to meet his thrusting as he reached a climax swiftly, spilling his seed inside her. 'I have never loved any man but you…'

Stefan lay with his head pressed against her breasts. For a moment he lay still, then he rolled away from her and lay on his back staring up at the ceiling.

'You were a virgin,' he said. 'There was no man before me.'

'No…' She lay with her eyes closed, feeling the sting of his anger now that his lust was done, the tears beginning to trickle down her cheeks. She had hoped that he would love her, but it was clear that, even now her innocence was proven, he did not love her. A shaft of pain went through her. Even though she had shown her love for him, he still did not honour her. She had loved him for so long now, but he had not wanted to marry her and he would never forgive her for forcing the marriage upon him. Suddenly, a great wave of shame washed over her. She was nothing to him and yet still she loved him, would always love him. But no, she must find the strength to send him from her, for she would not be used in this way by a man who did not truly love her. 'Leave me. I beg you, leave me.'

'Elona…'

Suddenly, from nowhere, anger surged up in her. She had done everything she could to please him, even playing the harlot to arouse him, and it was not enough. Shame and anger made her reckless. So be it! Let it be over. She would not beg for his love.

'Leave me,' she said again, her throat caught with tears. 'I would be alone. There is nothing between us and can never be. When I am rested, I shall leave this place and you will be rid of me.'

'No!' Stefan's cry was like that of a wounded beast. 'You shamed me before my father, you lied to force me to wed you—and you will honour those vows, Elona. Be warned, for I shall never let you go.'

'Even if I hate you for what you have done?' She stared up at him as he walked over to the tub and bent to pull on his clothes. What was she saying? All she desired was to be allowed to stay here, but she could not stay if he despised her. 'You cannot keep me here against my will. I shall return to France—'

'You are my wife and you will do as I bid you,' Stefan said.

'Try to leave and I shall fetch you back—and then I shall teach you obedience.'

Elona watched as he strode from the room. What was she to do now? She had believed that she would win him in the end, but now she saw that it was useless.

Her pride would not allow her to stay here to be used as his whore. She had longed for his love, but it was useless when he did not care for her. She should leave his house and go back to her father's manor in France—and she would just as soon as she had the opportunity!

Chapter Ten

It did not take Elona long to realise that an attempt to leave without her husband's permission would be useless. He could order her women not to obey her, prevent her from taking her possessions, and even imprison her if he chose. A sleepless night was enough to show her that she was powerless, at her husband's mercy.

Besides, how could she demand that Melise accompany her all the way back to France? It had taken many long weeks for the old woman to make the journey here and the return might kill her. For Melise's sake, she must stay for the time being. Perhaps in time Stefan might relent and let her go.

Bethany had told her that Stefan had gone hunting when she brought food to break her fast the next morning.

'Our stores of fresh meat are low, for we had sent much of what we had to the village,' the woman told her and looked at her mistress oddly as she added, 'They say that Sir Stefan was not in the best of moods this morning. He yelled at one of the servants and was brusque with Piers.'

Elona did not choose to enlighten her. The bloodstains on her linen must have told their own story, but she would not satisfy Bethany's curiosity.

'We have much to do,' she said. 'We have neglected our tasks here the past few days and must begin to prepare for winter. The apples, pears and what plums are left should be sorted; those good enough for preserving need to be peeled and cooked with spices and then sweetened with honey before they are stored in stone jars. Mary and Roberta will do what is necessary. You must make a start on turning out the linen chests, if you please.'

Having sent her women about their various tasks, Elona went in search of Father Fernando. She had neglected her lessons and was determined to begin again.

'I am glad that you have spared time for your studies, my lady,' the priest said, his chins wobbling as he nodded his head vigorously in a smile of welcome. 'My lord gave me the books you have chosen to use, and I think they will give you pleasure.'

When had Stefan given him the books? It must have been after he left her chamber the previous evening! He was clearly determined that she should stay here and for the moment it seemed that she had no choice but to obey him.

Yet she was not to be ill used. There would be no repeat of what had happened the previous night! Elona made her silent vow as she began her lessons; she was determined that she would force her husband to respect her somehow. He had believed her a whore and a liar, but he could no longer think it. She had given him the proof of her innocence the previous night.

Her mood was sombre when they began to read, but the stories of King Arthur and his knights were so enthralling that Elona ended the morning feeling very much happier than when she had begun it. For more than two hours she had been carried away by the tales of chivalry and love and it had restored her spirit.

After taking a little cold meat, bread and ale at midday, she and Julia began the task of mending some of the household linen. Most of it was in sore need of attention, and she made a note to ask Piers if they could not renew much of it. It was when she had put aside her work for the day and begun to think of changing her gown for the evening that Mary came to her.

Elona saw at once that she was deeply troubled and asked her what had happened to cause her such distress.

'I have been told that I am to marry Ulrich the carpenter and leave you, my lady.'

'Who told you that?' Elona was surprised and angry. 'I gave no such order, nor have I been informed of this.'

'It was Master Piers. He said that the order came from Sir Stefan. Ulrich's wife was killed and there is no other woman in the village to take her place.'

'And since you are a widow it seemed convenient, I suppose. Well, it does not suit me. I need you here.' Elona's eyes narrowed as she fought her rising temper. 'You do not wish to marry him?'

'No, my lady. I would rather stay here with you. I have no wish to marry again ever.'

'Then you shall not.'

Elona's temper had begun to boil as she set out in search of her husband. How could he give such an order without first consulting her wishes? Oh, he should discover that he could not treat her so scurvily! She had been too eager to please, but after his behaviour the previous night things were changed. She had been afraid that he would send her away, and had felt guilty because of her lies, but now he should learn that she would stay here only on her own terms.

Stefan saw Elona walking towards him as he stood in conversation with his steward. Something about the way she held herself warned him that she was angry—nay, furious! She had not been as angry as this since the day he had told her that she would have to do better if she wished to trick him. Immediately, he dismissed Piers. If she were about to demand her freedom, he would have privacy.

'My lord,' Elona began with a flash of fire from her lovely eyes, 'I pray you will give me a few moments of your time.'

How beautiful she looked! Stefan saw that the proud, haughty beauty he had first encountered in France had returned. She was no longer weighed down by guilt or remorse and he was glad of it. There was no shame in that lovely face, and why should there be? If anyone had cause to be ashamed, it was he for the way he had treated her the previous night.

'How may I serve you, Elona?'

'I have been told that Mary the Wise is to be given to Ulrich the carpenter in marriage and I forbid it. She is my serving woman and I do not give my permission for this marriage.'

'Do you not?' Stefan was so surprised at the reason for her anger that he was lost for an answer. Was such a trivial thing enough to cause this rage in her? 'May I ask why? It seems sensible—since he is in need of a wife and she hath no husband.'

'She wishes to remain here as one of my women. She is far too useful to me and I refuse to allow her to leave.'

'And what does Mistress Mary say?' A little smile touched

his mouth as he heard the ring of authority in her voice. It had been missing far too long and he had missed it sorely, had blamed himself for its loss.

'She does not wish to marry again.'

'Then that would seem to be an end to it.'

'You are saying that she will not be forced to accept him?' Elona was so taken aback that she stared foolishly. She had not expected him to give in so swiftly.

'It shall be as you wish. Ulrich may look for a wife in the next village.'

Elona watched him warily. He had given in too easily and, though she had gained her way, she was not placated. 'When will you allow me to return to my lands in France?'

Ah, now they were coming to what ailed her! 'I am afraid I cannot permit you to leave here, Elona. Baron Danewold has refused to surrender to the King. While he is at large, your safety can only be assured as long as you remain under my care.'

'I am safe enough. I am your wife and can be of no value to him.'

'He could not wed you while I live,' Stefan agreed, his tone calm and reasonable. 'But he has sworn revenge on us and would perhaps take delight in capturing or killing you. Since he is now outlawed, he can lose no more.'

'You could send an escort with me.'

'I fear I cannot spare the men.'

Elona looked at him suspiciously. She would swear that he was mocking her, amused by this little game. That glint in his eyes showed that he was enjoying himself.

'Do not imagine I shall allow what happened last night to happen again. I am not a whore and shall not be used so.'

The gleam of humour vanished. 'Indeed, you are not,

Elona. You are my lady wife and shall be given all the respect due to you. It was my intention to beg your pardon for my behaviour last night. I have misjudged you, wronged you, and I am sorry if I hurt or distressed you. I shall strive to make amends as best I can.'

'You were a savage brute,' Elona said, temper flaring. 'You do not know how to treat a lady. I suppose you have been used to taking what you want from women, but you shall not find me so accommodating again.'

'Shall I not, Elona?' The corners of Stefan's mouth would not quite stay still. Why did he not quite believe her protests? 'Would you have me beg for my wife's favours?'

'Oh, do not be so foolish!' she snapped. 'I am angry with you. Do not come to me, for my door will be locked.'

'Do you imagine that would keep me out if I were determined to enter?'

'You are a brute. Learn the art of love and then I may welcome you to my chamber, sir!'

Elona turned on her heel and stalked off. Why had she said such a foolish thing? The last thing she wanted was for Stefan to come to her bed again—wasn't it?

Stefan smiled as he watched her walk away. He had taken himself off for a hard day's hunting to ease the tortured confusion of his mind. His shame at the way that he had behaved to Elona had overwhelmed him so completely that he had compounded his foolishness by leaving her without a word of contrition. It was little wonder she was angry.

Even had she been the whore he'd named her, she had deserved better than harsh words and a hasty tumble between the covers. But she was innocent. He had realised it too late, his need too urgent to pull back, and then he had been overcome by the enormity of what he had done. The vile names he'd called her, the harsh manner of his possession, the hurt he must have inflicted in his haste to bed her.

It was only to be expected that she would hate him. He could not blame her for wanting to leave him—but he could not lose her now! She was his, his wife, his love, and his reason for living. He could never let her go. Somehow he must win her trust and confidence, if not her love.

He had hardly slept, rousing his men early to the hunt, glad of the need to seek provisions to ease his restless mind. He had been so sure that he had killed Elona's love for him. Why should she care for a man who had treated her so ill? If she insisted on leaving, in the end he must let her go, and he would never force her to accept him in her bed though already his body burned for her.

He had returned to the house that afternoon determined to see her, to beg her forgiveness, but Piers had detained him, and Elona had come to him. Not to demand her freedom, though she had done so as an afterthought, but on behalf of a serving woman.

It was not the action of a woman who hated. Had she hated him, she would not have thought of approaching him on such a matter. She was angry, but anger cooled and then…was it possible that she would find it in her heart to forgive him?

He had no right to expect it, yet something in her manner had given him hope. She had accused him of being a savage brute, of needing to learn the arts of love. Well, perhaps one day she would allow him to show her that he was not quite the clumsy oaf she thought him.

A little smile touched his mouth. He had believed all chance of happiness lost, but now he thought that it might not be so—all he needed was to have patience.

* * *

Elona had dressed with care that evening. She wore the tunic and surcote she had first worn for the King's banquet, her hair bound in a smooth coronet on the top of her head with silver and pearl pins, a cap of silver wires holding the veil that fell down her back past her waist. Her undergown had a long train that dragged on the floor behind her almost like a serpent's tail, and she wore the chain Stefan had given her about her throat.

She looked proud and beautiful, a queen amongst women, that any man might be proud to call his wife. And she was his! Stefan thought, his eyes devouring her as she walked slowly towards him.

It was a week since his hunting trip and Elona's angry outburst. Since then she had maintained a cool dignity in her manner when speaking to him. Stefan in his turn had behaved with polite courtesy, giving little or no indication of his feelings towards her. He had neither insisted on his rights as a husband nor apologised further for his behaviour. Instead, he had tried to please her in small ways.

A travelling minstrel had been welcomed to their hall and Stefan had paid him well to stay and sing love songs for them. One night they danced and Stefan led the company with Elona, treating her as if she were made of some precious material that must not be damaged. His nearness had seemed to affect her during the dance, but afterwards when he smiled at her, the cool smile was back in place.

He had asked their neighbours to dine with them; a genial knight, his plump, pretty wife and two young daughters. Elona had seemed pleased with the company and the daughters had stayed two days at Sanscombe before being escorted to their home. Arrangements had been made for them all to meet again soon for the winter fayre that would come to the villages.

'You look beautiful,' Stefan said, rising as she came to join him at the high table that night. 'I trust you are well, my lady?'

'Quite well, thank you.' Elona inclined her head. She had taken refuge in dignity, otherwise he found it all too easy to provoke her. 'My women have been mending your shirts, my lord. Indeed, they were in sore need of it. If you will send for the stuffs, we shall make you some new ones. You are in dire need of some refurbishment to your attire.'

'I am but a rough soldier,' Stefan replied, a twinkle in his eye. She had asked for any mending and he had given her a pile of his oldest shirts, some fit only for the rubbish, to keep her busy. 'You must order material for my shirts as you see fit, my lady.'

Elona sensed the mockery beneath his easy words and wondered if he had played a trick on her. 'Melise grows stronger every day,' she said softly enough so that only he could hear. 'I dare say she will be fit enough to travel soon.'

'Is she not happy with us? I thought that she had come to stay for the rest of her life.'

'You mock me, my lord!'

'Do I, Elona? Are you so very anxious to leave us? I had thought you found plenty to occupy you here?' If not, he must find her more mending!

'I dare say there is enough to keep me busy for a few weeks.'

'Oh, then the snows will be upon us and you would find it hard to travel. You should make up your mind to stay until the spring.'

'I shall leave before the snow comes!'

'But you cannot leave without seeing that we have enough provisions for the winter,' Stefan replied. 'We shall hunt again soon and your women will be needed to help salt the excess. My people do not have your skills. You would not have us starve this winter?'

'You will have more than enough to keep from starving.'

'But we must think of the villagers, Elona. You know that pigs and also a cow were lost. They will need several barrels of good salt pork to keep them from going hungry.'

'You have a silver tongue, sir,' she said, giving him a darkling glance.

'You surprise me with your compliment, Elona. I believed you thought me an ignorant oaf?'

'You are too clever for you own good, sir!'

'Indeed, I am a fool,' Stefan said and the smile had left his eyes. 'If I were not, I should have recognised what a precious treasure was mine and treated it with care.'

Elona saw the burning heat in his eyes and averted her head as her heart skipped a beat. How could she remain angry with him when he did everything to please her? He was courteous and gentle, his smile teasing her out of her moods, try as she might to retreat behind a mask of cool indifference.

It was useless to pretend to herself that she hated him. She had asked three times that she be allowed to return to France, but each time he found a new excuse. He did not intend that she should leave, and, if she looked into her heart, she did not want to go. Sanscombe Manor had become her home, its people her people. She enjoyed being mistress here and took pleasure in the improvements she and her women had made.

But how could she stay when he did not love her?

Oh, he had apologised for hurting her, and he had done all that he could to make up for his unkindness that night, but he did not love her. He had been forced to marry her against his will and nothing could change that.

'Father Fernando tells me that you make good progress with your studies, Elona.'

'I believe he is pleased with me,' she replied. 'I shall miss him when he leaves us next month.'

'He wishes to make a pilgrimage to the Holy Land. We cannot forbid him, Elona, for it is every man's right if he so wishes. I have told him his place will always be here if he wishes to return, and he has arranged for his replacement—a kindly man who will not try us too much if we do not always follow a strict doctrine.'

Elona nodded her agreement. It might be years before the priest came back to them, if he ever did. So much could happen on a long and dangerous journey.

'Your brother is to leave with Duke Richard when they set out on the crusade, I believe?'

'You had a letter from my stepmother this morning, I think?' Stefan's eyes were shadowed for a moment. 'I trust that she and my father are well?'

Was he still angry because of what had happened? She had believed that he had begun to forgive her for her lies, to accept what could not be changed—but that was surely anger deep in his eyes? She sensed a change in his mood.

'My lord?' She laid her hand on his arm and he shook his head, a wintry smile on his lips.

'Nay, Elona. I am not angry, merely thoughtful. My mind dwells in the past tonight for some reason.'

She accepted this and remained silent, then, seeing that he seemed to have withdrawn into himself, rose to her feet.

'You will excuse me, my lord? I am tired and would retire.'

Stefan's brooding gaze followed her as she left the table. She knew that he was watching her, but not what he was thinking or what had brought that expression to his eyes.

As she moved towards the stair that would take her to her own apartments, a man got up from his seat and slipped from the hall to follow her.

'Lady Elona, stay a moment, if you will. I would speak with you.'

She turned her head, frowning slightly as she saw that Will de Grenville had called to her. 'Oh, Will,' she said, feeling slightly uneasy. 'What is it you would say to me?'

'Only that I leave for France in the morning. Sir Stefan has given me a letter to the Duke and I have hopes that he will take me with him on his crusade. Then I may earn my knighthood.'

'I see…' Elona hesitated. 'I thought you wished to take service here? Would my husband not have you?' Was Stefan jealous of him even now?

'He offered me service if I wished for it, but asked what I truly wanted and then advised me to go to the Duke. I am more likely to win glory and wealth in fighting than in the peaceful existence your husband plans here.'

'And you leave in the morning—do you go alone?'

'No. I believe there are two youths from the village who have asked permission to go on the crusade and your lord has generously given leave. We shall travel together.'

She could go with them if she wished, Elona thought. One of her women could ride with her, the others follow with her baggage. If she took the chance to escape, surely Stefan would let her go?

'I wish you Godspeed, Will,' she said. 'I hope that you gain all you desire of life.'

'I can never do that,' he told her with a sad, sweet smile. 'You have given your heart elsewhere, Elona, and I shall never love another as I have loved you.'

Elona made him no answer as she turned away for there was nothing she could say. It was true that her heart belonged to another. Running away from Stefan would not change that, merely increase her sorrow.

Alone in her chamber, Elona sat looking out at the moon as it sailed through a clear sky. There would be frosts on the morrow, she thought, for winter was fast approaching. Her heart felt heavy as she combed her long hair and sighed for something that was as far away as the moon itself. She had dismissed her women after they had helped her prepare for the night, but was too restless to sleep.

She knew that she would not ask Stefan to release her again, and yet the years promised little happiness. She loved her husband desperately, but he did not love her. He desired her body, his eyes told her that, but he did not love her. Somehow she must learn to accept the hopelessness of her situation and accept the terms he offered.

Tears trickled down her cheeks. Why could he not love her as she loved him? She wiped away the tears with the back of her hand. Weeping would not help her.

'Why do you weep, my lady?'

Elona was startled by his soft voice so close to her. She had not heard him enter her chamber, but he had come through the door that led to his own bedchamber. He had not used it before and she had almost forgotten it was there, hidden as it was behind a heavy drape.

'I was thinking of my father and brother,' she lied instinctively. He must not know that she wept for him.

'You miss them both still?'

'I was happy while Pierre lived,' she said. 'After my brother's death, my father was often silent and withdrawn. Sometimes he forgot I was there, but I believe he loved me in his own way. Pierre's loss was a heavy blow to him and he never truly recovered from it.'

'And your mother died soon after you were born?'

'Yes. My father married again for the sake of his children. The Lady Elizabeth was very good to us. I think we were fortunate to have her.'

She had risen to her feet now, gazing into his face, her breast rising and falling as her breath quickened. The candles had burned low in their sconces and cast shadows over him so that it was difficult to see his face clearly.

'Your mother died soon after your birth, I believe?'

'For a long time I believed that I had killed her. But I know now that the birth made her frail of health and she died some months later. My father could not bear to be reminded of it and as soon as I was old enough he sent me away to our kinsman to be educated.'

'Surely he did not blame you for her death? The child is not to blame for the suffering it causes at its birth.'

'No matter,' Stefan said and shrugged. 'It was a long time ago. I mentioned it merely because it was something we had both experienced. I do not like to see you so unhappy, Elona.

Do you truly wish to leave us? Would it make you happy to return to your home for a few months?'

'Would you let me go?'

'If you gave me your word that you would return one day. I do not want to keep you a prisoner here, though I should not wish to lose you for ever.'

'Why?' Elona moved closer to him, straining to see his face in the flickering light. 'Surely you cannot wish to keep a woman who trapped you into marriage with her lies? Would it not be better to have the marriage annulled?'

'I hardly think that possible after the other night,' Stefan said and there was a faint smile on his lips. 'I was angry—as much with my father for believing me untrustworthy as with you for lying.'

'I am sorry I caused Sir Ralph to think ill of you. Shall I write and tell him the truth?'

'No—then I should be very angry. I do not beg for forgiveness of any man, even my father.'

'But it was my fault—'

'No matter. Had he not been so ready to despise me, he would have listened to me instead of demanding that I put right the wrong I had done you.'

'Yet still I would make amends. I lied and now you are bound to a woman you cannot love…'

'No, that is not so,' Stefan said and her heart caught. 'I think I wanted you from the first moment I saw you, but I did not know my own heart.'

'Stefan…' Was he saying this only to please her?

He hushed her with a finger to her lips. 'Let me finish, impatient one. I knew that I wanted you. I would have spoken much sooner, but my honour held me back. You were destined to be Alain's bride, and therefore forbidden to me. How could I speak when to do so would have robbed my own brother?'

'Alain did not want to marry me. Nor was there ever any promise between us,' Elona cried.

'I had given my promise to your father and to my stepmother. I do not take these things lightly, Elona.'

'I know…' She held her breath, knowing that she must tell him all. 'I thought that if I did not lie to your father I would lose you. I believed that, after you had delivered me to Banewulf, you would go away and I should never see you again.'

'It was my intention to speak to Alain, to discover if he would release you. I do not know what I might have done had he refused—for it was not until you were snatched from me, and then when you lied about the child, that I realised how much I wanted you. I could not bear to think that any other man had touched you.'

'I thought you hated me then. You were so angry.'

'Angry and jealous,' Stefan confirmed ruefully. 'I hated the man who had been your lover. I would have killed him if I could. For a while I wanted to kill you. It was because I was afraid that I might do you some harm that I left you at Banewulf. Believe me, I was tempted many times to come and fetch you. Only pride held me back.'

'I was so unhappy. I believed you would never send for me and I wanted to die. Alain saw me weeping and it was his idea that I should come here. I was sure you would send me away at once, but he said that you were not so foolish.'

'It seems he knew me better than I knew myself.' Stefan's eyes were dark with some strong emotion. 'And he was able to see that you were innocent because his judgement was clear. I was such a fool to believe ill of you. Can you find it in yourself to forgive me, Elona? I know I hurt you the other night. I have found it hard to forgive myself.'

'I was hurt that you should think me so low, Stefan—but as for the other…' She smiled up at him. 'I wanted you to take me, to make me yours. It was the reason I had them prepare a bath for you in my chamber, why I sent my ladies away. I hoped that it would make you forget your anger.'

'I forgot everything, including my honour,' Stefan admitted with a wry twist of his lips. 'You were right to brand me a savage, Elona—but it was because I wanted you too much to hold back. Your consideration for my comfort, your touch, had aroused me—and then, again, I lost my temper when I learned that your squire was here. I thought that you still loved him and I could not bear it. I shall try to make you happy next time—if you are willing to forgive me and begin anew?'

'Do you not know that all I want is for you to love me?' She had no pride left, for her heart and body longed to be as one with him.

'You must know that I do? Why else should I be driven mad with jealousy at the thought of another man touching you?'

'Then take me to you,' Elona said. 'Let us make this a true marriage, my lord.'

'My sweet temptress,' Stefan said as he moved towards her, clasping her against him in a passionate embrace. 'How I have burned for you, longed for this moment.'

His kiss was soft and tender, but beneath the gentleness was a hunger that he held in check. Elona was aware that he had himself on a tight leash as he led her to their couch. She stood meekly as he undressed her, letting him play the role he had chosen for himself. She had been his handmaiden, but this time he would be hers.

He knelt before her, kissing her navel as she stood naked and proud, her clothes lying in a heap on the floor. His tongue circled the perfect little indentation, moving slowly over the firm flat flesh to her breasts. His mouth closed over the peaked nipples, which were evidence of her arousal, nudging them with his tongue and lips and sucking at them delicately until she gasped with pleasure, her back arching, hair falling past her narrow waist.

He lay her down on the bed and began to discard his own clothes, ripping at the fastenings in his urgency to join her. In a moment he was there beside the bed, gazing down at her, the hot passion in his eyes, feasting on the creamy perfection of her body, and she was able to let her own eyes dwell on the hard suppleness of his.

Lean and honed to supreme fitness, Stefan's arms, chest and thighs were strongly muscled, his skin ridged in places by small scars that he had received in battle. As he lowered himself to the bed beside her, she traced one of the larger scars with the tip of her forefinger.

'You have been hurt many times, my lord?'

'They are nothing, Elona. When I thought you lost to me I received a far deeper wound.'

'Forgive me…' she began but his lips were on hers, cutting off her words. And then as his hands began to stroke and caress her, she forgot everything but the sweet sensations he was arousing in her. 'Stefan…'

'My lovely Elona…my wife…'

She had never felt such pleasure, never dreamed that her body could feel this way, could respond to his touch so readily. It was as if she were an instrument on which he played, making her body sing in perfect harmony. Their bodies seemed to fit together, lying side by side, his teasing lips and tongue making her writhe as the pleasure intensified to an almost unbearable pitch. If it did not end soon, she would die of it!

When he parted her thighs to allow his entry, she prepared herself for the inevitable pain she must feel, but this time Stefan did not thrust heedlessly into her. This time it was slow and easy, sensuous, her body opening in welcome to his hardness, her moistness enclosing him like a silken sheath.

She gasped with pleasure, her back arching to meet him now, yet still he held back, moving slowly and surely, bringing her with him as he climbed towards that moment of supreme ecstasy.

She cried his name aloud, her nails scoring his shoulders as she felt a spasm of something that was both pleasure and pain shoot through her. The next moment she felt the weight of his body on her and heard his deep breathing, the shudders that ran through him convulsively as she writhed beneath him, and she knew that he was as shaken by this thing that had happened between them.

''Tis no wonder they call it the little death,' Stefan murmured. 'I vow I died and woke in paradise.'

'You must not blaspheme,' she chided, but with a gurgle of delighted laughter for his words had echoed what was in her mind.

She expected that he would leave her as he had the first night, but instead he lay beside her, holding her close, stroking her back as if he could not bear to let her go. Was it possible that he did truly love her more than she had ever thought he would? Tears stung her eyes as she realised that she had been given so much that night, but she would not let them fall.

She felt a strange lassitude steal over her, closing her eyes as he whispered softly to her. He spoke of love, of their life together, and of the children they would have.

Elona slept. She felt at peace. Stefan spoke of love and she must believe him. She knew he wanted her, knew that their loving had given him pleasure, and that was as much as she could ask for. Perhaps he truly loved her. Only time would tell.

'Will you take me hunting with you tomorrow?' Elona asked as they were at supper a week later. 'I sometimes hunted with my brother in the forest at home.'

'If you wish it, my lady,' Stefan said and sipped his wine, his eyes thoughtful as they dwelt on her. 'But remember that we hunt for food and not for pleasure. I dare say your brother took you hawking, which is a very different thing.'

'We also hunted for deer and wild boar as you do, for my father also had a concession from the King to take so many deer each year, and our forest had herds of wild boar. In truth, I do not care so much for the kill, but the chase is always exciting.'

'Well, you need not be there at the kill,' Stefan said. 'Our men will see to that side of things and we may walk a little in the woods.'

The look in his eyes made her laugh, her cheeks a little pink, for she knew well enough what it meant. This past week he had come to her bed every night and she had learned to know him.

Life had become full of good things for Elona. She enjoyed the work she did, ordering her household, keeping her accounts, filling the shelves of the stillroom and visiting the villagers.

Already life had begun to return to normal there. New stone cottages were being built to replace those destroyed by the fire and a wall was being erected, with a warning bell to sound the alarm, to make it more difficult for the village to suffer a surprise attack in the future. Stefan was also training the villagers to defend themselves so that they were able to hold off an attacking force for long enough for help to reach them.

The man Ulrich had taken a wife from a village nearby, and his son had begun to learn his father's trade. It seemed to Elona that everything was almost perfect.

'We have only to hear that Danewold has been captured and we need fear nothing,' she said to Stefan, as she lay in his arms that night, content from his loving. 'It is for our people that I worry, in case he tries to harm them again. Is there nothing more that we can do to see that he is punished, my lord?'

'Did I not tell you? He has been captured…'

'And when was that?' Elona raised herself on one elbow to look at him, her eyes bright with suspicion in the glow of the candle. 'I believed he was captured all the time. You told me he was outlawed to keep me from leaving.'

'I would have told you anything to that end,' Stefan whispered as he pulled her down to him, so that she lay on top of him, her lips close to his as he began to kiss her. Little, teasing kisses that aroused her even though she had thought herself satiated from their last loving. 'Shall I never have enough of you, Elona?'

'I hope that you will not, my lord,' she said and laughed as, greatly daring, she straddled him. Seeing what she meant to do, he laughed and lifted her, his hands about her waist, letting her ease herself on to the hard shaft of his manhood, easing her silken moistness down to its root so slowly that he cried out with pleasure. Her hair fell over his face and he twisted his fingers in the scented tresses, holding her fast as he kissed her long and hard, and then, with one surging movement, swung her over on her back and took the dominant position. She laughed up at him, her love in her eyes, surrendering to him completely as she said, 'For I do not think I can ever have enough of you.'

'You are my love, my heart, my life, and I should die without you,' Stefan breathed, and Elona felt the sweetness of his words like honey. At last she believed. He loved her as much as she loved him. 'Never forget that I adore you, Elona. If God should take me from you…'

'Hush, my lord,' she begged him and pressed her lips to his.

He must not tempt fate, for his words had sent a cold shiver down her spine. Her happiness had seemed so complete and now she realised that it could change in an instant, for without Stefan her life would once again be empty.

Chapter Eleven

By the morning Elona had forgotten any foolish fears she might have had the previous night. Stefan was strong and healthy, as was she, and there was no reason why they should not have a long life together.

It was a crisp winter day; the air was chill but not yet bitter, a pale sun promising to break through later, and the earth hard beneath the horses' hooves.

'A good day for hunting, my lord,' Malachi the huntsman said as Stefan and Elona went out to join the small crowd of men awaiting them. 'We should have some good sport.'

'You have not forgot my orders?'

'No, my lord.'

Elona caught the excitement of the men. It was a day to remember, the clean crisp air like wine on the tongue.

The dogs were baying madly, straining at the leash as the runners set off ahead. They were to hunt wild boar rather than deer that day, for Stefan's men had already taken the permitted number of royal venison that year. Wild boar belonged to the lord of the manor, as did the other game in his woods.

Hunting the boar was different from stag hunting, for the dogs were not unleashed, at least until the boar was wounded and cornered. Their keen scent glands were useful for picking up the scent of the dangerous beasts and their baying for flushing the boars out of the undergrowth for the bowmen to shoot.

The horsemen rode at a canter, keeping pace with the dogs and the runners who had an easy loping movement that they could keep up for hours at a time. Hunting deer was a more thrilling chase, but it was pleasant enough in the forest, and although they found no scent for quite some time, Elona was content. For herself she would not have cared if they had not put up a quarry. However, hunting for food was a necessity rather than a pastime and when the dogs started to howl and strain at the leash, she knew what to expect. Clearly they had picked up a scent.

Suddenly, a boar plunged out of the thicket and charged towards the dogs and runners. It was a massive, fearsome beast with huge, sharp tusks and red eyes.

A bowman took aim, his arrow piercing the beast at the back of its neck, but, instead of falling, it plunged back into the forest and disappeared from sight. The runners would have gone after it, but three more wild pigs had broken out of the undergrowth and the bowmen and dogs were kept busy.

'Come, Elona,' Stefan said as the serious business of slaughtering began. 'We shall ride this way a little.'

She turned with him obediently, for the bloodletting held no appeal for her, though she understood that it must happen if they were not to starve that winter. Once the snows came there would be little fresh meat available and they would rely on the salted meat taken from this hunt. Such were the facts of life and a good housewife must be prepared to deal with whatever the huntsmen brought in.

'Shall we walk a little?' Stefan asked as they came upon a pretty glade. 'The men do not need me and we shall not ride into the forest again until next spring, for if I am not mistaken the weather will change soon.'

'Your weather here in England is much colder than in France. Often my father and brother were able to hunt throughout much of the winter. And that meant we had fresh meat most of the year, though we always salted several barrels just in case.'

'You were fortunate,' Stefan said. 'Here the game is plentiful in spring and summer, but the last time we hunted we took only one boar and a hind. I think we have done better today. You must have brought us luck, Elona.'

She smiled as he came to help her down, his hands lingering about her waist as he gazed into her eyes, then drew her close to his heart for a moment. He kissed her, and touched her face with his fingertips.

'I love you so much, my dearest wife.'

'And I love you.' She stretched up to touch her lips to his, and then as he let her go and she looked about her, she pointed to the other side of the clearing excitedly. 'Oh, look, Stefan, are they not filbert nuts? We have stumbled upon them quite by chance. I shall pick as many as I can for they will make good eating.'

'How will you gather them?'

'In my wimple,' she said. 'Will you unpin it for me, Stefan?'

She was wearing a simple covering, which she fashioned into a small pouch to carry the nuts. Stefan followed a few steps behind her as she ran across the clearing, amused at her determination to make the most of her find. She was happily pulling the small nuts from the bush when the grunting sound alerted Stefan. Something was hidden behind those bushes next to hers.

Suddenly, the wounded boar that the bowmen had not killed broke from the undergrowth. Behind it came a bowman and a runner with his dog, but neither of them were close enough to stop the boar charging—and Elona was in its path.

Nothing was more dangerous than a wild boar when wounded, which was why the dogs were kept leashed until the animal was cornered. They had no chance against those evil tusks and Elona had even less.

Stefan was unarmed. He could do nothing except what he did, which was to thrust Elona into the bush and turn to face the charging beast. With only his bare hands, he tried to ward it off, but he was caught by those cruel tusks as they tore viciously at his thigh, his scream of pain alerting the bowmen and the runner.

The runner released his dog, and the brave creature rushed to his master's defence, growling and attacking the boar from behind. Snarling and growling, the dog closed with the boar for a few seconds, diverting it from attacking Stefan, and as the two fought savagely, the bowman took careful aim. His arrow pierced the boar's neck. Maddened by the fresh pain, it tossed the dog to one side, where it lay bleeding and spent, and looked for the source of new danger, and then a second bowman had found a surer mark and an arrow pierced the beast's eye.

This time it staggered and fell, grunting and twitching until the huntsman dispatched it with his merciful knife. The wounded dog was also dispatched, for it had fought bravely but suffered grave injury and there was nothing to be done.

Elona had meantime scrambled to her feet and was bending over Stefan as he lay on the ground. The wound to his thigh was deep and bleeding profusely, his face pale as he struggled to fight the terrible faintness that threatened to rob him of his wits. He had other gashes on his hands and arms, but they were skin deep and not serious.

'He is losing too much blood,' the huntsman said. 'We must tie him above the wound, my lady, to stop the flow.'

'Stefan…' Elona's voice caught with tears as she saw that he was in terrible pain. 'You foolish, foolish man…'

'Would you have had me leave you to your fate, my love?' Even now there was a wry smile upon his lips.

'We must get him back to the house,' she said to the huntsman, fighting the tears and faintness that threatened her. She must be strong for his sake! 'That wound must be cauterised or he will die.'

Stefan's eyes were closed. She thought he must have lost consciousness as the huntsman tied a belt tightly above the wound, cutting off the crimson flow.

'It will hold for a while,' Cedric told her. 'We must do as you say, my lady, though the wound is deep.'

His face told her what he would not say. Men seldom recovered from such wounds.

'I shall do the cauterising,' Mary said once she had examined her master's wound. 'It must be done thoroughly or it will not serve.' Her eyes met Elona's. 'I shall need men to hold him, for he may wake—and the shock could kill him.'

'Stefan will not die,' Elona said. 'Do what you must, Mary.'

She signed to four strong men who were standing by, ready to take their places. 'You know what to do. Hold him well, for he will fight you.'

The iron had been heated over the fire until it was red hot. Mary glanced at Elona, pausing for a moment as though she feared what she must do, and then, at a nod from her mistress, she held it against the open wound.

The stench of burning flesh was terrible, but not so fearful as Stefan's scream of agony. He jerked violently, fighting against the unbearable agony as Mary continued to hold the iron against his flesh for what seemed an eternity. And then, mercifully, he fainted, his endurance at an end as his body gave its own response by robbing him of his senses.

'He is merely unconscious,' Mary said as Elona gave a sobbing cry. 'Fear not, my lady, he lives.'

'God be praised,' one of the men said and another made the sign of the cross over his breast. All four of them looked sick and shocked, and as Elona dismissed them she could hear them murmuring to each other of their fears that their master would die.

'What must we do now?' Elona asked of her women as the men departed. It had been agony to watch Stefan's suffering, but she would not spare herself anything. 'Do any of you know a remedy for the pain he will feel when he comes to himself?'

Melise had a remedy for a sleeping draught, which she warned must be used sparingly; if not, the sleep it induced would be permanent. Mary had something that had helped her husband when he was in fever, though, as she reminded Elona, it had not saved him.

'His life is in God's hands,' Elona said. 'We can only tend

him and pray that he recovers, but there are books in my lord's special chamber—and I believe that the good Father and I might find some remedy in them that may help us.'

'We must take turns in sitting with him,' Mary said, 'for he will need constant watching, and it is too much for one person alone. You have had a terrible shock, my lady. You should rest for a while.'

'You will call me if he wakes?'

'Yes, of course.'

'Then I shall leave him to your care for the moment. I have other tasks that I must perform.'

Elona went over to the bed, bending down to kiss Stefan's forehead as he lay with his eyes closed, his skin damp with sweat from the pain he had endured before he lost consciousness.

'Sleep well, my beloved husband,' she said. 'I shall come to you soon and my thoughts are always with you.'

Elona was frowning as she left the chamber. Piers would be waiting for his orders, as would the men. She must take charge of the household now, for Stefan might lie on his sickbed for many weeks—if he ever rose from it again. Her eyes were stinging with the tears she could not afford to let fall. Weeping would not save her husband nor oversee his affairs. She had to be strong for there was no other choice.

'My lady…' Piers came hurrying to her as she reached the great hall, his face working with grief and anxiety. 'What are we to do? If my lord should die…'

'My husband will not die,' Elona said. 'He may be ill for a long time, Piers, but we shall nurse him and he will recover. In the meantime, you will do all that was done before. His men must train every morning as they have always done. There will be no slacking just because Stefan cannot be there to watch them. I charge you to see that everything goes on as it must.'

Piers looked at her, wondering at how calm and yet how pale she looked. 'You need not fear that we shall shirk our duty, lady. What of the meat that was brought in from the hunt?'

'Half of it is to be taken to the village,' Elona instructed. 'The rest will be salted for the winter. I shall go to the kitchens now myself and set the work in train.'

'But you have other concerns…'

'My lord is being cared for for the moment,' Elona said. 'I know what he would have me do, and I must do it.'

'Yes, my lady—but he would not have you tire yourself.'

'Trust me to know when I must rest,' Elona said with a smile for his concern. 'After I have set the kitchen to work salting the meat, I shall write a letter to Sir Ralph and you will arrange for someone to deliver it, please.'

'A letter to Sir Stefan's father…' Piers looked at her uncertainly.

'I know that my husband does not always see eye to eye with his father,' Elona said, 'but Sir Ralph must be informed, though he need not trouble himself to come if he does not wish.'

Piers inclined his head. 'It shall be as you command, my lady.'

'Good.' Elona smiled wearily. 'And now I must see to the meat.'

'He is in fever,' Mary told her when she returned to her husband's chamber after washing and changing into a clean tunic and gown. 'He has not woken since the wound was cauterised.'

'Then he did not know I was not here,' Elona said and looked at her serving woman. 'And now you must rest, Mary, for I want you to share the nursing with me. Bethany and

Melise will help where they can, but my poor nurse is old and cannot do much other than sit or prepare one of her cures, and Bethany would be afraid if his condition were to worsen and not know what to do. You have had experience of such nursing.'

'I thought that my husband would recover,' Mary told her, her face grave. 'He seemed to heal and the fever eased, but then one day, he had an odd seizure and his death was sudden—as if something stopped his heart. The priest told me it was God's hand, but I have wondered if there might have been a reason for it—something I could have done to prevent it if I had only known what…' She shook her head sadly, for she had not done with grieving.

'We must pray for guidance,' Elona said. 'Do not think that I shall blame you if my husband dies, Mary. I know that you will use all the skill you have to save him, as I shall—but his fate is in God's hands.'

'Did you find anything that might help him?'

'Father Fernando is searching the manuscripts now. He says that there are several with remedies of treatment for wounds, and that Stefan brought them back with him from the Holy Land, intending to discover more about them. So far he had not had time to study them, but the priest will do so now.'

'He did not disapprove or say that you should not try to usurp God's privilege?'

'Father Fernando is not of that ilk,' Elona said. 'We are fortunate to have him still with us, for he is to leave us very soon now, and I know that if something can be sent for that will help, we shall discover it. And now you must leave us for a while. Go to your couch and rest.'

After Mary had departed, Elona took her stool closer to

the bed and reached out to hold Stefan's hand as it lay on the coverlet.

'I am here with you now, my dearest,' she said. 'Everything is being done as you would order it. There is nothing to worry you. We shall do all that we can to make you well and strong again.'

His hand moved restlessly in hers, twitching and jerking, his eyelids fluttering as he moaned with pain. Elona let go of his hand and picked up a cloth, rinsing it in the pan of cool water beside the bed. She bent over him, bathing his forehead and shoulders for he was very hot.

'Don't send me away…'

She was startled as she heard the feverish words and continued with her work of cooling him, slipping down the light coverlet to bathe more of his heated flesh.

'No one will send you away, dearest.'

'Killed my mother, but I did not mean to…' Stefan muttered. 'It wasn't my fault, Father…forgive me…'

Had it hurt him so very much to be sent away from his home as a child? It must have done if he still felt it so strongly that it played upon his mind. Elona's heart wrenched with pity for the child he had been, and for the man she loved lying so ill in his bed.

'It wasn't your fault, dearest,' she told him soothingly. 'The child is not to blame, for it does not ask to be born.'

'Elona…' Stefan's head moved restlessly on the pillow. 'Don't leave me…love you…need you…don't leave me…'

'I shall never leave you, my love,' Elona said and bent over him, placing her lips against his. Emotion caught at her throat and the tears ran down her cheeks, but she wiped them away. 'Never in this life…' Her voice caught on a sob. 'Don't leave me, my dearest. Fight…cling to life, for it can be so very sweet for us.'

She loved him so much and she did not know how she would bear it if he died. But he must not die. He should not die if there were any way to prevent it!

Elona sat with him throughout the night, and in the early hours Melise and Bethany came together and forced her to give up her place. She went to her chamber and allowed Julia to undress her and help her to bed, for in truth she was too weary to resist.

She slept for some hours and when she woke and broke her fast, Bethany told her that there was no change.

'Your lord is still in fever, my lady,' Bethany said. 'Mary gave him some of the draught she had prepared for him and it seemed to ease him for a while, but the fever still rages.'

'Yes, I am sure that it will,' Elona said. 'We must not expect a swift cure; my lord's wounds are terrible and the cauterising robbed him of his strength.'

'I do not know how Mary could have done it,' Bethany said with a little shudder. 'I should not have been able to face such a terrible thing.'

'It is given to some of us to bear what others may not,' Elona said. 'Mary tried to save her husband's life that way. It did not save him, but it has stopped the bleeding in Stefan's case and for that we must be grateful.'

Yet had it brought about the fever that was making him so ill? How could she know? Elona felt a wave of helplessness wash over her. She had never had to deal with such hurts as Stefan's and knew only what she had learned from Melise and her stepmother—but even Elizabeth would have been uncertain how to deal with such a wound.

Mary was dressing it when she entered the chamber, and she cried out as she saw the foul-smelling stuff that she was about to put on the puckered flesh.

'What is that, Mary?'

'It is something I learned from a wise woman once,' Mary said. 'It is merely herbs and roots, my lady. I know it hath a foul odour, but it will help to draw out the poisons and heal the flesh. I used it on my husband and the wound healed well.'

'And yet your husband died.' Elona hesitated, and then took a deep breath. 'Very well, try it, Mary. You told me that your husband did not die of his wound, but some strange malady that came on him after he seemed to recover, and I will trust you in this.'

'It was not Fredrich's wound or the fever that killed him,' Mary said. 'I have pondered on it many times, for he was laughing when I was with him, and then I left for a few seconds; when I returned, it was as if he had a seizure that left him short of breath and he died in my arms quite suddenly.'

Elona nodded. 'Perhaps one day the surgeons and apothecaries may understand many things that are not known now. All we can do is to use our skills and pray.'

She watched as Mary applied the salve, binding clean linen about Stefan's thigh. The woman then took the stained bandage and threw it into the fire.

'You burned that,' Elona said with a puzzled frown. 'Would it not have served again once it was washed?'

'I believe that the bindings carry poisons from a wound and that it is best to burn the disease in the fire, that way in the end it becomes weakened and dies.'

'That sounds almost like witchcraft,' Elona said and then, as she saw a flicker of fear in the other's face, 'No, no, I did not mean that you were a witch, Mary, of course I didn't. I am grateful for your help. Do not fear me. I am your friend and know that you are mine. It just seems strange.'

'I know only that bandages are best used fresh and burned afterwards,' Mary said. 'The wise woman who told me of this salve also told me that I must use only cloth that has first been boiled and dried, and that I must burn it afterwards or the poison will go back to the wound.'

Elona knew that some people would believe such rituals to be some kind of black art, and decided to tell no one else of Mary's methods of nursing, for she did not want her serving woman accused of witchcraft when she was trying so hard to save Stefan's life.

'Do whatever you must,' she said. 'Your secrets will be safe with me, Mary, and do not fear that I shall blame you if my husband dies. I know that it may happen, but I would try everything possible to save him if I can.'

'Pray for God's help,' Mary replied. 'We can do so little, my lady—and He can do so much.'

Elona made the sign of the cross over her breast and Mary did the same.

Stefan's fever went on for more than ten days, and then on the eleventh he opened his eyes and looked about him. Elona was fetching more water to bathe his heated body when she heard the sound of his voice and turned to look at him.

'Elona…am I ill?' He sounded hoarse and seemed puzzled to find himself lying in bed. 'What happened?'

She went to him at once, gazing down at him, her throat tight with emotion as she saw that his eyes were clear. The fever had gone. God be praised!

'We were hunting in the forest. I had found some filbert nuts and then a wounded boar attacked us. It would have charged at me, but you pushed me to one side and faced it yourself. You had a terrible wound in your thigh, which is still badly puckered and inflamed, but we cauterised it to stop the blood and have been tending you ever since.'

'Have I been in a fever? I cannot remember…' His voice trailed away and his eyes closed on a sighing breath. 'So tired…'

Elona bent over him, afraid that something terrible had happened. Was he going to die as Mary's husband had when it had seemed that he was recovering? She laid her hand on his brow and discovered that his skin was cool and dry. He was breathing easily, his sleep seeming natural and peaceful.

The door opened at that moment and Elona gave a cry of surprise when she saw who had entered the room.

'Sir Ralph,' she said. 'I did not expect you to come…'

'I came as soon as I could,' he answered with a frown. 'I parted on bad terms with my son, Elona, and I must put things right between us if I can. They tell me he is in fever—has he woken yet?'

'Just a moment ago, but I think he is sleeping now.'

'Then we shall leave him for a moment. Where may we talk, Elona? I have brought some things that may help him. There is a remedy for fever, which you may not need now, but also something that Alayne believes necessary for good recovery from wounds and serious illness of this kind.'

'Lady Alayne knows something of these things?' Elona stared at him in surprise, for she had not known that. She led him through to her chamber and invited him to sit, but he remained standing. 'We have been using simple things, though Mary has some knowledge of healing.'

'My wife is a natural healer,' Ralph said. 'We do not talk of it often, for there has been murmuring that she was a witch in the past and we have to be careful. She would have come herself, but she is needed at home. She gave me everything she thought necessary. There is a potion she would have Stefan drink once a day while he lies in bed—she says it prevents a reaction from too much inactivity and lying still. And she says that you should get him to move his legs as much as possible once he begins to recover.'

'That sounds strange,' Elona said. 'Why should he move—is not rest the best thing for a sick person?'

'Alayne says that she has observed a strange phenomena when a person has been ill and begins to recover, which leads to sudden death—but the risk of death is reduced with her cure and exercise.'

'Then we shall do as she bids us,' Elona said, 'for that was what happened to Mary's husband after he had recovered from the worst of his wound.'

'And now I would talk with you,' he said. 'I think that perhaps you were not quite honest with me, Elona—and I would have the truth if I may?'

'Yes, of course. It was always my intention to tell you one day. Did Alain tell you that there never was a child and that I had never lain with a man before my marriage?'

'No, he said nothing, but I guessed that it was a lie concerning the child before you left Banewulf. There had been no miscarriage and yet you were not with child, therefore it was more likely that it had been a mistake on your part. I was not sure whether you had lied or merely been deceived by a lack of your womanly flow?'

A hot flush burned Elona's cheeks, but she did not shirk

from even so personal a question, for this time she must be completely honest with him.

'It was a lie because I knew you would demand that Stefan married me,' Elona confessed, a look of shame in her eyes. 'Stefan behaved most honourably towards me the whole time. He would never have betrayed Lady Alayne's trust in that way. He is far too honourable a man.'

'That was what puzzled me afterwards,' Ralph admitted. 'I had always believed him so and yet he did not deny it. He allowed me to dictate to him when he knew his own men were more powerful than mine—that he could have defied me if he had chosen.' His brows rose. 'Why did he do that, Elona?'

'Because…because he loved me,' she said, a sob in her voice. 'He may not have behaved thus towards me after the wedding, but he was so angry—so jealous of the man he believed had been my lover. It was a terrible thing I did, and I have begged his pardon—as I now beg yours for causing trouble between you.'

'But why? If Stefan loved you…'

'I thought he would go away from Banewulf and that I should never see him again, that I might be forced to marry a man I did not love. I believed that his honour would come between us.'

'And you loved Stefan too much…' Ralph nodded his head. 'All is clear to me now. Alayne was sure it was so, but I was doubtful because my son showed no sign of loving you and I could not understand why he should wed you and leave you at Banewulf.'

'You told Lady Alayne of my wickedness? Does she despise me now?'

Ralph laughed and shook his head. 'My lady applauded your courage and said she would have done just the same in your place.'

Elona blushed and hung her head for a moment, then as she looked at him, she smiled. 'He has forgiven me and we are happy—or we were until this happened…' Her voice broke on a sob. 'I have been so afraid that he might die.'

'My son is a strong man. He has been wounded many times, though perhaps not as deeply as this—but you must continue to pray, Elona.'

'And to use the cures you have brought for us,' Elona said. 'I thank you for bringing them to us, sir.'

'I could do no less,' Ralph told her. 'I shall stay until my son is on his feet again, and do anything that I can to help you keep things running smoothly here.'

'Piers has tried to keep all as it was,' Elona told him. 'But if you could make sure that the men train as they ought I would be grateful. I know Stefan would not like them to become neglectful of their duties.'

'You may safely leave all to me,' Ralph said. 'But I keep you from your vigil. I have been told that you seldom leave his side except to rest or order the household.'

'We shall talk later, sir. I hope I have your forgiveness?'

'And my blessing, daughter.'

Ralph smiled at her as she turned away to return to Stefan's chamber.

Elona hurried to the bedside, but Stefan was sleeping. She took her place by his side, ready for when he should wake and need her.

'You should not have sent for my father,' Stefan said a few days later. He looked at her as she brought him a small vial and held it to his lips. 'Elona…ahhh.'

She smiled as he made a fuss about the medicine, which she knew tasted bitter, for she had tried a drop on her tongue.

'I did not send for your father,' she said. 'I sent word that you had been injured and he came as soon as he was able. It was his wish to come, and he brought you things that have helped to ease you.'

'Alayne was always a good healer,' Stefan said with a grimace. 'I remember being ill once as a child and having her tend me—but she never sweetens her dose with honey.'

'You make too much fuss,' Elona told him. 'Are you doing the exercise I told you she advised?'

Stefan pulled a face at her. 'Were I not so weak, I would get out of this bed and train with my men—if they train at all! I'll have their hides if I discover they had been slacking while I was ill.'

'You are a bad patient,' Elona told him. 'Indeed, you are not patient at all. Have I not told you that Piers has kept them working? Your father told me he was surprised to discover that the men have been training every day just as they ought. In fact, everything is in order and you have no need to concern yourself.'

'Good, then he may go home and leave us to ourselves,' Stefan said and she realised that he had trapped her again. 'I do not know why he bothered to come.'

'Because you are his son and he did not wish the quarrel between you to go on without attempting to mend it.'

'It is mended,' Stefan said. 'He may go home with an easy conscience.'

'I believe he means to stay for a while,' Elona replied, refusing to bend. 'He says that there was never a chance to get to know you when you were younger and…'

'Had he not sent me away so young, there might have been.'

'But that was not his fault,' Elona told him with a smile, for this time he had fallen into her trap. 'Your father's kinsman told him that it was time you had your training and he did what was best for you. It was not that he wished to part from his son, but merely a custom that he followed.'

Stefan glared at her, but said nothing. In his heart he knew that she was right, had known it since he grew to manhood, and Alain's feeling of being tied to his mother's skirts had made him realise that he might have been more fortunate in his education than he'd realised.

'Will you not see your father? He asks every day if you are well enough to receive him.'

'When you let me up from this bed, wife, I shall see my father.'

'Very well, you may get up today,' Elona said and smiled at him. 'You are not strong enough to walk downstairs yet, but you may sit in my chamber in my chair, and your father shall visit you there.'

He glared at her again. 'I think you learn too swiftly, Elona.'

'Of what do you speak, my lord?' she asked innocently.

'You know well enough,' he said and growled low in his throat. 'Very well, it shall be as you wish—but I warn you, when I am myself you shall pay for this, Elona. I know how to treat a scold.'

'Indeed, you wrong me, my lord,' she said and laughed softly. 'I am the most obedient of wives.'

'Huh!' He pulled a wry face, but she saw that he was amused. 'I have taught you too well, lady, but the battle is not over yet. Believe me, I shall have more lessons for you to learn when I am well again.'

'And I shall be most eager to learn them, my lord.' She laughed as his eyes sparked, her heart lifting, for he was truly getting stronger again—and, providing he did not have a sudden seizure, she had every confidence that he would soon be well.

'I have never told you the truth, because I thought you did not know the circumstances of your mother's death and I did not wish to cause you pain,' Ralph told him as they sat together in Elona's chamber. 'Your mother was ill after she gave birth to you, but it was not weakness from her illness that killed her—she was poisoned by a physician I employed.'

'Poisoned?' Stefan was astonished. He had heard nothing of this. 'You mean he was an ignorant fool and killed her by mistake or, no…I see from your expression that he did it on purpose? Why?'

'Because she had discovered that he was incompetent,' Ralph told him and looked grave. 'We had become estranged, because of her illness—and because we were too young when we married. Berenice was too young to be married at all, and I…I did not love her as I ought. She was young and silly and I was impatient. I have regretted the breach. For years it haunted me, for I believed that if I had taken more care of her she would not have died.'

'What did you do to him?'

'He remained in my service for some time, for I did not know the truth. It was Alayne who first suspected it and she accused him of it—and he tried to kill her in a rage, but this time he was discovered.' Ralph's mouth hardened. 'He was tried before a council of my men and punished for his crimes, believe me.'

'I would have killed him with my bare hands.'

'You were but a child,' Ralph said. 'The death you would have given him had you been a man was more merciful than my men decreed, for he had been the source of much pain and many deaths amongst them and they had no mercy.'

Stefan nodded, understanding. 'Then he was well punished. I shall say a mass for my mother's soul.'

'It has been done many times,' Ralph told him, 'but another cannot hurt. And now I ask you to forgive me if I hurt you by sending you away when you were but a child.'

'Elona has spoken to you of this?'

'She did not need to,' Ralph answered with a smile. 'Alayne has taken me to task over it many times. She would have brought you home, but you were doing well with your studies and I believed it was the best way. I think Alain suffered for being allowed to remain at home. He loves his mother dearly and would not hurt her for the world, but he needs to be free—to find himself, to prove himself.'

'Yes, he has told me this,' Stefan said. 'I believe it is his intention to leave for the Holy Land soon?'

'He will do so, but for the moment the Duke keeps him at his court. He writes to his mother and to me, and I believe he is frustrated by the delay. Your brother cannot wait to prove himself as much a man as you, and indeed I do not blame him. I have been proud of your deeds, Stefan—and your reputation.'

'You were swift enough to believe ill of me.'

'And swifter to realise I had wronged you,' his father admitted ruefully. 'Had you wished, you could have ridden off with your men and I could have done little to stop you.'

'That might have caused bloodshed. I could not raise a hand in anger to my own father.'

'No, I realise that now that I begin to know you better,' Ralph said. 'But that did not prevent you simply riding away, for I would not have used force to keep you. You stayed for another reason, did you not?'

'To have deserted Elona would have shamed her,' Stefan said. 'I thought that she was carrying a child—though I was not sure whose child it might be. I believed she might have had a lover or perhaps been ravished by the brutes that took her, and I could not abandon her.'

'Yet you did not send for her? The letter Alain brought to Elona was not from you, I think?'

'I was too stubborn and proud. I have to thank my brother for understanding me better than I could myself.'

'Alain has his mother's insight,' Ralph said. 'In a woman, such traits are good and often useful, but in a man...' He shook his head. 'To tell the truth, I fear for him, Stefan. I think he may find the world too harsh for a man of his nature. You are more like me and I thank God for it.' The sincerity in his voice could not be denied and at last the shadows of doubt fell away from Stefan's mind, never to return.

'I think you worry too much,' Stefan said. 'There is strength in Alain, though it has not yet been tried, but when the time comes—'

They both turned as someone knocked at the door and then Elona entered, carrying a sealed document.

'This comes from the King,' she said. 'His messenger says that it is urgent and awaits your reply, Stefan. I told him you had been ill, but he insisted that I bring it to you.'

'I will see it,' Stefan said and took it from her, breaking the seal. He read it swiftly and then more slowly. 'Baron Dane-wold accuses me of treason against the King. I am called to court to answer the charges.'

'But how can this be? Why should the King think you guilty of treason?'

'Because he knows that I have been his son's man for many years. He fears Richard and therefore he is wary of any that come from Richard's court. Henry is an old man, my love. He knows that the time left to him is short, and that is why he listens to those who pour poisonous words into his ear.'

'But you have sworn loyalty to him now that you have returned to England.'

'Indeed, I have. Henry is our rightful King while he lives, and I would do nothing to harm him, though I would support Richard if there were a struggle between him and his brother John.' Stefan drew a heavy breath. 'It is a monstrous lie, yet I must go to answer it. If I do not, the King will think I am guilty.'

'But you cannot go,' Elona cried. 'You are far too weak. The journey would kill you.'

'I must answer a summons from the King.'

'But it may be the death of you. Please, my husband, I beg you not to do this foolish thing.'

'I shall go in your stead,' Ralph said. 'He will listen to me, for I have served him faithfully on many occasions.'

'He may arrest you in my stead,' Stefan said. 'But go if you wish with a message from me. Tell him that I am laid prone upon my sickbed after a wound that laid me low for weeks, but that I shall come to him in one month and then I will answer any charges against me. On this I give my solemn word before God.'

'No!' Elona cried. 'You will not be well enough in a month, Stefan. You cannot travel for many months.'

Stefan looked at her and the expression in his eyes told her that he would not listen. 'Go to the King, Father. Tell him that I shall answer in one month or he will hear of my death…'

Chapter Twelve

Elona watched Stefan fighting with Dickon, who was the only one of his men who could be persuaded to train with him. His leg pained him so much that he stumbled when he tried to lunge at his opponent and cursed, and the other men had refused to put him to so much agony. Only Dickon seemed unafraid of his cursing and his rages.

She caught her breath as she saw him stumble again; his language was not fit for the stables and Elona clenched her hands, curling the nails into the palms to keep from crying out. It was ten days since the King's message had arrived, and Stefan had insisted on beginning to exercise with his men. He had made a remarkable recovery, but his leg was not yet fully healed and the pain made him sweat as he forced himself to do things that he should not have thought of for weeks or months.

He leaned on his sword, shaking his head as Dickon asked him if he had had enough for one day.

'I must be ready to meet all challenges in a month,' he answered. 'If the King will not listen, I may prove my innocence only by combat.'

He could not think to fight Danewold? Elona wanted to cry out her protest, but she dared not. His temper was at boiling point and any protest from her was labelled as nagging and dismissed brusquely. He would have none of her fussing, but she had noticed that he continued to take the medicine that Alayne had sent to make him stronger.

She knew that he would force himself through any pain in order to defend himself against the charge, and she could only pray that the King would listen and not demand that he choose trial by combat.

Stefan swung himself into the saddle, wincing with the pain. He was able to walk without stumbling now, but Elona knew that he suffered terribly, and that he had little hope of winning in hand-to-hand combat. His strength was nowhere near what it had been, and might not be for months to come.

She looked nervously at Dickon as he came to help her mount her palfrey. She had feared that Stefan would refuse to let her accompany him, but he had seemed to relent towards her the previous night, and for a moment he had been as he was before the boar dealt him such a deathly wound.

'If I denied you, you would probably defy me and follow without a proper escort,' he told her with a wry smile. 'Besides, I would have you with me, my dearest one. I have been harsh with you of late, but I could not rest as you begged me. I have but one chance, Elona, to prove my innocence by fighting.'

'Yes, I know,' she said, holding back the tears that threatened. 'It is just that it hurts me to see you in such pain.'

'At least I did not need to do your exercises,' he said, a gleam in his eyes. 'And my strength returns daily. Fear not, in time I shall be as well as ever, my love.'

If he was given time, she thought, but kept her fears inside. Stefan must do whatever was necessary and she would not help his cause by weeping. If she begged and pleaded it would unman him, and he needed all his courage for the trial ahead.

He turned now and saw she was mounted, smiling at her as he gave the order to move off. 'Courage, my lady,' he told her. 'God is just and I am innocent, therefore I must win my cause.'

'Oh, Alayne,' Elona cried as Sir Ralph and his wife came to meet her in the palace courtyard. Stefan had been arrested as soon as they arrived at court, and she had been left alone with his men to find lodgings for herself. 'I am so glad to see you—and Sir Ralph.'

'I came as soon as I knew what was happening,' Alayne said, 'for I knew that you would need me. Besides, Alain is on his way to court. His letter told me that he was due to arrive in England a day or so ago with messages from Duke Richard to King Henry, and I had hoped that I might see him here.'

'Stefan has been arrested…'

'Yes, but he will not be imprisoned,' Sir Ralph told her. 'I have spoken to his Majesty and it is my opinion that he knows the charges are false and yet he must appear to show fairness. Stefan accused Danewold of killing his people and of abducting you, and now he has been accused of treason. If Henry is to punish one, he must also try the other.'

'Of what is Stefan accused?'

'That he plotted with Duke Richard to overthrow the King and that he came to England for that purpose.'

'That is a lie! He came because he wished for peace—to make a new life and have a family. Surely the King does not believe such lies?'

'Henry is a fair man,' Ralph told her. 'Stefan must answer the charges, but I believe that all will go well for him.'

'But he is not strong enough to fight for himself,' Elona said. 'He has been training, pushing himself to the limit, but he is in so much pain, and he cannot fight as he did—may not again.'

'I have thought of that,' Sir Ralph said and smiled. 'When the King decrees that he must fight to prove his innocence, I shall offer myself as his champion.'

'You will fight in his stead?' Elona stared at him, her eyes wide. 'But it will be a fight to the death…'

'I shall show mercy to my opponent, never fear.'

'But…' Elona looked at Alayne and saw the concern in her eyes. She gave no sign of her anxiety, but Elona felt it. Sir Ralph was still strong and handsome, but he was not a young man and it was a long time since he had fought in truth, though he trained often. 'You are generous, sir—but Stefan would not ask it of you.'

'He is my son,' Ralph told her. 'I would give my life for his if need be—but I can still fight and beat most men half my age.'

Elona could not deny him, for in truth she did not know what he was capable of, nor did she care to offer what must be an insult by doubting his word. She could only pray that it did not come to such a challenge.

Elona was permitted to be present at the trial. She and Alayne sat at the back of the hall and listened as the charges were presented and refuted, waiting with bated breath for the King's answer. It came after some seconds of almost unbearable agony, and it made the two women look at each other in dismay.

'You shall prove your innocence by trial of combat, Sir Stefan—do you accept?'

'Yes, sire,' Stefan's voice rang out strong and true, unafraid. 'I do accept your challenge.'

'Baron Danewold has put up a champion,' the King said. 'You will meet Boris the Boar tomorrow at the hour of nine in the courtyard. It will be a fight to the death, but mercy may be shown if the victor is willing.'

'I accept, sire.'

'Hold!' Sir Ralph's voice rang out in the hall as he walked forward. 'I claim the right to fight as my son's champion. He is but just risen from his sickbed and may name a champion if he so chooses.'

'Aye, that is true.' Sir Orlando stood up in the hall. 'Sir Stefan may choose a champion. It is his right. I also am prepared to fight for him. He once saved my life and I would give mine willingly for his.'

'Nay Father…Orlando…' Stefan began, but before he could say more another voice rang out and a younger man came striding to stand beside his brother and father.

'I claim my right to fight as Sir Stefan's champion,' Alain cried in ringing tones. 'My father is older and not as strong as he once was, though he will likely be angry that I say it. I am my brother's champion. He gave me that right with this sword, for he told me to take it and make him proud of his brother. I shall defend him against all challengers.' He held the magnificent sword Stefan had given him aloft for all to see.

Stefan was silent for a moment, and then he smiled oddly.

'I thank both my brother and my father for the love they show me,' he said. 'It is true that I am not yet recovered from my sickbed and, if the King permits it, I name Alain as my true champion.'

Elona heard Alayne's indrawn breath, and knew that she feared for her son as much as her husband. She reached for her hand, holding it to comfort her as the older woman had earlier done for her.

'Alain is a brave man,' she whispered, 'and strong. I am sure he will win tomorrow.'

Alayne nodded her head, but her face was pale and Elona felt for her. They got up together and went out of the hall. Alain was being congratulated by many of the knights, for his brave speech had aroused admiration and respect.

'I am sorry that your son must risk his life,' Elona said as they went out into the chill air. 'Yet I am glad that he is to fight rather than Sir Ralph, though he would not like to hear me say it.'

'He would have done his best and perhaps he might have won,' Alayne told her. 'There was a time when none could have beaten him in a tourney, but it is many years since he has fought other than to train with his men.'

'Yes, I thought it must be so,' Elona said and smiled. 'Yet it showed love for Stefan in the offer made so bravely. I am grateful to Alain for taking his place, though I know you fear for him.'

'I must not show my fear,' Alayne said and lifted her head proudly. 'It would hurt him if he knew that I was distressed, and I must not weaken his resolve. I have kept him too long at home with me, but I loved him so much and I wanted to have him always with us.'

'Yet a man must prove himself,' Elona said. 'It shamed Alain that he had not done the things that fell to Stefan's lot.'

'Yes, I know,' Alayne said and sighed. 'And he must have

his way. I can only spend the night in prayer and hope that God is kind.'

'You love him as any mother would her son…'

'As you will yours,' Alayne told her. 'And, if I am not mistaken, you are already carrying Stefan's child—does he know?'

Elona shook her head. 'I could not tell him, knowing that he must push himself to this meeting with the King. If I had, he might not have found the strength to do it.'

'Let us go to the chapel and give thanks,' Alayne said, taking her hand. 'For my son must win this challenge or Stefan's guilt is proven and it will all be in vain. We shall lose them both at a stroke.'

Elona had not seen her husband all night, for he had kept a vigil in the chapel with Alain, praying for right and justice to prevail. She had hardly slept, for her fear that something would go wrong lay like a shadow over her.

Alain was young and untried in battle, though he had been the victor in more than one tourney. Supposing he should fail? His failure would be taken as a sign that Stefan was guilty and he would be executed for treason against the King.

But now the long night was over and she and Alayne sat together with their sewing in the house close by the palace gates, which Sir Ralph had secured for them. Neither of them had any interest in the work, but they made a pretence of it to calm their nerves. Yet as the hour crept on and nothing was heard, they both began to pace the room, their nerves stretched almost beyond bearing.

What was happening? Had Alain won his fight—or would he fail and thus prove Stefan guilty of treason? Neither woman could speak of what she feared, but both were in agony.

And then, when they felt they could bear it no more, they heard the sound of heavy footsteps and in a moment Sir Ralph entered the chamber where they sat.

'All is well,' Alayne said after one glance at her husband's face, and then burst into tears. 'Forgive me…I am foolish to weep now that all is well.'

'My beloved,' Ralph said and took her in his arms. 'I came as soon as I could, for I knew you would be in agony.'

'Alain won?' Elona's heart leaped. 'Is he hurt or injured?'

'He will no doubt have a few bruises. But he is well enough,' the proud father said with a huge smile. 'Danewold's champion was a huge bear of a man, strong and fearsome, but he had no intelligence. Alain gave him a lesson in swordplay and then disarmed him. I have seldom seen a man fight with more skill or determination and yet show mercy. I was so proud of him—so very proud.'

'He has proved himself,' Elona said. 'For to save your brother's life is surely enough to gain any man his knighthood?'

'The King insisted upon it,' Ralph said. 'I do not think Alain truly wanted it, for he believes he must earn his spurs in battle—but from this day forth he will be known as Sir Alain de Banewulf.'

'He did not come back with you?'

'They would not let him,' Ralph said. 'There is to be feasting and I was at last released to bring you both to the great hall. Both Alain and Stefan are being made much of by their friends, and I fear that they are being forced to drink more wine than is their wont.'

'Then we must go to them and join in the festivities,' Alayne said. 'I would have my son know how proud we are of him this day…'

'What will happen to Baron Danewold now?' Elona asked.

'He will cause trouble for neither you nor Stefan again,' Ralph said. 'Had he surrendered to the King and not brought false charges, he might have been banished for a period of years, but now…he will pay the final penalty.'

Elona was silent. The laws were severe and she knew that only good fortune and Alain's strong right arm had saved Stefan from a similar fate.

Elona smiled as Stefan stirred and groaned. He had slept soundly since his men had carried him to their chamber, laying him in his bed to sleep off the excess of the previous night. Knowing his abstemious habits, she had been surprised to see him drinking freely of the wine the courtiers forced on both him and Alain that night, but supposed that he must have allowed his relief and pleasure in his brother's victory to go to his head.

'Are you feeling ill, my lord?' she asked as he opened his eyes and looked at her. 'I fear that you indulged in a little too much wine last night.'

'I took some of Alayne's medicine before the banquet,' Stefan told her. 'And it seemed to act strangely with the wine. I should not otherwise have drunk so much. I must ask you to forgive me for my behaviour, Elona, for I cannot remember what happened after they gave me the first glass of wine.'

'There was nothing to forgive,' Elona said. 'In truth I was glad to see you enjoying yourself with Alain—and you slept well. The best sleep you have had in many weeks, my lord.'

'Yes, and I feel better for it,' Stefan said. 'At least, my leg does not pain me as much as it has of late, but my head feels as if a thousand cymbals are crashing inside it.'

'Alayne gave me this for you…'

'Nay, I'll take no more of her cures for the moment,' Stefan said. 'The headache will pass and I must begin to live without such cures to help me.'

'Stay in bed and rest a little longer,' Elona said as he threw back the covers. 'There is no need for you to force yourself to work harder than you can now that your innocence is proven.'

'Thanks to my brother,' Stefan said and smiled at her. 'Did my father tell you? Alain fought like a man possessed. I have never seen a display of better skill. I pitied Danewold's champion, for he was beaten from the beginning and never stood a chance.'

'You did not know that Alain could fight so skilfully?'

'He claims it was the sword I gave him. He said that once he was handed his sword by his squire he felt as if he had the strength of ten men and knew that he could not be vanquished.'

'It was a magnificent sword. I saw it when he held it aloft in the great hall of the palace.' Elona looked at him curiously. 'Does it have magical powers, Stefan?'

'It's previous owner claimed it was so, but I never found it gave me any special power,' Stefan said and smiled. 'It was too light for me. My sword is much heavier.'

'Then perhaps the magic was in Alain's mind?'

'Yes, I think it may have been,' Stefan said after some consideration. 'He was determined to win to save my life and to gain glory for himself—and he achieved both. Besides, I do not think he needed a magic sword to win against that oaf. I might have beaten him even as I am.'

'Just why did you allow Alain to fight for you?' Elona asked. 'I was afraid that you would refuse both your father and your brother's offer to stand as your champion.'

'I would have refused my father,' Stefan said. 'Orlando too, for I know that he has plans to marry if the lady will have him.' A little smile touched his mouth. 'Think you Marguerite would entertain his suit?'

'I believe she might,' Elona said and smiled in answer to the teasing look he gave her. 'But what made you accept your brother's offer when you would have refused the others? Alain was but an untried youth…'

'I could not refuse Alain, for I knew that he would consider it an insult. He would have thought that I did not trust him to win for me, and that would have wounded him. Besides…' He looked at her lovingly. 'I thought of you, Elona. My leg is not yet healed enough to be certain that I would have won. Despite all that I endured I could not make it so, and I knew that it would break your heart if I died—and I wanted to live for you and our child.'

'Our child?' She looked into his eyes as he rose from the bed and came to her. 'You knew that I carried your child?'

'You would not tell me because you knew it would worry me,' Stefan told her. 'But others were not so careful of their tongues. Your women scolded me for upsetting you at such a time. Bethany told me that I did not deserve you. Mary told me that I was a fool to throw away all that I should hold dear—and in truth I did not wish to fight. I left the Duke's service and came home because I wished to live in peace and raise a family of my own.'

'Because you had no family life when you were young?'

'How well you know me,' Stefan said and bent to touch his lips to hers. 'I was starved of affection when I was a child. Harald of Wotten was a good man, but he believed that young lads should be treated harshly to make them stronger of mind and body.'

'And what of our children? Shall you send our sons away for their education?'

'Not at so tender an age,' Stefan said. 'I know that it is the custom and that I was fortunate to receive such a good training at my kinsman's hands, but our sons shall learn first from me, and then, when they are old enough to understand, they shall go or stay as they choose.'

Elona smiled up at him, her heart overflowing with love. 'That is exactly as I would want for them,' she said. 'For if they learn honour and compassion from their father, they are halfway to becoming worthy men.'

'And they will learn how to love from you,' he said, tipping her chin up so that he could kiss her lips. 'Between us, we shall give our children all that is necessary to make them happy, Elona.'

'As I am happy with you, my love.'

A teasing light came to his eyes. 'I have not forgot your scolding tongue, Elona, nor that I promised to teach you how to respect your husband. I dared not spend what little energy I had in your arms, or I should not have been here to meet the King's challenge—but I am feeling much stronger now. There will be nothing to stop me chastising you when we return home.'

'I am ready to take my punishment, my lord,' she said and a gurgle of laughter bubbled up inside her; she knew that somehow this last day and night Stefan had turned a corner. He was truly mending and soon would be as strong as ever. 'For I know that you will treat fairly with me, my lord—my most beloved and honourable knight.'

'I think that my brother will surpass me,' Stefan said. 'I have behaved with chivalry and honour, though there are things I have done that I would prefer to forget. But I believe that Alain will be a true knight, perhaps the truest in Christendom, and I look forward to hearing of his fame.'

'His fame has already begun,' Elona said and reached up to touch his cheek with loving fingers. 'When Alain was so kind to me in my despair I thought him a true knight and I shall always be grateful to him for what he did for you, Stefan.'

'I am grateful for the love he bears me—and for my father's love,' Stefan told her and there was a look almost of humility in his eyes at that moment. 'It is a most precious gift, Elona, and one I never hoped to have.'

'You are more than worthy of their love,' she said, pressing her lips to his in a sweet kiss that promised so much more. 'And of mine…'

'You have given me a rare gift,' Stefan told his wife as he looked down at her and the children she held in her arms. 'I would have been happy with a daughter—but two healthy boys! Had I known that we should have twin sons, I should have been mad with fear for your life, Elona.'

'Then it is as well that you did not,' she said and smiled at him. 'As you see, I have managed it quite well.'

Stefan knew that the birth of his sons had caused her much pain, but the physician he had brought from court to care for her was certain that, because there were two of them, they were smaller and therefore easier to birth than one large child. Yet his fear for her life had caused Stefan much grief and he was glad to accept the advice of his physician, who had told him ways to avoid having another child too soon.

'I love you so much, my dearest,' Stefan said and bent to kiss her. 'I think I must have died if I had lost you.'

'You did not lose me, nor shall you,' Elona told him. 'Before my good nurse died, she read my fortune and told me that we should have two sons and a daughter, and that we shall both live to a great age in happiness and content.'

'I wish I might have rewarded her for such a blessing,' Stefan said. 'You miss her still, I think?'

'She was the mother I lost,' Elona said. 'But she was old and tired, and now I have you and my children. What shall we call them, Stefan?'

'I should like to name one of them for my father,' Stefan said. 'For I believe that would please him.'

'And the other shall be named for my father,' Elona said and gave the babes to their nurse. 'And now, my love, tell me what you have been doing since I was brought to bed?'

'I hunted for deer,' Stefan said. 'And then I wrestled with one of my men—I fear he beat me, but at least it was a close thing. A month ago I would not have made a match of it. I grow stronger every day.'

'But you are truly well again?'

'Yes, my love. I am truly well.'

'Then I am content,' Elona told him. 'Forgive me, but I am a little tired and would sleep, my lord.'

'Yes, you must sleep,' he agreed. 'Now that I have seen you and know that all is well, I shall go and send the news to my father. I am sure that both he and Alayne will want to see you as soon as you are churched.'

Elona's eyelids were heavy. She felt the lightest of kisses on her forehead and was aware that he had gone out, closing the door behind him. She gave a sigh of content.

Stefan was almost himself again, and she had given him the sons they both desired. She had a loving family and would be glad to see Alayne once more, and to hear news of her son if there was any to hear.

Sir Alain was with Duke Richard and soon now the crusade against Saladin would begin. She would pray that her brother-in-law gained all the glory he desired and returned to them safely, for she would never forget the part that he had played in her happiness.

'May God bless and keep you,' she murmured as she drifted into a peaceful sleep. 'I hope that you too will find content one day…'

* * * * *

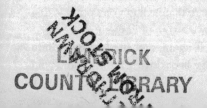

WIN A TWO-NIGHT WEEKEND BREAK
with
OLD ENGLISH INNS
a more enchanting choice

Mills & Boon® has teamed up with Old English Inns to offer you the chance to win a weekend away with a friend or partner with two nights' dinner, bed and breakfast at an Old English Inn of your choice.

Each and every inn has their own special charm and delightful surroundings – historic buildings, cosy bedrooms, oak-beamed bars and restaurants, freshly cooked food, fine wines and real cask ales – perfect for a quick get away!

With the emphasis on relaxation, the traditional inns and hotels offer a warm and friendly welcome and, above all, excellent value for money! Perfect for walking, cycling, sightseeing, visiting historic houses and gardens and golf breaks.

To be in with a chance to win, call FREE on

0800 917 3085

quoting "Romance"

Terms & Conditions

1. The offer entitles two people sharing a standard twin or double room to 2 nights' accommodation including breakfast and dinner. 2. Offer subject to availability. 3. Single supplements may apply. 4. All rates are based on current rack rates and could be subject to change during the promotion. 5. Must be booked through central reservations on 0800 917 3085, not with hotel direct. 6. Excludes Bank Holidays. 7. Offer valid until 30th September 2005. 8. OEI reserve the right to remove/change the hotels during the promotion. 9. Cannot be used in conjunction with any other offer. 10. Applies to new bookings only. 11. Calls will be recorded for training purposes.

www.millsandboon.co.uk

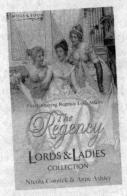

FREE!

2 Books
and a surprise gift!

We would like to take this opportunity to thank you for reading this Mills & Boon® book by offering you the chance to take TWO more specially selected titles from the Historical Romance™ series absolutely FREE! We're also making this offer to introduce you to the benefits of the Reader Service™—

- ★ **FREE home delivery**
- ★ **FREE gifts and competitions**
- ★ **FREE monthly Newsletter**
- ★ **Exclusive Reader Service offers**
- ★ **Books available before they're in the shops**

Accepting these FREE books and gift places you under no obligation to buy, you may cancel at any time, even after receiving your free shipment. Simply complete your details below and return the entire page to the address below. You don't even need a stamp!

YES! Please send me 2 free Historical Romance books and a surprise gift. I understand that unless you hear from me, I will receive 4 superb new titles every month for just £3.65 each, postage and packing free. I am under no obligation to purchase any books and may cancel my subscription at any time. The free books and gift will be mine to keep in any case.

H5ZEF